2

MIDNIGHT FAE
ACADEMY

USA TODAY BESTSELLING AUTHOR

LEXI C. FOSS

Midnight Fae Academy: Book Two

Copyright © 2020 Lexi C. Foss

Editing by: Outthink Editing, LLC

Proofreading by: Katie Schmahl, Jean Bachen, & Julie Robertson

Cover Design: Lori Grundy, Cover Reveal Designs

Interior Designs: CyberWitch Press & Cover Reveal Designs

Published by: Ninja Newt Publishing, LLC

Print Edition

ISBN: 978-1-68530-156-9

"NO?" AFLORA REPEATED. "*NO?* I'M PRETTY sure that's not your call to make, Zeph."

"I'll just bite you again," Shade interjected, sounding bored already by the discussion. But I caught the hint of hurt in his icy gaze. He very much disliked this line of thought. For once, I agreed with him.

Kols, however, remained quiet.

I glanced at him, expecting to see rage but catching a glimmer of intrigue instead. "You can't possibly be considering this, Kols."

"It'd solve a lot of problems," he admitted with a shrug.

"Yes, it would solve several problems," Aflora agreed as she stood on shaking legs.

"And create a thousand more," I inserted, folding my arms.

Kols gave me a look I knew well. The one that told me he was up to something. Then he returned his focus to Aflora. "Can you undo the Earth Fae bond?" he asked, the question making me realize his intent.

He wanted to test her resolve and see how far she'd go.

Which meant he didn't actually want to dismantle the bond.

Thank fuck for that.

We didn't go through all this bullshit just to undo it.

The bonds existed for a reason. If Aflora fractured our ties, she'd implode, and none of us would allow that to happen to her. She belonged to us. End of discussion.

"Um." She winced, causing me to narrow my gaze. *That*, right there, told me she didn't actually want to do this. Something else was driving her to suggest this insanity. "I'm not sure, but I'm going to try."

"No, you're not," I replied, done with this conversation. "You're not going to do anything."

"Again, that's not for you to decide," she bit back.

I grabbed the back of her neck and tugged her to me. "You're upset. I get it. You don't trust us. Fine. But those are not reasons to break a blood vow. Relationships require work. And I'll be damned if I let you just Quandary-magic your way out of this, pixie flower."

Midnight Fae Academy

Book One

Book Two

To Jen, for introducing me to the wonderful world of reverse harem, thereby allowing me to create Shade, Kols, Zeph… and that other guy. ;)

MIDNIGHT FAE
ACADEMY
BOOK TWO

PROLOGUE

AFLORA

EARTH FAE RESIDE IN A WORLD of peace and flowers. We value life. We encourage growth. We adore vitality and prosperity.

That was the world I grew up in—a universe warmed by the sun and caressed by love.

Now I'm trapped in the darkness, fighting for my existence among a horde of treacherous Midnight Fae. Trust does not exist here. Hearts are often broken. And mate bonds mean nothing to the male fae who reside in this realm.

Those are the lessons I've learned these last few months during my captivity in the Midnight Fae realm.

They promised to teach me how to control my growing dark powers.

They promised to keep me safe.

I naively started to believe them.

Then they lied.

The cold black stone beneath my bare feet is evidence of their betrayal.

The looming cell with iron bars and a cold-faced gargoyle define my fate.

But I won't take this lying down.

If it's a fight they want, I'll give them one. I'm not going down alone. I refuse. They got me into this mess. It's only fair to invite them to the party of chaos.

I'll bite my tongue.

Bide my time.

And destroy them just like they destroyed me.

The jail door clinks shut while two of my mates watch with merciless expressions. I don't bother meeting their cold gazes. I already know what I'll find—unapologetic righteousness.

In the end, I'll burn those smug grins right off their faces.

I'm no longer the meek little Earth Fae they held captive here before.

Now I understand their rules.

And as soon as I free myself from the magic of these bindings, we'll play.

Prepare to bow to the queen, boys. I'm coming for you.

CHAPTER ONE

KOLS

AFLORA REFUSED TO LOOK AT ME.

Not that I could blame her.

She thought I'd betrayed her.

That knowledge hurt me almost as much as her resulting shiver to the dungeon air. Shade's shirt and boxers did little to keep her warm, but it was more than her lack of proper clothes. It was her soul reacting to the wrongness of her surroundings.

Elemental Fae weren't meant to stay underground for long periods of time. It'd only been a few minutes since our descent, but I caught the unease radiating from her shoulders. It rivaled my own, because I had no idea what to expect. The news of her trial arrived first thing this morning, and the Council was set to meet within the hour to discuss her fate.

I had no clue what this supposed recording revealed. Hell, I could be facing my own execution, for all I knew. But I doubted it. Otherwise, I'd be in chains right next to Aflora.

Which meant there was still hope.

It all depended on what Shade had told the Council.

I rubbed a hand over my face as the iron bars locked behind Aflora, the gargoyle overhead watching her with severe distaste. "Don't harm her," I told the stone creature. "She's still a guest until the Council deems otherwise."

Aflora snorted before settling on a stone bench, her eyes continuing to avoid mine.

There were things I wanted to say but couldn't with our surrounding audience. So I merely said, "Someone will return should a test of your abilities be required for the trial. Otherwise, you will be notified when the Council reaches a decision."

I met Zeph's gaze as I turned, his green orbs giving nothing away. We'd discuss this more once we were away from all the surveillance cameras and lost our two Warrior Blood guards.

Aflora didn't reply or acknowledge my comments, her stature prim and proper as we left her alone in her cell.

Too bad I couldn't force her into a temporary dream to communicate with her, but we didn't have time for that. So instead, I walked with purpose up the stairs, past the Council Chambers, and into a corridor that led to a room where I could speak with Zeph in private.

The pair of Warrior Blood guards remained at the dungeon entrance, their job to ensure Aflora didn't escape. That alone told me the Council had no idea how powerful she was. If they did, they'd put a lot more than two fae on watch.

Zeph closed the door behind us, his first comment a string of curses that ended in Shade's name. "Did they let you hear the rest of the recording?"

I shook my head. "Only the bit you overheard with her calling for her own extermination." I ran a hand over my face once, fatigue weighing down my shoulders. "We need a backup plan. Because if this goes south…" I trailed off, not wanting to finish that statement out loud.

"Breaking her out won't be hard. Those two nitwits on the stairs will go down in a single spell. But we'll need to alter the security footage."

Yeah, we were on the same page. I'd already begun to think about whom I could bribe to clear the tapes. "Where will we hide her?"

"That's the part I haven't figured out. We can't trust anyone. Not even her Elemental Fae."

True. If they learned about her growing power, they'd have no choice but to end her life. "Fucking Shade," I muttered, livid all over again. "What the hell was he thinking? He has to know this is going to bite him in the ass, too."

"Maybe that's what he wants." Zeph scratched the dark stubble dotting his jaw. "His motives all seem to revolve around creating chaos. If the Council finds out what happened last night—"

The door opened to reveal my father on the other side, his expression one of relief. "Oh, good, you're already here." He joined us without asking, his gold eyes narrowing at Zeph just enough to indicate he still wasn't pleased with the Warrior Blood, before fixating on me. "Is the recording true? Is her power growing out of control?"

"I haven't heard it all yet to comment," I answered carefully.

Disapproval radiated from my father. "You've spent the last few months supervising her. Surely you can make an assessment regarding her power."

"Yes. From what I've observed, her power level remains the same as the first day she arrived." Not exactly a lie. She was born with Quandary Blood abilities; she just hadn't used them much until her forced enrollment at Midnight Fae Academy. And last night, she sort of exploded because of that contained power.

So, yeah, she was losing control. But the quad-bond mating ritual we'd performed as a result of her outburst should help ground her. Maybe.

Which opened a whole new realm of consequences.

We'd solve those problems another day.

One issue at a time.

The first one being to free Aflora from the dungeon.

"Then why is she claiming a need to be exterminated?" my father challenged.

I considered his query and quickly formulated a safe reply. "From what little I've heard of the recording, it was a hypothetical statement—*if* she proves too powerful, she needs to be removed. Aflora feels very strongly about protecting her Earth Fae."

My father studied me for a long moment, his gaze narrowing. "So what caused the inferno in her room at the Elite Residence on campus?"

Fucking gargoyle, I seethed. My brother, Tray, wouldn't report the incident. Neither would his mate, Ella. Which left the damn stone guardian at the front door. "That was my fault. I had a little too much aggression after my duel with Shade and released it inappropriately. I'll repair the quarters myself." By using magic, of course.

The tick in my father's jaw suggested that he suspected I wasn't providing the whole truth, but he eventually conceded with a stiff nod. "The Earth Fae is your ascension trial. I trust you to see it through appropriately."

"And I am," I promised him. I just wasn't doing it the way he'd originally intended. What with accidentally mating the girl during sex and biting her soon after to initiate the Midnight Fae bond.

My father left without another word, never once acknowledging Zeph other than that initial glance. Normally, it would irritate me. Today, I had other, more important matters to address.

"He knows you're lying," Zeph said before I could speak. "But I don't think there's anything incriminating on the tapes, or he'd be angry, not just disappointed."

A fair assessment. If there was anything about the quad-bond on the recording, my father would have reacted

6

differently. Such as throwing my ass in the dungeon and Zeph into an execution chamber. "Whatever it is, it had to be enough to call an emergency meeting and require her detainment."

"That wouldn't be hard. The Council often overreacts."

I snorted. "You would say that."

"Just as you wouldn't," he returned, his tone lacking his usual teasing disdain. He seemed as tired as I was. Likely because we both didn't do much sleeping last night, having enjoyed the new connection with Aflora a little too much.

Palming the back of my neck, I blew out a long breath and looked at the ceiling. "She thinks we betrayed her, Zeph."

"She'll get over it." He clearly didn't share my concern. "Go prepare for the Council meeting. If the findings are dire and she's truly in jeopardy, text me a note about possibly missing a few classes this week. If she's fine, let me know when you'll be back on campus. I'll react accordingly."

I bobbed my head in agreement. "Okay. And if you see Shade before I do, punch him in the face for me."

Zeph grunted, his green eyes blazing with vengeful power. "If I see him first, there won't be much left of his face for you to hit."

"Good." Because the fucker deserved a beatdown for whatever game he'd engaged us all in now.

I just hoped Aflora wouldn't pay the ultimate price for his newest diversion.

CHAPTER TWO

AFLORA

"I DON'T SUPPOSE you can fetch me a glass of water?" I asked the gargoyle.

He snorted in reply.

"I didn't think so," I murmured, sighing as I relaxed into the stone wall at my back.

This place was hell. My own personal purgatory. Earth Fae didn't belong underground. Not that it mattered. I couldn't access my source with this choker around my neck anyway.

Closing my eyes, I returned to my task of trying to unlock it with my mind. The magic caressing my skin itched at my conscious, the cloaking mechanism one that seemed to warm the bonds emanating from my heart.

I tugged on one of them, and a familiar woodsy scent touched my nose. *Zeph.*

Yanking on the other strand filled my essence with rich spice and power. *Kols.*

And the final cord released a wave of peppermint, the refreshing taste one craves first thing in the morning. *Shade.*

I frowned. *Why is the collar connected to them? To hide our links?*

That would explain Zeph's haste this morning in forcing the contraption on me. He wanted to guarantee no one would find out about our bonds.

"I need you to put this on, and we need to run. Now."

His words replayed in my head, causing me to scowl even harder than before. I'd stupidly believed he wanted to help me. Had thought he might even care about my welfare.

But those jackholes only cared about themselves.

Hence my current predicament.

Ignoring my anger, I refocused on the enchantment circling my skin and plucked at some of the other magical strings. They all seemed to be suffocating my powers, which explained the tingling sensation rioting through my spirit. It was a miracle in itself that I could access enough of my essence to investigate the spells on the collar. Undoing them would be another task entirely.

"Ah, there you are." Shade's voice warmed my face, his hands soon following as he materialized in front of me.

I jumped to my feet, my fists ready to meet his face, when he grabbed my wrists with ease and backed me into the wall. The gargoyle didn't seem to care at all, his beady red eyes focused on a space over my head instead of on the Midnight Fae forcing a thigh between mine.

"The Council is about to convene. Do you have any special requests on how I should address them on your behalf?" he asked, his ice-blue eyes capturing and holding mine.

I spat at him rather than reply.

Like I'd trust him to speak on my behalf.

Willow stump, I thought, furious.

His eyebrow inched upward as he released one of my wrists to wipe the spittle away from his face. I used the opportunity to try to shove him away, but he caught my wrist again with ease, holding both above my head beneath one of his palms.

"Are you asking me to spit on them, Aflora?" He cocked his head in an almost playful manner. "Because I'm pretty sure that won't go over well."

"Go to hell," I told him.

"Already there, baby," he replied.

Holy Elements, I hated this male. He'd bitten me against my will, trapped me in this world, nearly convinced me to somewhat trust him, and had me thrown into a jail cell again. "Did you record everything last night?" I asked him, my lip curling into a snarl. "Including the part about our qua—"

His mouth caught mine, his tongue pushing inside before I could think to respond. Fury boiled inside me, my reaction coming a second later in the form of a bite that caused his blood to spill over our lips.

I spat it on the ground instead of swallowing, our residual dreams teaching me the consequences of imbibing his essence.

Fire lit his gaze, causing the ice to melt around his irises into a pool of bright blue flames. "Careful, Aflora, or we'll end up giving the Council quite the show." He cocked his chin toward the corner, just above the gargoyle's head. "They're watching us right now. Listening, too. So if you have something you want to say, do it now."

His eyes flared with warning, some sort of hidden message brewing in his azure depths.

Had they sent him down here to torment me while they observed?

Was I supposed to admit something?

Remain quiet?

Fight him?

I didn't know.

"It would help if I knew what I was on trial for," I said, narrowing my gaze.

"You don't remember what you told me last night?" he countered, his lips curling. "I suppose the sex was pretty intense in comparison."

Sex? We didn't have sex. He'd used his thigh to force my climax. Then Zeph and Kols had taken over my dreams afterward.

What are you trying to tell me? I wondered, some of my ire cooling in favor of confusion. "I told you I should be exterminated."

"Yes, *if* your power can't be controlled," he replied, his emphasis on the word *if* making me frown. "Do you have anything you wish to add to that statement?"

"What would I add?" I countered.

"That's why I'm here." His thumb stroked my wrist. "Is there anything you want me to say on your behalf?"

"I don't want you to speak on my behalf."

"That's not how our rules work."

"Well, your rules are archaic."

"Perhaps, but that's a discussion for another day, Aflora. I need to know if there's anything else you want me to tell them. That's why I'm down here—at the Council's request—and why some of them are watching us right now."

There it was, a reiteration of a warning.

They can hear and see us.

Okay.

I expected that.

But why did it concern him? Because he didn't want me to mention the quad-bond? How would that impact him? Everyone knew we were mates already. Kols and Zeph were the ones who'd suffer if I mentioned what happened last night.

Well, and me.

However, I didn't matter to any of them.

Just as Kols and Zeph didn't matter to Shade.

So why would he care?

"If you have nothing to add, then I'll handle it from here," Shade said, his voice lower as his thumb continued to massage my wrist. "I know exactly what happened last night, little rose. But don't worry. I won't go into specifics

11

on how good you feel around my cock."

My brow started to furrow. "What—"

His lips caressed mine. "It's okay, sweetheart. They won't ask for specifics. They just want clarification on the recording. I know what you meant, and I'll make sure they do, too."

Another riddle.

Another game.

Another way to betray me.

"Like I'd ever trust you to speak on my behalf," I whispered.

He smiled. "There's my fiery mate." His lips went to my ear, his voice dropping to a whisper as he added, "Don't lose her, Aflora. We have many more trials to dance through together." His teeth skimmed my throat in a display of Midnight Fae affection before he released me, his eyes glazed with power. "Wish me luck, little rose. I'm about to either exonerate you or ensure your demise. Personally, I hope for the former. It'd be such a loss of talent otherwise."

He disappeared into a wave of smoke before I could reply, causing me to growl in annoyance at the empty space around me.

Then I focused on the camera. "You're a bunch of archaic flower petals," I muttered. "When you're ready to join me in the present, I'll give you a statement. Until then, go fluff yourselves."

I started to pace, my mind rattling with notions of Shade's intentions. Whatever his goals, they were self-fulfilling at best.

Which meant I needed to be ready for a fight.

Something that would be hard considering my lack of sleep last night—thanks to my jackhole mates.

That was probably why I couldn't focus enough to unweave the power from my neck. Well, that, and inexperience.

Sighing, I collapsed onto the floor mattress and

pounded my fist into the soft material while envisioning three different male faces. They were probably watching me and chuckling, which only made me strike the fabric harder.

They continued to underestimate me.

That would change today.

I lay back on the makeshift bed and closed my eyes.

Time to tackle this collar, I told myself. *Once you're free, they'll never know what hit them.*

CHAPTER THREE

SHADE

"ANY LOSS OF LIFE IS UNACCEPTABLE. If I can't be controlled, I should be exterminated." Aflora's voice played throughout the Council Chambers, followed by my recorded response.

"That's a very narrow view, Aflora. What if you could learn control?"

Several snorts replied to that question while I maintained my calm demeanor against the wall, one leg crossed over the other, hands in my pockets. My father wanted me to sit beside him. I'd sooner accept a position in hell.

"I've been trying that since I arrived," Aflora replied, the rest of her sentence altered for the purposes of this meeting. I'd play along only to an extent. Which was why I'd doctored the tape before handing it over.

Convince them you're playing by the rules, and they'll give you more freedom.

Not exactly a prophecy, but solid advice. As *he* had been right about everything thus far, I chose to listen to him.

Because now more than ever, I needed the flexibility to blend into the shadows and help Aflora hide the truth.

"Yes, and now you have a support system to rely on." Another doctored section of the recording, this one easier than the other since it was my response.

"I have no one to rely on." Aflora sounded so disgruntled. Not that I blamed her. "You never tell me anything of importance. Zeph is the realm's worst teacher. And Kols hates me. Some support system."

"Yeah, he's a shit teacher." I smirked, just as I had when I originally spoke those words. "But Kols doesn't hate you, and I tell you important things all the time. You just don't hear me."

"Right."

"Here, I'll make it better, little rose. Just close your eyes and—" The recording cut off, causing several gazes to swing my way.

I shrugged. "What can I say? She's a gorgeous woman." I allowed them to form their own opinions on what had happened next. If they wanted to judge me, I welcomed it. Because that would deflect them all from the truth of what actually occurred after her last word.

When I told her about Kols's grandfather ordering the slaughter of the Quandary Bloods.

And admitted I knew about her heritage before we met.

Two very important details I did not want to share with the Council.

"That's it? That's the entirety of the recording?" King Malik demanded.

"Oh, there's more," I drawled. "But it's mostly just grunts and moans. Without the visuals, it lacks the finesse of the moment."

Kols narrowed his gaze at me, his golden orbs flashing with disdain.

Yeah, I could have given him a heads-up about my intentions. But I didn't want him to develop a false sense of leadership over me. I played by my own rules, no one else's. It would be best for us all if he learned that lesson now.

"So she believes herself to be an abomination." Tadmir's white hair flickered with blue flames, the only outward indication of his current mood. "That's enough for me. Kill the girl. It'll free up Shadow for the mating bond, and he can carry out the agreement between our families."

I remained quiet, not trusting myself to reply to that out loud.

Kols wasn't so restrained, his tone underlined in authority as he replied, "Aflora didn't call herself an abomination. She's just being a martyr because she cares about her people. If anything, that only marks her as a worthy queen to the Earth Fae throne."

The blue flickers grew around Tadmir's head. "There must be a reason she wants to be exterminated." His beady black eyes turned to me. "Where's the beginning of the recording?"

"Nonexistent," I lied. "We began the discussion in the hallway, out of range. I guided her into my room mid-conversation to catch at least part of her words for the use of the Council." Complete and utter bullshit, which only Kols seemed to know. Fortunately, he kept his royal mouth shut.

"What led to her proclamation?" Chern, ever the wise fae, played right into my hands the way I'd hoped he would.

Sangré Bloods could be so predictable sometimes in their penchant for logic. Today, that worked in my favor beautifully.

"She was upset about my little tiff with Kols." I met and held the prince's burning gold eyes. "She didn't appreciate the flare of power our duel created and was lecturing me about the loss of life in the LethaForest."

Releasing Kols's gaze, I took in the room of blank stares.

Idiots.

"She's an Earth Fae," I reminded them all. "She values

all life, including the destroyed burning thwomps."

I lifted a shoulder, done with my mouthful of untruths.

Though, I did mention the dead trees to her during that conversation.

And technically, her extermination reply followed right after.

So it wasn't all a lie, just a bit jumbled.

Kols's jaw ticked, but he didn't correct me. The duel had been his brilliant cover story for what really happened between the four of us last night. I'd only enhanced his explanation and also provided the Council with a different rabbit to chase, just in case they came back to question the destruction in the LethaForest.

"And that led to her calling for her own death?" Chern prompted, his gray eyes intelligent.

"Yes, because I told her sometimes things die, and she launched into a debate on her own powers and fate. Then she said if she can't be controlled, she should be exterminated. I believe she meant it hypothetically, but I thought it wise to share the recording with my father. It was this Council, after all, that demanded I report back any findings no matter how small. I'm merely complying with the edict."

There. Flowery bullshit for the table. Isn't it beautiful? I thought, fighting a smile.

King Malik didn't appear all that impressed.

Neither did Tadmir.

I mean, honestly. Did they really expect me to waltz in here and request the death of my mate? I suppressed a snort. That would never happen.

"That was the request of the Council," my father agreed, his tone flat. "And the recording itself is incriminating."

True. But my explanation exonerated her without fail. I just needed them to believe me. Which was the only potential weak point in my strategy.

And exactly why I had a backup plan should the Council vote negatively against Aflora.

"You've spent the most time with her, Kolstov." King Malik turned toward his son. "What are your opinions on the matter?"

"As I mentioned earlier, Aflora puts her people above herself. If she truly believed herself to be a danger to them, she'd demand her execution."

Clever wording, I mused.

"What I heard on the recording is exactly the kind of statement she'd say to me," he continued. "But it remains an *if* scenario, not a resolute one. To exterminate her now would be a false preemptive measure without proper merit and likely earn retaliation from the Elemental Fae."

All very logical without an ounce of emotion.

If we were alone, I'd applaud him for the outward stoicism.

"She's your ascension trial," King Malik replied. "If that's your decision, I stand behind it."

Oh, if you only knew what Kols had been doing to his little "ascension trial" yesterday around this time, you wouldn't be so quick to agree, I thought.

Outwardly, I remained as calm and cool as Kols, never once showing an opinion either way. The Council thought I only cared about fucking Aflora. I preferred it that way. Made things easier.

"So we just send her back to the Academy?" Tadmir's tone matched the embers floating around his oval-shaped head, his annoyance piqued.

"A hypothetical conversation is not grounds for execution." Chern rubbed his bald head, the designs along his scalp flaring with magic. "We should continue to monitor her developments through Kolstov's reports."

Kols's jaw ticked once more, the only indication of his discomfort.

Yes, young prince, how does it feel to lie to the room of your intended peers? To know that the truth would have you ousted from that precious throne and potentially killed in the process? I wondered.

I almost pitied him.

That cuff around his wrist might hide his truth from the room, but he'd made his bed when he chose to invite Aflora to play between his sheets.

Of course, destiny wrote that act into the cards long ago.

And there was no escaping fate.

I yawned as the Councilmen began their usual debates, with Tadmir on one side, Chern on the other, and my father and Malik in between while Svart remained dutifully silent. Some of the Seconds spoke up, but most were in agreement that Aflora should be allowed to return to the Academy with Prince Kolstov as her warden.

There were so many innuendos on the tip of my tongue regarding Kolstov's method of guardianship, but I swallowed each one.

"Continue to report back anything useful," my father told me after the meeting adjourned. "It doesn't matter how small."

"Sure," I replied, acting as though his request didn't faze me in the slightest.

My goal was to convince him I resided on his side, that my duty was to him and the Council. Because I needed him to stop watching my every move.

The pride in his eyes now suggested that perhaps I'd won some favor with him, that maybe he would remove the surveillance he had on me at the Academy. I'd know soon enough, as I'd spent the last few months skillfully avoiding them.

That was one of the many benefits of my bloodline— my ability to detect *paths*.

If only I could find the quickest way out of this new mess.

Alas, the prophecy stood, and things were about to become a whole hell of a lot worse before they ever improved.

Ah, my poor, darling Aflora. This is only the beginning. Please don't hate me too much.

CHAPTER FOUR

AFLORA

"WE REALLY NEED TO STOP meeting like this, little rose," a deep voice murmured into my ear.

I sighed, not wanting to move, my body cocooned in a blanket of comforting warmth. Yet something about those words nagged at me, dragging me back to a reality I didn't want to face.

To the hard mattress beneath me.

To the stale air of a dungeon.

To the beady red eyes of the supervising gargoyle.

I sprang upward, my head aching with the desire to return to my dreamless sleep. *Ugh.* The exhaustion had won while I was messing with the magic around my neck, leaving me in the same position as before—powerless.

Shade's palm ran up my side in a soothing gesture undermined by lies. Leaping to my feet, I backed away from him. He remained on the mattress, his athletic form balanced on his elbow. "The Council concluded that your theoretical commentary was not enough to require action, and I've been instructed to return you to the Academy. So whenever you're ready, let me know."

I gaped at him. "Theoretical commentary?"

"Yes. I explained to them how you were merely theorizing what should be done if your powers were to grow out of control. As they haven't actually proved uncontrollable, the Council saw no reason to act." He lifted a shoulder. "Classes resume tomorrow—well, later today, really—as scheduled."

"I'm... I'm free?"

"Not really. The Academy is just a fancier prison, in my opinion." He pushed off the ground and landed deftly on his feet. "Shall we, princess?" He extended his hand with the offer, his dark brow waggling in a taunting manner.

"Is this a joke?"

"If you think it is, then my ego's wounded. Because I swear I'm funnier than that."

I stared at him.

He stared back.

Time ticked on between us with his hand dangling in the air.

The gargoyle huffed in agitation, his stone wings beating rapidly as he shoved through the door and left it wide open in his wake.

Either I was dreaming or Shade had told me the truth.

"Take a chance," he dared, a sinful promise teasing the edges of his lips. "I promise not to bite you today."

"I think it's a little late for promises," I muttered, stepping around him to reach the door.

Shade caught me by the waist, pulling me back against him. "I said you were free." His lips brushed my ear with the whispered words. "I said nothing about using doors."

"Wh—"

The world shifted around us in a thick gray cloud, causing my stomach to roll with uncertainty.

Then the scent of fresh-cut grass tickled my nostrils.

Followed by flowers in bloom.

And the kiss of a morning sun.

I'm dreaming, I thought, spinning in a circle as the inky smog evaporated into a blue sky. Plush green blades met my bare feet, the sensation of earth breathing life into my being and sending me to the ground in a sob of unfiltered joy.

Earth.

I'm surrounded by earth.

The essence beckoned me to play, but the mechanism around my neck halted my reaction, yanking me back to a reality of pain and suffering. I clawed at the offending leather, longing to be rid of it, and screamed in frustration.

This was the definition of hell—being surrounded by the element I craved just to be cut off from it because of black foreign magic.

More torture.

More games.

More wicked intent.

I growled, ready to kill the being who did this to me. I lunged for him, only to find myself caught up in his much stronger arms, his lips at my ear. "Breathe."

The single command had me snarling. "*I hate you.*" It came out hoarse, my emotions spilling from my pores in ripples of convoluted fury.

"I didn't put that device around your neck," he reminded me in a calm tone that only infuriated me more. "But you have the tools to undo it. So stop freaking out and use your Quandary Blood to unweave the magic around your source." He released me and took a step back.

I spun around, ready to slap him, when his comment registered.

You have the tools to undo it.

He was right.

I did.

Assuming I didn't fall asleep again.

Frowning, I prodded at the spells enchanting my collar once more and found them waiting eagerly for my manipulation. Odd. They hadn't done that in the dungeon.

Why could I see them more easily now?

"The cells are laced with protective spells that make magic difficult to access," Shade said, reading either my mind or the confusion on my face. "You should find your Quandary Blood skills are much easier to access, even with that thing choking the life out of your magical spirit."

He took another step away from me, his back meeting the trunk of a nearby tree.

"Just try to remember how to put the spell back together. We can't have Kols or Zeph finding out that you can circumvent their little masterpiece, yeah?" He slid down to the ground, still braced against the tree, and closed his eyes. "I'll just be over here having a nap while you play."

I blinked at him. "A nap?"

"Mmm," he mumbled, clasping his hands in his lap. "You're not the only one who requires beauty sleep, little rose."

"Wait, where are we?" I asked, taking in the array of fields and trees and flowers around us. "In the human world?"

He snorted. "I have no idea where we are. While trying to return you to the Academy, my exhaustion kicked in and we accidentally ended up here. Too bad, really. It's so bright. Alas, I didn't want to risk getting us more lost, so we decided to nap here for the day before trying again. I'm sure Kols will understand. He has a room to fix, after all."

"Do you always talk in riddles?"

"Only when I'm tired." He yawned dramatically. "And, man, am I tired. Hope you don't mind spending some time here, Aflora. Sorry for my lack of coordination and direction."

He didn't sound apologetic at all.

But that was the point.

He'd purposely brought me here and was telling me the lie he intended to give everyone else.

My fingers unfurled from the fists at my sides, realization threatening to breach the icy confines of my heart. *He brought me here to play with my earth.*

He'd given me the gift of the sun. The grass. Trees with real leaves. Flowers in full bloom. And while he wouldn't tell me where we were, he'd also provided me with subtle instructions on what to do.

All in his cryptic little way.

I studied the chiseled features of his handsome face and caught the slight twitch of his lips—the only outward sign he was pleased. Then his expression slowly fell into one of contentment, his closed eyes unmoving. "Use your Quandary Blood to set your earth source free, little rose," he murmured. "I've always favored floral scents."

Me, too, I thought, slowly kneeling once more as I engaged the part of my spirit that loved solving puzzles. It felt so foreign and yet familiar. A conundrum of energy that I didn't quite understand, but I applied it to the collar around my neck and slowly picked at the various strands of magic. I didn't touch the ones tied to my Midnight Fae mates but focused on the black web surrounding my elemental gifts. Pulses of the source peeked at me from below the dark strings, demanding freedom.

It was an intricate dance woven through my mind, the powers blending in a manner that surpassed logical form. This shouldn't feel right, but it did. The essence mingled inside me, my problem-solving skills mating with my love for the earth as a spark of light stirred behind my eyes.

There, I thought, seeing the source of my elemental power beckoning me forward. I followed it knowingly, bathing in the rays of welcome it shined through my spirit, and lifted my eyelids to find myself rolling across the earth in a blanket of flowers.

An exuberant giggle bubbled from my chest, happiness kissing my soul after what felt like months of despair.

This was my rightful place.

My home.

My earth.

A breeze trickled through the trees, sending me their

warm welcome as more blossoms sprouted from the grass in an array of my favorite colors.

The dark one is watching, one of the trees whispered, drawing my attention to where Shade lounged beneath the green limbs. His eyes were indeed open, his expression amused.

"You remind me of a nymph," he said softly, his voice deep and soothing. "A gorgeous little nymph."

"I've heard that word used to describe Earth Fae before. It's appropriate."

His lips twitched, his eyes falling closed once more. "Wake me when the sun falls, little rose." He fell into true sleep then, his breaths even as he remained seated against the tree trunk with his legs crossed at the ankles.

I let him rest while I explored the meadow, my heart soaring with the song of beauty and nature's grace.

This place wasn't part of the Human Realm, the life surrounding me unfamiliar with mortal essences. So it was a fae world of some kind, but I couldn't determine which one. Every time I asked, the trees whispered of something different, something new, distracting me from my questions and urging me to exhaust my earth essence instead.

I created a myriad of plant life, played with the grassy roots and soil, and luxuriated in the foliage of life.

By the time the sun began to descend, I felt full of vitality, my soul thriving in a way I hadn't felt in far too long.

All because Shade brought me here to play.

Under the excuse of having lost his way back to an Academy he'd shadowed to thousands of times before.

Maybe this was his way of apologizing.

Maybe this was all just a trick, a last dance with life before death consumed me.

I couldn't know for sure, my faith in him nonexistent.

But that didn't stop the inkling of gratitude from entering my heart. He'd given me a gift. I just didn't know his intentions for it.

He stirred as night graced the horizon, his arms stretching overhead as he took in the twilight meadow. His lips curled. "This is beautiful, Aflora."

A compliment.

Not a taunt.

Or it didn't sound like one, anyway.

I remained cocooned in my sea of flowers as he stood, his head cocking to the side upon finding me beneath a shield of earth. He stepped forward, only for one of my tree roots to lift and stop his path. "Impressive," he replied, eyeing the obstacle before shadowing around it to appear at my side.

I considered wrapping a vine around him to secure him to the earth, but he knelt beside me and plucked a flower from my hair. He brought it to his nose and inhaled deeply, then released a sigh.

"Unfortunately, we need to return to the Academy, or they'll send Warrior Bloods after us. My excuse will only get us so far." Rather than hold out a hand to demand we leave, he sat down and settled into the flower bed I'd created. "For your own safety, you need to rewrite the spell, Aflora." His blue gaze met mine. "But maybe you can weave it in a way that allows for a little flexibility in the restraint."

Another riddle.

Another clue.

A suggestion.

"And maybe we can come back here in the future," he added, his knuckles brushing my cheek.

"That implies I can trust your word, which I know I can't."

"You can't?" He arched a brow. "Why not, Aflora? I've never lied to you."

"Your actions are louder than your supposed truths."

"My actions," he mused, his hand falling from my face to the flower petals around him. "You mean how I doctored the recording to save you from the Council's

27

wrath? How I brought you to this special place to give you a day of freedom at the expense of my own?" He phrased both as questions. "Are those not actions in your favor?"

"You gave them the recording."

"An altered version of it, yes."

"Why?" I demanded. "You had me essentially arrested for what purposes?"

He scrutinized me for so long that I was surprised when he actually replied, "To lull the Council into a false sense of security. If they think I'm playing by their rules, they'll give more freedom—something we could all use at the moment. I also wanted to distract them from looking into the explosion of power from the other night. Kols's little story about the duel wasn't going to satisfy my father. He knows I'm not the losing sort."

His explanation shocked me for a multitude of reasons, not the least of which being that he'd actually given me a factual reply. The question was, did I believe him?

"You believe actions prove integrity," he continued, arching a brow. "Then ask me to bring you back here in the future. We'll see what happens. In the interim, I need you to enchant your collar again. But if you want to program in a backdoor to access your earth, I'll look the other way and pretend not to notice."

He stood and wiped his palms against his pants.

"I'm fucking starving," he added, abruptly changing the subject. "Did you happen to make anything edible around here? Like fruit?"

My lips curled at the thought of home and the Elemental Fae Queen's favorite peach trees. "No. But I can." It was one of the only human fruits I knew how to create, thanks to Queen Claire's obsession with the juicy treat.

Shade faced me, his expression expectant.

So I gave him what he wanted by calling the seeds to the soil and expediting the growth through my access from the source.

He watched in fascination as the tree grew, the branches sprouting with leaves first and then luscious circles of fruit. He plucked one off the tree and took a bite, his moan of approval holding an erotic appeal that I pretended not to hear.

"Fuck, this is delicious." He leaned once more against the tree he'd used for his nap and devoured the peach. Then he walked over and snatched another one.

"Throw the pit over there," I instructed him, pointing with my finger to where I wanted it.

He did as I requested, and I used the core to create another tree. "Earth is a continuous cycle of life."

"While Midnight Fae are known for the darkness of death," he returned, his blue eyes alight with knowledge. "But Quandary Bloods are rumored to be more than just dark magic. They're conduits of The Source. The one that controls all others, I mean. That's how many of them were able to hide during the mass extermination—they assimilated as other types of fae. Even Earth Fae. Or that's the theory, anyway."

"Are you saying that not all Quandary Bloods perished?"

"I think your existence answers that question, little rose," he replied before finishing off his second peach. "Now we have to stop stalling. If we don't return soon, we'll be back where we started—in the dungeon—and we can't have that. Not after I went through the hassle of having that tape altered to suit our needs." He pushed off his tree, hopped over the root I'd left in the ground, and came to stand over me. "Snap the magic in place and let's go."

He made it sound so easy.

Which, now that I knew how to unravel the spell, actually was pretty simple to put back together. But the confident manner in which he spoke made me wonder how he knew it would be such a quick task.

"Do you know any Quandary Bloods, Shade?" I asked

him while I mentally began the process of closing off my connection to the earth source.

"Now you're asking interesting questions," he praised, his gaze alight with mischief. "If I told you yes, would you believe me?"

"Maybe."

"Then maybe I do. I mean, I know you."

"Other than me," I clarified.

He merely smiled, his hand finding mine as he pulled me to him and pressed a quick kiss to the corner of my mouth. "Did you create a way to access your earth through the spell?"

I took a page out of his book and didn't reply other than to grin.

"My perfect mate," he whispered, pressing his forehead to mine. "Hold on tight, little rose. I suspect we're about to endure a rough Academy welcome."

CHAPTER FIVE

SHADE

IF I WASN'T HOLDING AFLORA, I would have ducked.

For her, I took the punch waiting for me upon our arrival.

"Your actions are louder than your supposed truths," she'd said.

How's that for an action, princess? I thought now as I shifted my jaw to ease the pain.

When Kols went for round two with my face, I shadowed myself—and Aflora—to the other side of his royal suite.

The gargoyle chose that moment to appear with a screeching sound, his distaste at my Death Blood presence causing a shrieking alarm to blare throughout the audacious four-bedroom apartment. I blasted the damn thing with a silencing spell by issuing a command from my mind, causing it to sputter and collapse on the ground in a cluster of rocky wings.

Its red eyes breathed fire as it came for me in all its stone-filled glory.

Determined little badass, I thought, trapping it beneath a net of shadows I conjured with a flick of my wrist.

Its lips parted in a bellow that my silencing enchantment fortunately caught.

I smirked at the tiny idiot. "Not so tough now, are you?"

Rage blazed from its gaze, just as it did from Kols's gold irises as he charged across the living area.

"This isn't beneficial conversation," I pointed out, ready to shadow again.

Only, Aflora stepped in front of me and slammed her fist into Kols's jaw as soon as he was within distance.

My lips actually parted.

"Razzleberries," she breathed, shaking out her hand with a hiss of pain.

Kols's residual anger subsided beneath a wave of shock tinged with dismay as he prodded his jaw with two fingers. "You hit me."

Her shoulders tightened and her chin lifted. "You threw me in a cell."

"To protect you, Aflora," he growled.

A laugh bubbled out of her as she shook her long waves of black hair. "I felt very safe there. Thanks, Prince Kolstov." She turned on her heel to leave, and he caught her wrist.

"What was I supposed to do, Aflora?" he demanded. "Shade's the one who gave them the recording, not me."

I snorted. "Don't bring me into this."

"Are you fucking kidding me? This is *your* fault," he seethed. "And where the fuck have you been? You were supposed to bring her directly here."

"Oh, was I?" I pretended to think. "I suppose that order didn't register correctly."

"Where did you take her?" Another command. One of these days, he'd realize that I didn't consider myself one of his precious subjects to be dictated to.

"Let go of me," Aflora interjected, twisting her arm.

He tightened his grip. "Where did he take you?"

She gave him a defiant look. "While trying to return me

to the Academy, his exhaustion kicked in and we ended up in an unknown location. He didn't want to risk getting us more lost, so we stayed there for the day while he napped. Now I'm here. Happy?"

Kols's jaw ticked while my lips canted into a delighted smirk. My clever little mate had used my riddled explanation without even blinking. "Exactly," I agreed just as Zeph burst into the suite.

His gaze narrowed, a flash of anger crossing his features as he headed right for me.

Great.

"What the fuck were you thinking, Death Blood?"

"That my father would never believe Kols's little duel story and I needed to give him something to distract him," I replied coolly. "It worked."

Zeph paused midstep, his calculative gaze raking over me as he considered the reason. That was one thing I liked about the Warrior Blood—he preferred logic over emotion. Some of his fury melted, but not completely, his green irises whirling with notes of annoyance. "A warning would have been fucking appreciated."

"A warning could have impacted the fate of events." They weren't meant to know my intentions. Not yet. And I refused to alter the scope of Aflora's path just to appease her other mates.

"Fate of events," Kols repeated, his voice holding a mocking quality. "What are you, a Fortune Fae now?"

I merely smiled. "Do I look like a Fortune Fae?"

He scoffed. "You do love your—"

"Aflora!" Ella ran into the room, her blue eyes rimmed with relief. "Thank God you're okay."

God, I thought. *How human.*

Ella stopped short at seeing Kols's death grip on Aflora's arm, her expression going from relieved to livid in less than a second. "Let her go, jackass," she snapped.

Both his eyebrows flew upward. "Excuse me?"

She poked him in the chest, her petite form raging. "It

wasn't enough that you destroyed all her things, so now you're going to manhandle her? Fuck you, *Prince.*"

The fiery little Halfling just went up a peg, in my opinion.

"Destroyed my things?" Aflora repeated, her brow furrowing. "What do you mean? He had me locked up, but only for a few hours."

"You didn't tell her about the little tantrum you threw in her bedroom?" Ella sounded like she was ready to kill Kolstov, something I wouldn't mind watching unfold. He'd have a hard time protecting himself, what with her being his twin's mate and all.

How fun, I mused, folding my arms and settling in for the show.

At least until I saw Aflora's lower lip give a subtle wobble as she whispered, "You destroyed my room?"

"Technically, it's my room," he muttered, killing any sense of amusement I felt over the situation. Because that was precisely the wrong thing to say.

"You're un-fucking-believable!" Ella screamed, causing Tray to run out into the living room.

"What the fuck did you do, Kols?" he demanded, looking at his mate in dismay.

But my eyes were on Aflora, on the way she held her head high despite the heartbreak radiating from her eyes. "He's right. It's his room, his suite, his world. What an amazing king you'll be someday, Prince Kolstov. Now, if you wouldn't mind releasing me, I would very much like to take a shower. Assuming I still have a working bathroom that I'm allowed to use."

"Fuck, Aflora. I—"

"You can use mine," Ella cut in, her expression radiating murder. "Let her go, asshole, or I'll make you let her go."

"I suggest you listen to my mate," Tray added, his features as cold as ice.

Kols considered the room before grumbling out a curse and releasing Aflora's arm. "We need to talk," he told her.

"Have a shower and get dressed. We'll talk on our way to Defense Without Magic class."

"And what's she supposed to wear?" Ella asked, arching a light blonde brow. "*You destroyed all her clothes.*"

Aflora flinched.

Kols ground his teeth together in annoyance. "I'll buy her new ones."

"Damn right you will," Ella agreed. "Today. But I'm taking her shopping, not you."

"She has class," Kols argued, his golden irises flaring with power. "And she can't leave the Academy without supervision."

"Then I'll be her 'babysitter.'" Ella was not backing down, and I sort of loved her for it. Aflora needed a strong friend, one capable of keeping up with her own feisty side. It seemed this little pixie of a female was the perfect partner for her.

"She almost killed you in an academic setting, Isabella," Kols reminded her in a harsh tone. "You're not suitable to guard her."

"God, she's not a monster, Kolstov! She doesn't need to be watched twenty-four seven."

"I'm also standing right here, and I'm capable of making my own decisions," Aflora interjected, silencing the room. "I need clothes. If Prince Kolstov doesn't trust me to purchase them by myself, then he can supervise. I'm not afraid. I'm not a damsel. I'm not a threat. But I am tired of this debate. I want to take a shower. And I would really like to eat something at some point, assuming I'm still allowed to eat Prince Kolstov's food."

She issued him a challenging glare with that last comment, and his jaw clenched.

At this point, the guy was going to grind all his teeth into dust by midnight.

"I can make you breakfast while you take a shower," Zeph said.

Aflora looked at him, her blue eyes flaring with power.

"The last time I accepted a gift from you, it paralyzed my powers and I ended up in a dungeon. So, no, thank you. I would rather eat a burning thwomp."

He scoffed. "That's just childish, Aflora."

"You say that like your opinion matters to me." She cocked her head. "It doesn't." She dismissed him in favor of Ella. "May I please use your bathroom?"

"Yep. And you can borrow some of my clothes, too. Then we'll go shopping and have brunch somewhere."

"Again—"

"I'll go with them," Tray said, cutting off his brother's likely complaint about Aflora leaving the Academy without a *guard*.

"Have you all forgotten that you have class today?" Zeph asked, his tone holding an edge to it. "*My* class."

"Oh, I haven't forgotten," Ella quipped, her lips curling. "Consider this our notice that we're taking a free day."

He folded his thick arms over his crisp white button-down shirt. "You can't just take a free day."

"Stop. Just stop." Tray looked between Kols and Zeph, his black eyes simmering with fire. "I don't know what the fuck has gotten into the two of you, but figure it out and fix it. This bullying bullshit isn't you." He refocused on Aflora. "Come on. I'll show you that not all of us are assholes around here."

She gave him a nod, took a step, and then paused before glancing back at me. "Thank you for today," she said softly.

"Anytime," I told her, meaning it. "Actions prove integrity, right?" It was my way of letting her know my offer still stood. All she needed to do was ask, and I'd whisk her back to that field in a heartbeat.

She studied me for a long moment, her gaze filled with distrust. But she nodded in understanding.

That look alone told me she wouldn't request a return visit to our secret place until she possessed an inkling of hope that I might follow through. Which she didn't have at this moment. That gave me a goal to achieve.

I *wanted* her to trust me. To rely on me. To believe I always had her best interests at heart. Because I did. Everything I'd done these last few months was for her; she just couldn't see it because of the way fate had unfolded. But one day, she'd piece together the riddle I'd left for her and finally understand our purpose together.

Our fates were woven together through an event that occurred many, many years before our births.

Telling her wouldn't work.

She had to see it for herself, to learn her path on her own, to accept her destiny in this wicked world.

I'd keep pushing her because I had to. I'd hold her when she cried. I'd cherish her every breath and strengthen her from the shadows.

Because this was only our beginning.

And I refused for us to ever end.

She must have seen some of that knowledge in my expression, because her eyes narrowed just a bit. Then she gave another little nod and turned to follow Ella out of the room.

"Well, that went splendidly," Kols muttered.

"Were you expecting different results from your brutish approach?" I asked him, arching a brow.

"You're the last person I need or want advice from," he replied.

Well, that's just too bad, I thought. *Because I'm about to lay into you anyway, Prince Jackass.*

"You can blame her for the mating bond all you want," I told him, switching topics to the true issue at hand. "However, we all know Elemental Fae bonds require two willing participants to form, especially on that level. But maybe that's your chosen path to leadership—blame others for your faults rather than own them. In which case, I agree with Aflora's commentary about your future rule, *Your Highness.*" I gave him a mock bow with the derogatory words.

Then I glanced at an unamused Zeph.

I couldn't even get started on his issues.

"If you'll both excuse me, I have a class to prepare for. Hopefully, this one won't end in a needless death of a familiar." My comment was pointed at the dick who'd killed Aflora's falcon just because he couldn't control his own yearnings.

And these two idiots thought I was the volatile one.

I shook my head and disappeared into a cloud of smoke before they could reply.

If they didn't get their shit together soon, I'd have to consult my grandmother about the future again. Just to find out what might happen to the end objective if I accidentally killed one or two of Aflora's mates. Because at this point, it was a fair expectation that I might have to end them.

CHAPTER SIX

ZEPH

FUCK.

I knew Aflora would be upset, but I hadn't anticipated it bothering me.

Not like this.

I rubbed my fist over my chest, frowning at the hallway she'd just walked down moments ago with Tray and Ella. Shade's words didn't bother me. Aflora's, however, did.

You say that like your opinion matters to me. It doesn't.

Did she truly mean that? Or was she just being a brat?

I wanted to think it was the latter, but her overall demeanor punctuated the former. She'd *dismissed* us, her distrust evident. "What the hell was I supposed to do?" I wondered out loud. "Tell her the guards were coming?"

Kols's brow furrowed. "What the hell are you talking about?"

"Yesterday. The arrest. Was I supposed to warn her?" I actually wanted to know. Our plan was hasty but solid. We needed her in the choker before the Warrior Bloods captured her, or the Council would sense the mating bonds

39

on her. And that would lead to a whole world of questions we weren't ready to answer. "There hadn't been time to explain."

"We also needed her shock to look real," Kols pointed out. "It was the only way."

I considered that, my frown deepening. "Similar to Shade saying our knowing would have deviated from the path he intended us to walk down." He'd referred to it as fate, but I read through his statement. "Our anger at Shade—"

"Is probably similar to how Aflora feels about us," Kols finished for me.

"Only worse. She was all alone in that cell, uncertain of her fate. And we did nothing to convince her we were doing this to protect her."

"Which explains her hating us now." He palmed the back of his neck, giving the tendons a squeeze before glaring up at the ceiling and shaking his head. "Fuck."

"Yeah," I muttered. "*Fuck.*"

We shared a long look, a thousand words traveling between us without any defined meaning. But the end thought was the same—we had to fix this.

"I need to give her a free pass today," I said.

"And I need to not press the shopping trip issue."

I nodded, agreeing. "I'm giving you a pass today, too, so you can clean up *her* room."

Kols grimaced. "That just came out. I shouldn't have said it."

"Obviously," I deadpanned. "What the fuck is wrong with us? We're not this bad with women."

"It's *her*," Kols growled. "She's… she's…"

"Gorgeous," I suggested.

"Yeah, but it's more than that. She infuriates me just by existing. And not because of anything she's done, she's just so…" He trailed off on another growl.

"Irresistible. Headstrong. Powerful. Forbidden. I can play this game all day, Kols."

His lips twitched. "Sexy. Intelligent. Pretty much perfect, aside from the whole off-limits part."

"She's also ours," I added, arching a brow. "And we're doing a shit job of making her understand what that means." Which, to be fair, was all pretty fucking new. We'd also had the minor detail of her imprisonment to deal with before we could talk to her about what happened in the LethaForest.

"What do you suggest we do to help her along?" Kols asked, a glimmer of amusement brightening his golden irises.

"Well, for starters, we need to convince her to forgive us." Which would be a challenge in and of itself. *I would rather eat a burning thwomp.*

Ouch.

"Yeah, that'll be fun." He ran his fingers through his auburn hair, gripping the ends and blowing out a breath. "I'll start with her room."

"And I'll figure something out." Not only did I have her holding the collar trickery against me, but her falcon's temporary death, too. Both were done with good intentions, albeit harsh ones. Although, I doubted she'd accept the logical reasons.

We'd burned through her trust.

Now we had to earn it back.

Easier said than done.

"I don't recommend breakfast," Kols said, his lips twitching.

"Yeah, clearly not." Maybe I'd try for dinner, just to poke fun at her statement. However, she probably wouldn't find humor in anything I did right now. I also wasn't the humorous sort. "I need to get to class. Maybe I can kick Shade's ass today as a demonstration." Just the notion of it cheered me up considerably.

Kols snorted. "Hit him hard for me."

"That, I can do." Meanwhile, I'd figure out how to fix this with Aflora. Because yeah, my earlier assumption that she'd just get over it was obviously wrong.

And it was going to take a lot more than a meager apology to work my way back into her good graces.

CHAPTER SEVEN

AFLORA

"DON'T I NEED A NEW WAND, TOO?" I asked after the AcaWard figments finished wrapping up all my purchases into boxes. Ella had chosen the expedited shipping method so the items would go directly to the Academy, freeing up our hands for the afternoon.

"Kols didn't destroy your wand," Tray replied, leaning against the wall with a bored expression. "It's impossible to do since they're gifts from the source and conduits of our magic, not actual items. He probably has it somewhere. I'll ask him for it when we get back."

"Oh." I suppressed the urge to grimace for the thousandth time today.

Kols destroyed all my things.

Because he hates me.

Because we're mated.

I swallowed the feelings whirling around in my throat, compliments of my churning stomach. I didn't want Ella or Tray to see the mess I was inside, so I'd spent the better half of our day holding myself together and pretending not to care about what Kols had done.

Yet my heart fractured a little more each time.

Technically, it's my room.

What a lovely reminder of my lack of a place in this world. My presence was deemed temporary, a life to be snuffed out at the earliest sign of trouble.

Except the Council had let me go because Shade doctored the tapes. Which implied Kols had gone along with his explanation.

Why?

I didn't understand their choices. We all knew I was an abomination and a threat, but none of them took the opportunity to turn me in. Maybe because they feared the Council's reaction to our quad-bond.

Frowning, I accepted the cloak hanging before me on some invisible hook and draped it over my shoulders to cover my skirt and blouse combo. My new boots hit me at my knees and added a few inches to my height. The outfit proved suitable for our plans this afternoon, which included food and drinks. Apparently, Tray knew of a little place in the village that catered to all types of fae appetites, not just Midnight Fae. They even carried spritemead on tap.

A little jolt of excitement zipped through me at the reminder, helping to distract me from my more morose thoughts.

Kolstov could rot with the willow stumps for the afternoon.

I had other plans.

Lifting my head high, I looked at Ella and Tray. "I think that's everything."

"All your books have been sent on as well," Tray said, his arm automatically lifting to accommodate Ella as she sidled up to his side.

"Thanks, Nacht." She brushed her mouth against his square jaw, and he caught her mouth with his own for a sweet kiss before nuzzling her neck.

The two of them fit together like two petals on a perfect

flower. My heart gave a little pang that I swiftly ignored, not willing to let my not-so-perfect *mates* sour my mood once more.

I was done moping.

Not that I'd really ever started.

So Kols burned all my things. They weren't even mine to begin with. Just like the room. Let him throw his inferno tantrums and destroy the items his family had bought. Fine. It didn't matter.

They betrayed me. Locked me up. Didn't tell me what the hell was going on.

Okay, also fine. They could play their games with themselves from now on because I was done.

No more mates.

No more dreams.

No more anything.

Totally not practical resolutions, but I'd figure them out. Somehow.

"I need a spritemead," I announced, interrupting Ella and Tray's adorable little moment.

He stopped nibbling her jaw to smirk at me. "Then I know just the place."

The packages all whirled around us in a wave of magic before sailing straight through a solid wall toward whatever enchanted express would take them back to the Academy. Hopefully, they would remain untouched until my return. Not likely, but I'd deal with that later.

Along with all the other issues in my life.

For now, I wanted to indulge my Elemental Fae tastes.

The walk through town revealed a lot of cloak-clad fae wandering the streets in pursuit of a late midnight lunch, just like us. But the tavern Tray led us to wasn't overcrowded with patrons, leaving several booths open near the windows for us to pick from. The wooden tables were dark in color and adorned with candles that illuminated the darker interior. No ceiling lights or lamps, just fire, and the occasional torch near the corner bar.

Slightly spooky, but oddly homey because of the fireplace in the opposite corner lined with bookshelves. A gargoyle crawled up onto our table, his expression bored. "What'll it be?"

"Three spritemeads, please," Ella said. "And some menus."

"Yeah, yeah," the stone creature grumbled before jumping down with a loud crunch as his stone feet met the marble floor.

I winced, thinking that sounded rather painful, but his wings crinkled at his back as he strutted off toward the bar. He seemed to weave pretty easily between the array of high-top tables and stools, so it must not have hurt at all.

"Three spritemeads, hmm?" Tray asked.

"Aflora swears it's good, so we're going to find out."

"I've already tried spritemead," he replied, touching his index finger to the tip of her nose from across the table. He'd chosen one side of the booth, while we shared the opposite bench.

"And is it good?" she pressed.

"I guess you'll find out soon enough." He winked at her. "But I'm getting a proper beer to go with mine."

"Proper beer," she echoed, glancing at me and wrinkling her nose. "He likes human beer from Germany best. I'm not a fan of any of it."

"I'm not a fan of human drinks in general," I replied. "No offense."

"None taken. But hot chocolate is divine."

"On that, I agree." We had our own version as Elemental Fae, but it was similar enough. Just with a few additional spices.

Three pints of spritemead appeared before us on the table with an array of menus cascading across the top. Tray slammed his palm on the top of them to stop the colorful array of papers from flying to the floor, their windy arrival kicking up quite the little tornado across our booth. It disappeared with a flourish, but not before brushing the hair from our faces and leaving us all with a windswept kiss across our foreheads.

"Well, that's different," I breathed.

Tray snorted. "That's a gargoyle being an asshole." He glared over his shoulder at the stone creature in question. "Find a new occupation if you don't want to wait tables."

"Oh, it's my fault. He's in a mood from having to man the counter for me while I whipped up some stir-fry in the back." A woman with long white hair and dark green eyes seemed to appear beside us, her features young yet oddly old at the same time. Like she'd lived a long life and had seen a lot, too. But there wasn't a single wrinkle marring her otherwise lovely face. How interesting.

"Hey, Anrika," Tray drawled, his easy grin creasing into a pair of dimples that seemed to make Ella swoon a little. Or maybe it was the way he seemed to know everyone. He'd addressed all the figments by name in AcaWard as well, despite them being invisible. "How's the family?"

"You mean Seif?" she asked, snorting. "He's reckless and stubborn and just like his father."

"Which is why you adore them both."

"Absolutely." Her expression radiated pride. "But yeah, he's good. I'll tell him you were asking after him. He's been a bit busy lately with his errant Omega. She's giving him hell, which, of course, means I approve."

"Omega?" I repeated, frowning. "Like a Fortune Fae?"

"Yeah, Seif chose the seer life over his dark magic and blood. Crazy, right?" Tray winked at Anrika as he spoke.

I took a sip of my spritemead as Anrika replied, "He's always had a mind of his own, that one. But Gina'll be a good match once he calms her down."

I coughed, the liquid going down the wrong pipe, causing Ella to thump me on the back. Three sets of eyes looked at me in confusion, Tray arching a brow. "Not up to your standards, princess?"

"No, not that," I managed to say, my voice hoarse from the drink flowing in an inappropriate direction. I cleared my throat twice before asking, "Gina?"

"Yeah, that's his reluctant mate's name. I've not met her yet. Why? The name mean something to you?"

The vision of a coffee shop and a dark-haired Fortune Fae sprang into my mind. *Gina,* she'd told me. Just before adding something about our paths crossing as a happenstance of fate.

"It's going to be an interesting year for you, Aflora," she'd said.

I hadn't thought much of it at the time.

But now…

"You're in his thoughts now, after all."

I blinked and found all three of them staring at me expectantly. "Uh, I may have met a Fortune Fae named Gina recently. In a coffee shop in the Human Realm."

"Huh, well, I'll be," Anrika murmured, a distant gleam giving her that elderly aura once more. Such a strange contrast to her otherwise youthful features. Like her age was somehow trapped in a young Midnight Fae form.

Of course, all the Midnight Fae appeared young. They stopped physically aging in their twenties. This woman could be thousands of years old. Perhaps that was the reason I caught such an ancient quality to her appearance.

It would probably be rude to ask, so I didn't.

"You're Aflora," she said suddenly, that odd aura disappearing in a flash, replaced by her young self once more. "Ah, yes, I've heard all about you."

"From Gina?" I asked, slightly taken aback by her age-shifting trick. *Am I the only one seeing that?*

"Oh, no. From a very old friend." Her eyes sparkled. "I'm most excited to have you here, sweetheart. And I imagine you're in the mood for something from home, yes?"

A very old friend? I wondered. However, she'd asked me a question. Etiquette dictated I needed to answer that first. "Yes, please. I would love a proper sandwich."

"I have just what you're looking for," she beamed. "Wings for Tray, yes?"

"Always."

I almost asked what wings were, when Anrika asked, "And what about you, Ella darling? Wings, too?"

"Sure. It's been a while since I had some good buffalo sauce."

"Anrika's wings are the best," Tray vowed.

"Yeah?" A glimmer of humor entered Ella's gaze. "All right. I trust you."

Anrika clapped her hands, causing the menus to disappear before we ever had a chance to read them. "I'll be back in a shuffle," she announced, vanishing into a cloud of glitter that left me coughing in her wake.

Tray laughed.

As did Ella. "Well, she's fun. Why haven't you brought me here before if her wings are so amazing?"

"Because we've been on our tour of chicken around the kingdoms, Isabella. I had to save the best for last."

"Uh-huh." She gave him a fond look before glancing at me. "He has a thing for chicken wings. It goes back to our very first date, actually."

"Ah, that was a fun night. Your first visit to the Midnight Fae realm."

"Fun? I wanted to kill you that night."

"But you didn't. You even let me kiss you. Twice."

Ella grumbled something unflattering at him before adding, "I didn't like Tray much when we first met. He was kind of a dick."

Tray snorted. "She misunderstood my intentions."

"Because you were an asshole."

He lifted a shoulder. "My plan worked in the end, didn't it? You're mine."

"Yeah, yeah," she scoffed, rolling her big blue eyes. But I caught the happiness radiating beneath her expression, her absolute joy at having him in her life.

They really were a fine couple.

Very unlike me and my mates.

Whom I refused to think about.

49

No. No. No.

"So her son is a Fortune Fae?" Ella asked Tray, providing a fantastic distraction from my mind. "Like one of the Midnight Fae Alphas I learned about last year?"

"Yep. He chose to abstain from blood and magic all his life and turned Fortune Fae as a result. An Alpha, as you said. Fangs and all." He bared his teeth at Ella, causing her to snort.

"Still don't understand why you *vampires* don't have fangs," she muttered.

"Actually, I've never understood that either," I admitted. "Anatomically speaking, it makes sense since Midnight Fae drink blood."

"Exactly," Ella said, waving a hand in finality.

"Our incisors are sharp enough without the additional fang point," Tray drawled.

"Yet Midnight Fae males who don't drink blood end up getting fangs as a Fortune Fae Alpha. Yeah, that makes sense." The way Ella said it implied it didn't make sense at all. Which I agreed with her on. Then again, I had pointed ears and that seemed silly, too. They served no purpose, and I heard just as well as any other fae.

"Fortune Fae are a different breed of puzzles," Tray murmured.

"So what happens to female Midnight Fae who reject their dark source?" Ella asked, frowning. "We never covered that in class."

"Because they become Norms," he replied. "Not as exciting."

"What's a Norm?" Ella asked.

A type of Fortune Fae, I thought, while Tray dove into a political lesson that more than intrigued his mate. She peppered him with questions that took up the majority of our meal, which was fine by me. I sat by and listened while I enjoyed my sandwich—which was indeed a proper one with shrooms and all the fixings. Anrika brought me a second spritemead without asking if I wanted one, giving me a wink before disappearing into glitter once more. The magic reminded me a bit of Shade's, only he preferred the dark smog to happy confetti.

I sipped my drink while thinking about him and his promise before he left.

Anytime.

A hopeful part of me wanted to believe that he meant it. The intelligent part of me refused.

None of the guys could be trusted.

That much I knew with certainty.

Yet, Shade had given me a glimpse of home today. Had even coached me a bit on how to handle my collar.

Not the signs of a male who wanted to hurt me.

"Ready?" Tray asked, drawing me from my thoughts. "It's an hour before dawn, and Kols is probably ready to come find us."

I glanced out the windows and noticed the mostly vacant streets.

"Oh." I hadn't realized how late it'd gotten. We'd spent a good chunk of the midnight hours in this tavern, indulging in food and conversation. And spritemead. "I would very much like to come back here." *Wait...* I wanted to find out what Anrika had meant about her old friend.

I glanced around for the woman and frowned at the empty surroundings. "Ah, we're the last ones here."

"Yeah, Anrika closed up an hour ago," Tray said with a chuckle. "She left right after giving you that last mug of spritemead. Told her irritated pet to see us out." He gestured with his chin toward the stone-faced gargoyle standing absolutely still by the door. All eighteen inches of him seemed to bristle with irritation without actually moving. Impressive.

"Pet," it muttered, the stones grating with astute annoyance. "Leave."

Tray smirked. "Sure."

We exited the booth, and Tray bent to pat the little gargoyle on the head. "Have a good night, little guy."

The thing growled in reply, the sound far more ferocious than any being that size should be able to make. Ella squeaked and practically shoved Tray out into the cool air of the night, with me right behind them.

He bent over laughing, clearly having indulged in more than a few beers and spritemeads combined.

Oh, but we all had.

What a fun night.

I actually felt warm. Sort of like I was floating on a cloud. I started to hum as we walked, the song one my mother taught me long ago. A sad little ballad with words I didn't quite understand, but ones I'd memorized nonetheless.

It wasn't until I hit the second verse that I realized both Ella and Tray were gaping at me. "What?" I asked, my cheeks heating at their open perusal. "My voice isn't that bad."

"No, it's the song. It's haunting," Ella whispered.

"It's forbidden," Tray corrected. "Where did you learn those words?"

"What?" I asked, startled by his sudden vehemence. "How could a children's ballad be forbidden?"

"Because you're singing about spells used to realign the source," he replied, glancing around as if to make sure no one else heard. "We need to go." He moved with urgency toward the cloakroom I'd used with Zeph a little over two months ago during my first week in this realm. Only, we all already wore our cloaks this time because of the cooler weather.

Tray activated the portal and took us directly to the crow field at the Academy.

A few students watched our arrival with interest but didn't stand in our way or try to speak with us. Which was good because Tray didn't appear in the mood for conversation. He practically stormed down the obsidian sidewalk, past the burning thwomps and bare bushes, ignoring all the writhing snakes along the various posts and fences, and led us up the stairs into the Elite Residence.

The doors parted with a flourish, not needing a code because of whatever Tray did with his hand. And up the master staircase we went to the third floor.

"What's wrong with you?" Ella demanded as we approached the gargoyle at the end of the hall. Apparently, Kols had undone whatever spell Shade had cast over the creature. Its beady red eyes glared upon seeing me, as if blaming me for the earlier incident.

Join the club, I thought at it. *Everyone in this place seems to think I'm at fault for something.*

"We'll talk in the suite," Tray muttered, his voice holding an edge to it.

Ella frowned at him. "Fine."

Great.

There went my happy evening. All because of a song. I shook my head and followed them inside, ready to face whatever else waited to be thrown my way. Because at this point, what was one more mark on my record?

CHAPTER EIGHT

KOLS

I GLARED DOWN AT THE MESSAGE from Emelyn, not in the mood to deal with her bullshit. Alas, I had no choice but to appease the bitch. I couldn't risk her finding out I mate-bonded Aflora. Not because I cared about Emelyn's emotional reaction—which, I imagined, would be violent considering I was supposed to mate *her*, not Aflora—but because I knew Emelyn would go straight to her father with the information.

And he would go to my father.

Sighing, I typed out a response regarding her outfit question and hit Send. Then added, *Not that we're going together*. Because no, we were not attending the Blood Gala as a couple.

Talk to your father, she replied. *He's the one mandating we make a public appearance, Prince.*

I rolled my eyes because I heard the derisive snort on the end of that sentence. *Consider it done. We're not going.*

Good, she shot back.

Good, I repeated at her.

Then I put my phone down on the coffee table and ran my fingers through my hair. "Fuck," I muttered, exhausted. My father had been trying to force my hand with Emelyn Jyn for several years. Neither of us was keen on the arrangement, nor did we have much say in it.

Her father, Lima, was Malik Nacht's right-hand man. They'd established the agreement between our families years ago, deciding that crossing the birth lines would produce one hell of an heir.

Sure, Emelyn and I would create a powerful child.

But that required us to fuck, which would never happen.

She despised me almost as much as I despised her. And there was only one female I wanted in my bed right now—the one walking through the door with my brother and his mate. Mmm, I loved her legs in that skirt and boots combo. But I didn't particularly care for the wary expression upon finding me sitting in the living area.

Aflora was not going to forgive me easily. I hadn't betrayed her trust, at least not intentionally. However, her blue eyes said I'd destroyed every bridge we'd built, landing me near the top of her dislike list.

I cleared my throat and stood. "Your packages arrived and have been put away."

"By you?" she asked, sounding displeased at the prospect.

"Yes, but you can reorganize however you want."

She lifted her chin a notch upward, lengthening her regal neck. "I will."

Yep. Definitely not going to forgive me anytime soon.

Tray cleared his throat before I could reply, not that I really had a response. "Aflora, sing again."

My brow furrowed at the bizarre request. "What?"

"Quiet," he snapped at me, focusing on my gorgeous mate instead. "Sing again."

She cleared her throat. "It's just a ballad my mom taught me."

He nodded. "And I want Kols to hear it. Please."

Uh... I looked at Ella for an explanation, but her concerned gaze was on Aflora. My mate twisted her hands in front of her and cleared her throat. Then she began to hum, and I swore my heart stopped at the hypnotic sound.

I gaped at her, amazed by the sweet notes leaving her mouth. *Ballad* was an understatement. Aflora resembled a siren, her voice tugging at my very soul.

Mine, I thought. *This beautiful creature is mine.*

Except she hated me at the moment.

We weren't supposed to be together.

And our little mating quad might end up killing us all in the end.

Minor details.

I nearly snorted at my mental gymnastics, only Tray's intense expression caught my attention. He was trying to tell me something with his gaze. I frowned, not understanding.

Aflora was a gifted singer. So what?

Except then her words began to register.

The ancient language she spoke was one I'd only heard in whispers throughout my upbringing. It was an ancient dialect of Midnight Fae that supposedly died with the Quandary Bloods.

The Council had maintained hints of the spells in our historical documents. Particularly, the most violent of potential enchantments.

Which was what she uttered now—a string of promises to realign the source through an incantation only Quandary Bloods understood. It sounded so hypnotically beautiful coming from her mouth. I could almost feel myself slipping into her thrall, willing her to carry out the threat lurking behind her bewitching melody.

"Aflora," I breathed, stepping toward her as if to pull her into my arms.

But then the music stopped, and her blue eyes clouded over in distrust, her own feet carrying her backward and into Ella's side.

I blinked. *Right.* Tray and Ella didn't know about my attachment to Aflora. And I needed to keep it that way to protect them, because if they found out about what happened the other night, they'd be forced to speak to the Council or face severe punishments for conspiring to hide us.

This whole thing was a fucking mess.

"Who taught you that song?" Tray demanded, his dark gaze hard.

Aflora swallowed. "My mother did, many years ago."

Tray glanced at me, his brown brow cocked upward. I stared back at him, telling him with my expression that I'd handle it. This was my job, not his. I'd go to Exos and Cyrus, see if they could give me some history on her background. The Earth Fae she grew up with was part of their mating circle. Maybe he'd know something useful.

"How could Aflora know a forbidden song about the realignment of power?" Ella asked, telling me that Tray had explained what the song meant before they arrived. Great. I hoped he was at least quiet about it.

"Maybe her mother heard it from someone," I suggested, thinking on my feet. "And she didn't understand the meaning, so she hummed it to Aflora as a little girl. The Elemental Fae wouldn't recognize it, so her mother wouldn't have thought much of it."

"Sure. That's one theory," Tray said, still looking at me.

I dared him with my gaze to voice another. The tick in his jaw told me he wanted to, but not in front of Ella and Aflora. Likely because his speculation would be damning to my mate. Not that he knew we'd mated.

Well, he suspected it.

While he hadn't expressly admitted it, I knew he was aware that I'd slept with Aflora. My twin had taken one look at the aftermath of her room, glowered at me, and stalked off. There was really only one thing that could have made me react like that, and it'd come from a very emotional place, brought on by sleeping with Aflora.

I only hoped he didn't suspect the bond, or we'd be in a world of hurt. Not because I didn't trust him, but because he'd end up risking himself and Ella to protect my actions. And I couldn't let him suffer on my behalf.

I cleared my throat. "Look. It's been a long fucking night. Hell, it's been a long fucking week. We can worry about the song later. Just... don't hum or repeat the words in public, yeah?" That part was directed at Aflora.

She nodded in reply, then pulled her cloak around her like a blanket. Or maybe she considered it a shield. Regardless, there wasn't much we could do right now. I explained that to Tray with another look, one he conceded to with a nod.

Then I refocused on Aflora. "Come on. I want to show you what I did to your room." I didn't wait for her to acknowledge my request, just turned and headed to the hallway off to the left of the living area.

I passed the study area, guest room, and Tray's quarters and paused at Aflora's upgraded door. She appeared a minute later, her shoulders bowed a little as she met me alone in the corridor. Ella had probably told her to yell if I caused any trouble.

Given the tension in the air, that wouldn't take much.

With a whispered spell, I called for the new key I'd created earlier and sent it to hover in front of her. Her blue irises swirled with power as she studied it. "What's this?"

"Your key," I told her. "It's programmed to recognize your magic. I tied it to your wand, which is on your bed inside."

"Why do I need a key?"

"Because I put a lock on your door, and that"—I gestured to the ornate metal rotating in the air between us—"is the only thing that can open it."

Her ebony lashes flickered. "You made me a lock?"

"Yes."

"One you can't override?" She sounded disbelieving.

"Yes," I repeated. "I never should have said it was my

room. An excuse won't make up for it, so instead, all I'll say is I'm sorry and I hope you'll accept my apology in the form of reinforced privacy."

She gaped at me. "You're apologizing?"

"Yes," I said for a third time.

"Really?"

"Do you want me to go onto my knees, too?" I asked her. "Beg a little?"

Her lips twitched. "Actually—"

"No." The only way I'd kneel for her was if she spread her legs and welcomed my tongue between her thighs. I allowed her to see that knowledge in my gaze, the very real fire burning inside me just for her. *My mate.*

Fuck, that was going to take some getting used to.

Yet I couldn't deny how right it felt between us. Maybe because of her Elemental Fae influence. We were level-three bonded, which, in her world, made it pretty fucking permanent. As did my bite as a Midnight Fae.

Yeah, Aflora and I were tied together indefinitely.

Whether we liked it or not.

Her vibrant eyes held mine for a beat, then she swallowed and grabbed the key to try it in the door. Magic hummed around us, the mechanism searching out Aflora's identity before allowing her entry. "It's similar to a gargoyle but without the added nuisance," I explained softly.

"What happens if I misplace the key?" she asked as the wood whispered open.

"There's a spell you can use to call it to you, like the one I just recited." I spoke the incantation again, this time slower, and she murmured it back to me, which caused her key to jump out of the door and hover in front of her face again.

She smiled at it. "That's handy."

"I'm glad you approve."

Her amusement dimmed a little, whether at my words or the thought of entering her room, I wasn't sure. But I suspected it was the latter when she steeled her spine and stepped through the threshold. I waited by the entrance, not wanting to disrupt her perusal of the room.

She set her key on the nightstand, admired the new bed, draped her cloak over the blue comforter—the same shade as her eyes—and then focused on the shimmering magic near her window.

I waited for her reaction, unsure of what she'd think of the enhancement. "What is this?" she asked, squatting down beside the makeshift pot.

"It's, uh, a gift," I replied, palming the back of my neck. "Our flowers and general vegetation are a bit different here, but Mistress Marigold said this will bloom with a fairy plant if properly cared for. And so, I bought you one." It seemed lame now, like some sort of lackluster apology present. But it'd felt right when I was working on redecorating the room.

"Mistress Marigold?" Aflora glanced at me. "Who's that?"

"One of the Academy caretakers." I swallowed the lump growing in my throat, irritated by its presence. Since when did I feel nervous around females?

Ridiculous.

With a shake of my head, I focused on my surroundings instead of on Aflora.

"Mistress Marigold is in charge of the residence halls. After I finished cleaning everything up in here, I consulted with her on ways to make it a little more Elemental Fae friendly. She suggested the plant. So I ordered it. But if you don't like it, I can take it back. Actually, if there's anything you don't like, just let me know. I'll return it. This is your space. You choose."

And, wow, since when did I fucking ramble?

This chick was giving me a headache just by existing.

I winced. Yeah. Not the best thought. Right. "I'm going to bed," I announced. Some sleep would help me sort out my behavior. Maybe a hand job, too. With thoughts of Aflora.

Ah, fuck. Just the notion of it had me hardening in my

pants. *This mating business sucks!*

"Kols!" she called after me. I'd already gotten to the door of my room, my feet carrying me away from her as if I were running from a fire.

I paused and didn't look at her. "Yeah?"

"Thank you," she whispered, the two words making me cringe.

I didn't do this for her gratitude. I did this because... well, I couldn't say why I went through all the trouble I did today other than I wanted to make it up to her. An apology of sorts to right a handful of wrongs. And I doubted I'd even achieved that. But at least she seemed to like it.

Rather than reply, I just nodded, not trusting myself to speak, and disappeared into my quarters.

I needed some sleep.

Tomorrow, I'd dig into her past.

Starting by meeting with a pair of Elemental Fae Kings.

I sent a notification off to Cyrus, knowing it might be a few hours before he caught it. His kind weren't as big into technology as Midnight Fae, but someone would pass along my request.

Then we'd chat.

Likely in the Human Realm.

At least I'd get some much-needed blood. Sex, not so much.

I winced and picked up my phone again and shot Zeph a text. *Celibacy isn't my thing.*

His response arrived a minute later. *No shit.*

Come over. He would know why I sent the text.

Just as I understood his response. *Be there in five.*

Playing with each other didn't break any mating rules, particularly as we were all set in this quad together. Besides, if Aflora wanted to come over and join us, we'd both be game. But something told me it would be a while before she'd even consider the opportunity.

Which meant we would just need to work that much harder to convince her.

I always did adore a challenge, especially a forbidden one. As did Zeph. Together we'd break her resolve. Not just in her dreams, but also in her bed, with our mouths and tongues and hands. Until she couldn't stand the thought of breathing without us. And then we'd truly make her ours.

Because fuck the consequences.

Aflora was already mine.

CHAPTER NINE

AFLORA

I SAT IN MY MIDNIGHT FAE POLITICS CLASSROOM, trying to ignore the whispers around me.

Everyone knew about my arrest, but the reasons behind it were all wrong.

Some said I attacked Kols.

Others claimed I'd lost my shit after Zeph killed Clove, and stated I tried to burn down the Elite Residence.

"Kolstov is fine," I heard someone say behind me in response to someone else's comment about me trying to kill him. "Altrina saw him in the Human Realm last night, working his magic on a pair of mortals."

My teeth clenched. *Is that where he ran off to?* I wondered.

I hadn't seen him since the night he gave me the key to my renovated room. Not that I'd really gone looking for him. I needed a few days just to decompress and was thankful my mates had allowed me the time alone. But when I woke up for classes and heard from Ella that Kols still wasn't back, I'd begun to wonder where he went.

Is he meeting with the Council about me?

Has he told his father about our mating?

Is he trying to find a way to undo what happened?

The thoughts had run rampant through my mind, making me uneasy and distrusting. I kept waiting for a horde of Warrior Bloods to descend upon the Academy and take me back to that dungeon. However, the primary assault I'd received so far was in the form of rumors.

And now this.

"Sounds like Kols," another girl replied. "I swear he's fucked his way through half the mortal population."

"Well, if I had my fate promised to a chick like Emelyn, I'd do the same." That came from a male in the back of the room.

"You could only be so lucky, Slag," a prim female sniped with a flip of her long blonde hair over her shoulder. "And if I were Emelyn, I wouldn't want to be anywhere near Prince Kolstov's cock. He's a walking disease. I hear he even fucks Halflings."

Someone snorted. "You're confusing Kols with Tray."

"Oh, no, it's a Nacht family tradition at this point." The prim fae practically purred the words, her penchant for cruelty written into the sharp angles of her too-perfect face. "I mean, Tray took the Halfling human mutt as his mate, and his brother has no doubt fucked the Elemental abomination. To each his own, I suppose."

"Aw, are you not getting enough dick in your life, Justine?" Ella asked, her expression one of mock concern. "Is that why you have to focus on others? Live vicariously through those you envy? That's a shame."

A flicker of magic singed the air, but Ella caught it easily with her wand and returned it to the sender just as our headmaster entered.

"Isabella Cinder!" Headmaster Vayera snapped, her cloak billowing around her in a flurry of annoyance. "What do you think you're doing?"

"Practicing defensive arts," Ella replied, not at all contrite.

"Not in my classroom, you're not." Headmaster Vayera pointed to the door with a sharp black nail. "Out."

"It was one spell," Ella argued.

"*Out!*" she shouted, not bothering to give Ella a chance to explain.

"Ella was just protecting herself," I interjected. "Justine started it."

"I did not!" the blonde perfectionist fae retorted, sounding affronted.

"Oh, come on," Slag drawled. "We all saw you send that firefly at the Halfling. Aflora's right, Headmaster. Ella was just protecting herself."

Headmaster Vayera pulsed with irritation, her beady blue eyes searching the room. "Anyone else care to add to this delightful discussion?"

"Ella insulted—"

"That was a rhetorical question, Corrine," Headmaster Vayera cut in, then took out her wand to wave it through the air with a muttered spell. Thick texts landed on each of our desks, all opening to various sections littered with legal jargon.

Groans filtered through the air.

"You will read and decipher each point, then present your section to the class by midnight. There will be no break today, as it's clear you all enjoyed your fresh air a little too much yesterday and the day before. We'll have a quiz instead that will cover all of the presentations, so I suggest you pay attention and be thorough in your translation."

Ugh, academic punishment, I thought glancing down at my section regarding Paradox Fae time manipulation laws. This wasn't even related to Midnight Fae at all. Well, except for the bit about how it was illegal to work with a Paradox Fae to change a timeline. But that was the case in all the realms.

I blew out a breath that turned into a vibration between my lips. Ella snorted in response.

And so began our very long day of reading, deciphering, and articulating into essay form. Because yeah, that was the test method Headmaster Vayera selected.

"She's just evil," Ella said as we entered the residence hall several hours later.

Tray stood waiting for her at the stairs, his eyebrow cocking upward at her statement. "Who?"

"Headmaster Vayera." Ella drew out the *a* on a long groan. "She made us read Midnight Fae ordinances, Tray. Then she quizzed us on it afterward, and it was awful."

His lips quirked upward. "Sounds like my childhood."

"Ugh, not the same." She walked into his open arms and accepted his hug. "It felt like law school," she mumbled into his chest. "Not that I've been, but it's the hell I imagined."

"Mmm," he hummed, holding her close and kissing the top of her head. "Need me to make it better, baby?"

And that was my cue to keep moving. "You two have fun," I called, racing up the steps to the third floor and heading toward the gargoyle at the end.

"Sir Kristoff," I greeted.

"Abomination," he returned in his chilly tone. It didn't help that the stones churned together in his mouth every time he spoke.

At least he allowed me to enter. I suspected if he had a choice, he'd close off all the doors and keep me trapped in a room with no entrance or exit. Similar to his *master*.

I scowled at the memory of the Council dungeon and moved through the threshold into the suite. Kols and Zeph were inside, their attention snapping to me as their conversation came to a halt.

"Don't stop talking on my account," I said, noting Kols's flushed appearance.

Blood, I realized. *It's from drinking blood.* Zeph had the same look about him, suggesting they'd both gone into the Human Realm for a snack. And probably sex.

Fine.

Just fine.

We were mates, but we hadn't discussed anything about

being committed. I mean, they betrayed me not twelve hours after biting me. So. What did that say about our *bond?*

I snorted and stomped off to my room, not wanting to talk to either of them. If they wanted to seek pleasure elsewhere, I couldn't stop them. I didn't even want to sleep with them anyway.

At least I knew why my dreams were vacant the last few nights. It wasn't out of respect for me or their way of giving me time. No, they were too busy playing with mortal females and using them for blood and pleasure.

My bedroom door slammed behind me.

"Not my business," I muttered to myself.

Who was I to even judge anyway? I had three mates. There was one of me. Of course, I wouldn't be enough to satisfy them. Not that they'd bothered to try. But I didn't want them to anyway, so this worked out well for all parties involved. They could mess around and leave me alone, and maybe we'd find a way to break this link between us.

I was a Quandary Blood, right? My gift literally unraveled magic. Why not try it on the mating connection?

I hung my cloak in my closet and stared at my reflection in the mirror Kols had affixed to the back of the door.

"What's the point of any of this?" I asked myself. "Why am I even here?"

Because Shade had bitten me.

I narrowed my gaze.

Shade.

I hadn't heard from him in a few days either. Had he joined the guys in their little human orgy? Doubtful. So where was he? Why hadn't he reached out?

"Stop it," I chastised myself while taking off my blouse and skirt. "Just. Stop."

The guys didn't matter. My future did. Whatever that meant.

I put on a pair of flannel shorts and a soft white T-shirt, then shut the closet and walked over to flop onto my bed. "Enough," I muttered into my pillow. "Enough. Enough.

Enough."

CHAPTER TEN

ZEPH

I CLEARED MY THROAT, attempting to dispel some of the tension in the air caused by Aflora's abrupt entrance and subsequent exit.

"She's still pissed," Kols noted, vying for the role of Captain Obvious.

"She needs to get over it," I replied. "We gave her three days to cool off. Now she's just acting like a brat."

Kols gave me a look. "We destroyed her trust."

"By protecting her," I pointed out.

"But she doesn't get that."

"Because she's being a brat and choosing not to talk to us. Instead, she's stomping around and throwing a fit." As if she overheard me, a door slammed from her room, causing me to roll my eyes. "It's as though she wants me to spank her."

Kols grunted. "Yeah, good luck with that."

"She'd be wet for me in a second and you know it."

"And she'd hate you every step of the way." Kols shook his head. "Seriously, we fucked up. It's going to take time to fix that."

"Something we don't have on our side."

"Well, tell her that," Kols said, gesturing to the hallway. "Let me know how it goes."

I huffed out a breath. It would go well until she came all over my cock. Then she'd go right back to hating me. While the former would be enjoyable, the latter wouldn't help us move forward.

My elbows fell to my thighs as I leaned forward. "This is ridiculous. All we've done is to help her."

"She doesn't see it that way."

"Clearly." And while I could admit to some fault in the matter of the approach, she wasn't exactly giving us a chance to explain.

Or maybe I hadn't tried hard enough to be heard.

Or really at all, I thought to myself.

But that wasn't the point. "Tell me what Sol said." Kols had been in the middle of detailing his meeting with the Elemental Fae when Aflora stomped into the room. I'd been about to suggest she join us for the discussion, but her little temper tantrum reaction to seeing us in the living area had me biting my tongue.

Kols cleared his throat. "Right. Well, first, he threatened to kill me."

"You told him about the mating?"

"No. He sensed it. Not sure he approves."

I smirked. "I bet not. But he can't do anything about it."

"That's exactly what I said. Then I asked him to help me help her."

"And?"

"He told me to fuck off." Kols picked up his beer and took a long swig. "So Cyrus stepped in and reminded Sol how I helped them with their Chancellor problem by providing dark-magic texts. And Exos commented on how working together would only help Aflora, not hurt her. As her Earth mate, I'm duty-bound to protect her and yada yada, so eventually Sol caved."

He stood up to retrieve his suit jacket and pulled something from the pocket. "These are Aflora's parents." He handed me an old-fashioned-painting-styled photograph, one depicting a couple staring down at the baby in the female's arms.

"Is that baby Aflora?"

"Yep." Kols snagged his beer bottle by the neck and enjoyed another swallow while remaining on his feet.

I studied the photo. "She looks so much like her mother." Gorgeous. Dark hair. Pale complexion. Beautiful smile. I felt my own lips curve at the sight, my heart warming a little at an innocent Aflora being loved on by her parents. Did they know then what a powerful child they'd created? I imagined they did.

"Do you recognize them?" Kols asked.

I studied both parents and slowly shook my head. "No. Should I?"

"No. I was just curious."

"Wouldn't you already know what they look like through all your royal training?" I meant the question earnestly. Kols had grown up studying fae politics. Surely he'd seen a photo of the Elemental Fae royals at some point.

"Elemental Fae are not known for capturing photos. They prefer to live life and enjoy the moment, and they balk at technology."

"So why did her parents have a photo?"

"Exactly," Kols replied, collapsing in the recliner once more. "Sol said that a lot of things about Aflora's childhood were abnormal, including that photo. And when I asked him about the ballad, he recognized it. Aflora used to hum it often when she was younger, usually in moments of happiness."

"But he didn't recognize it otherwise?"

"Nope. None of them had ever heard it before, so it's not like some Elemental Fae nursery rhyme."

"Well, that's something at least." It would cause a lot of

political strife if our kind found out that the little Elemental Fae were running around humming about how to realign the source of dark magic.

"It's still troubling, and what I dislike even more is that Sol couldn't tell me anything about Aflora's grandparents. She's a descendant of the royal Earth Fae line. How do they not know anything about those who came before her parents?"

I frowned. "Do they not believe in keeping records, in addition to their dislike of technology?"

Kols snorted. "I asked the same thing. Sol didn't appreciate the comment."

"It's a fair statement."

"I agree, as did Cyrus. He felt it very strange that not much is known about the Earth Fae royal line. They rely so much on whom the source has favored that they don't focus much beyond that. And while they know the names of her ancestors, they couldn't say much about them. Everyone who would have known them died in the plague that abomination caused."

"Their former Chancellor?" I asked, seeking clarification. There were several abominations throughout our history, but she was the latest to cause issues among the realms.

"Yeah. Elana."

I considered that. "Do you think she took out the Earth Fae on purpose?" I wondered out loud. "I mean, she targeted their element first. What if she did it to erase the history?"

"Why attack Aflora as a girl, then?"

"To cover up her actions?" I suggested.

Kols finished his beer in silence, contemplating my comments. Then his head bobbed side to side slowly. "Doesn't feel right."

While I agreed with his assessment, I still said, "But it's worth keeping in mind."

"True." He set his empty bottle on the end table. "All

right. So we know she has Quandary Blood in her. We know her lineage doesn't have great records. And we know her powers are unraveling."

"She feels grounded right now," I replied, sensing my mate-bond with her. It tugged at my heart a little, mostly because I could feel her displeasure. Knowing I helped cause that emotion irked me. But I couldn't change anything we'd done. It was all to keep her safe, whether she realized that or not.

"She does," Kols agreed. "We need to keep her that way."

"Is that why you fed while in the Human Realm?" I asked, arching a brow.

"You're just as well fed as I am."

"I ordered a catering service," I admitted. Digesting food infused with blood wasn't the same as feeding from a neck, but it did the trick and rejuvenated my magic.

"How was it?" Kols asked, genuine curiosity in his gaze.

"Different. Not nearly as enjoyable as biting Aflora."

His lips curled. "I doubt much is as enjoyable as biting Aflora."

"Did you think of her while you fed?"

"No. I didn't want to make it intimate, and feeding without sex is hard enough already."

I nodded, understanding. "Did you just enchant them?"

"Pretty much. They'll have a memory of a heavy make-out session that left them light-headed afterward." He lifted a shoulder. "There were a few other Midnight Fae roaming about, so I created a glamour for them as well. Have to keep up appearances and all that."

"It worked," I told him. "I overheard a few of them gossiping about it outside."

"Good." Then he frowned. "Do you think it got back to Aflora?"

"Probably."

"Do you think it'll bother her?"

"That her mate was seen in the Human Realm fucking

around with mortals?" I asked. "Would it bother you if we heard Aflora was doing that?"

He scowled. "She doesn't need blood."

"What about sex?"

"Are you trying to piss me off?" he demanded.

"No, I'm trying to get you to see the obvious, idiot," I replied. "Your reaction right now is your answer."

He started to snap something back, only to pause, then he growled in annoyance. "Fuck."

"Yeah." I understood because I wouldn't like hearing that about Aflora at all. In fact, I'd probably find the human who dared to touch her, and kill him. She might not feel like she was mine yet, but that didn't make it any less true. I claimed her the moment my incisors met the plump flesh of her breasts. She just hadn't accepted it yet.

"I suppose that's another apology for my list," Kols muttered.

"Maybe we should just give her a dozen orgasms instead. Most women prefer that to flowers."

Kols snorted. "She's an Earth Fae. You know she prefers the flowers."

"Only because she doesn't know any better," I mused, finally taking a sip of my own beer. "I'll happily show her when she's ready."

"In her dreams?" He sounded hopeful, but I turned him down with a look.

"No more dreams for her. Not until we've worked this all out." It was what I'd said the other night, and I stood by it. We needed our mate to trust us before I could continue her sexual education. Otherwise, I risked pushing her too far, and I didn't want to chance harming our already fractured bond.

"Ugh," Kols groaned, his head falling back against the chair. "You have no idea how much I want to fuck right now."

"You always want to fuck," I pointed out. "And I'm very aware of that."

He grunted. "Dick."

"Not a good way to woo me into some temporary relief, Kolstov."

"I'm not getting on my knees again," he said, glancing at me. His reference to the other night in his room had my lips quirking upward in amusement.

"Then I guess you're not getting fucked," I replied.

"I said I want to fuck, not be fucked."

"Semantics."

"You're an ass," he chastised, standing up and tossing his bottle into a nearby trash can. "I'm having a date with my hand tonight. You can fuck off."

"Enjoy," I murmured, not moving from the couch.

"You can go now."

"I'm good."

He shook his head and grumbled a curse under his breath, then focused on the kitchen. "Leftover pizza?" he asked, changing the subject.

"Sure."

"Good."

I watched as he worked, the banter between us reminding me of an easier time between us—a time I wasn't sure we'd ever experience again. However, as he pulled a box out of the refrigerator and slid the contents onto a tray, I started to entertain the notion of a different kind of future. One where we were friends like before, only closer.

Because of Aflora.

Or maybe it would all go up in flames and burn us all to the ground.

I rubbed a hand over my face and shut my eyes, the vision of a dark-haired beauty with cerulean magic flashing in my mind.

What am I going to do with you? I thought at her, aware that she couldn't actually hear me. That wasn't how the initial bond stages worked. I could sense her and manipulate her dreams with magic, but I couldn't yet access her mind.

Soon, though.

Soon.

CHAPTER ELEVEN

AFLORA

I STARED AT THE BLACK ROSE on my seat before glancing across the room at Shade. He winked and returned to his conversation with one of the other Death Bloods. Then the flower disappeared into a purple mist, the illusion gone.

"How romantic," Emelyn drawled, having witnessed the entire exchange from her spot a few seats over. "He sends you dead flowers as gifts."

"Shall I do the same for you, *my beloved?*" Kols asked as he took the chair beside mine.

Emelyn narrowed her black eyes at him and ignored the offer. "Why does your father still think we're going to the Blood Gala together, *darling fiancé?*"

Blood Gala? I repeated to myself as I took my seat.

"I told you I'd handle it," he replied with a hint of annoyance.

"Is that what you were doing while gallivanting all over the mortal realm, fucking everything with two legs?" she asked, her long lashes batting demurely at him. But the violence radiating from her dark irises told a very different story. One I understood very well as my stomach clenched with her words.

Murderous, I mused. *That* was how I felt as a result of her statement.

I wanted to throttle Kols for being so disrespectful to our bond.

Which was ridiculous.

I had to get over this. We weren't exclusive. We didn't even like each other. Maybe I'd tell him later about my idea to use my Quandary Blood gifts to unravel the mating. He'd probably jump at the chance, what with all his other obligations. Including the female staring at him now, waiting for his response.

He didn't give her one.

Rude.

Headmaster Zankry cleared his throat from the front of the room, his hazel eyes boasting a bluish color today. They tended to change with his mood. Green meant angry. Black correlated with irritation. Brown indicated boredom. And blue typically suggested excitement.

Which meant he had a dangerous task for us to complete today.

I wondered if anyone else noticed that his class plans matched his irises or if they were all too busy talking to each other to pay attention.

"Aflora," Kols murmured.

I ignored him. Just like I did during breakfast when he asked me to wait for him before going to class. I didn't see the point, so I'd gone on ahead. He'd caught me at the entrance to the academic building but had wisely stayed quiet.

It seemed that bout of wisdom had come to an end.

Fortunately, Headmaster Zankry cut in with his trademark clearing of the throat to signal for our required attention. Black tendrils of power slithered like a snake up and down his arms, his Malefic magic on full display. "I hope you all followed the course assignment list and read the chapter on hallucinogen charms, because that's our task for today."

Excited murmurs broke out in the room, causing the hairs along my arms to rise.

Oh, I'd read the chapter all right.

He wanted us to play with optical magic, the kind that disrupted the mind and created dangerous illusions. If not properly deflected, the opponent could be rendered completely useless in seconds.

"And I'll be matching you all through a compatibility enchantment," Headmaster Zankry continued. Magic swirled through the air, the strands reminding me of that day in Advanced Conjuring class when Headmaster Irwin linked me to Shade for the entirety of the course.

His ice-blue eyes caught mine from across the room, his lips curling as if to confirm he had the same thought. The notion of being tied to him again didn't upset me like it did that first day. Actually, I really wouldn't mind—

"Oh, you have got to be fucking kidding me," Emelyn snapped as the ropes connected my wrist to hers.

My eyebrows lifted in surprise.

"How is *she* compatible to my magic?" Emelyn demanded, taking the thought right out of my mind. Because we were nothing alike. At all. The only thing we had in common was Kols. Sort of.

"No shit," a male said from across the room. It was the guy Shade always seemed to hang out with during classes. His name started with an *A*. Ajax, maybe? "There is nothing compatible between me and the friggin' Midnight Fae Prince." He held up his wrist, the magic strand attached to Kols.

My Elite Blood mate snorted. "I think your enchantment needs some work, Headmaster."

Shade just yawned, his magic cord linked to Stiggis. The latter appeared thrilled to be tied to my Death Blood mate. He clearly hadn't forgiven Shade for turning his back on the mating to his sister, Cordelia.

It was like everyone in the room was tied to someone they disliked, making them the opposite of "compatible."

The dark-haired fae snapped his fingers from the front of the room, forcing our attention back to him. "I said nothing about these being pairings based on friendship qualities. This class is about dueling and offensive magic. Now stop messing around and get to work."

Kols glanced warily at me before he stood. The warning in his eyes was clear. *Don't give anything away*, he was telling me.

I didn't dignify the look with a response and instead watched as our desks disappeared into mist, the room shifting forms to resemble a gymnasium-sized arena with marks along the floor. The first time this happened, I'd gaped at the transformation.

Now, I'd expected it and waited until it was done before allowing the illuminated cord to guide me to the appropriate sparring ring. As soon as Emelyn and I were in position, the magic vanished and she readied her wand.

The spell left her lips before I even had a chance to prepare. Bright red flames engulfed me, the heat shocking the hell out of my system. It felt *real*. It *burned*. My knees buckled on instinct, my hands frantically seeking a wand that didn't exist. Somehow, she'd cloaked it. I couldn't find it. I searched futilely while the fire ate through my clothing, leaving me naked and hot and mortified as everyone turned to watch me fail.

Then they all evaporated into a cloud of smoke, the infamous death fields in the Spirit Kingdom taking their place.

Screams.

Terror.

Death.

I couldn't breathe. This place had haunted my nightmares as a child. Every Earth Fae feared this place—the one where plagued souls went to die.

And I had firsthand experience battling at the entrance in soul form. Sort of. In a weird metaphorical way.

This isn't real, I promised myself, closing my eyes. *This isn't happening.*

And then I heard a whisper against my ear that had me spinning on my heels. Just my name, but it sounded unmistakably like my father.

Impossible.

"...forest," he whispered, the words before it lost to a subtle breeze scented of pine and lavender. "My sweet, beautiful flower. I've missed you. Meet me, my darling. Meet me soon. Join us. Come home."

I whirled in a circle, searching for the source of those words, my heart in my throat. "Dad?" I shook my head. No. It couldn't be him. This was all a game. A trick. A mind illusion, one I needed to break. But I couldn't. Not without my wand.

Then I recalled Zeph's earlier training. Conduits were used to focus control and weren't the source of magic. That came from within.

I searched inside, fighting to untangle the spell Emelyn had woven through my aura. All around me, trees wept, her newest attack an illusion of killing the element I held dear— my precious earth.

Flowers wilted.

Branches burned.

Leaves fell like tears against the ground.

And all the while, my father's spirit hovered nearby, murmuring words I didn't understand. A warning, maybe. But no. This was all tied to Emelyn's cruelty, her wicked intent to destroy me in the harshest manner possible by attacking everything I cherished, including my memories of parents I barely had the chance to know.

She'd taken the mean-girl act too far, had made this personal and shown her vicious nature.

Vindictive.

Evil.

Bully.

I crossed my arms and pretended to cower on the floor, then fought the binds she held on my mind, unweaving them one at a time while carefully keeping my magic hidden. I didn't want her to feel my approach, preferring to take her by surprise.

"Meet me," my father whispered once more.

His voice was a shock to my system, causing tears to well behind my eyes.

I focused on that link next, ripping the anchor out of my heart, unable to take another second of his torment. *He's not real. Not real. Not real. Not real!*

Power blasted out of me, the focal point on Emelyn. I threw her vision into the death fields of the Spirit Kingdom, forcing her to see and feel every spirit's pain of being trapped there. She thought to use it against me, not realizing I knew more about that realm than most Elemental Fae. I'd been taken there by a horrendous abomination who tried to plague my entire kind. I'd stood at the gates, blocking their entry in spirit form while I fought to dismantle her powerful hold and thwart her attempts at accessing the earth source.

I knew pain.

I knew death.

I knew torture.

And I allowed Emelyn to feel every ounce of it now, my anger singeing the air around me.

She deserved this. How dare she try to hurt me. To make me believe for even a second that my father might still be alive. It was wrong. Unacceptable. She—

"*Aflora!*" A wave of defensive magic accompanied my name, the source coming from beside me and knocking me off my feet.

I blinked, unsure of when I'd stood up to begin with, or even how I'd managed it. And at some point, I'd returned to the reality of the gymnasium-style classroom, but now I gaped up at a seriously pissed-off fae prince.

"That was fucking hot," Shade praised as he stepped into my line of sight. Kols glowered at him, which only made Shade smirk. "What? Powerful females don't turn you on?"

The fae prince didn't appear at all amused. "I'll handle it," he said, the words confusing me.

"You'd better," Headmaster Zankry stated. "Or she won't be permitted in my class again."

"Emelyn started it," Shade drawled. "Can't punish one fae and not the other."

"I can when one is knocked out cold and the other is just dazed," Headmaster Zankry retorted.

"I said, I'll handle it," Kols repeated through his teeth. He held out his hand, his gold irises narrowing down at me. "Come. Now."

Part of me wanted to tell him to fuzz right off. But as I glanced around the room and noticed everyone staring at me, I decided not to make matters worse by fighting him.

Pressing my palm against his, I allowed him to yank me forward, my body tingling at his touch. *What magic did he use to pull me out of that spell?* I wondered, electricity humming beneath my skin. It felt like a web of heat encasing my body from head to toe. A static net of sorts, yet my legs moved without any trouble as he guided me out of the Malefic Blood Education Building and back to the Elite Residence.

I didn't speak.

Neither did he.

But I felt Shade following, his presence a security blanket against my senses.

It was strange to realize I felt secure around the male who'd forced me into this mess to begin with and nervous around the one who claimed to want to help me.

They had all hurt me.

Betrayed me in some way.

Yet Shade was the one I sought now as I allowed Kols to guide me upstairs. I glanced behind me, needing to reassure myself that my Death Blood mate still trailed after us. His ice-blue eyes met mine as he winked, completely unfazed by the anger vibrating off the Midnight Fae Prince.

As soon as we were inside Kols's suite, he released me, and the weblike sensation left, bringing me to my knees as a burst of energy puffed out of me.

"Dick," Shade snapped before bending down beside me to press his palm to my lower back. "Are you okay, little rose?" he asked softly, his other hand going to my cheek to tilt my face toward him.

"What happened?" The words were hoarse, my throat suddenly parched.

"Kols cast a cocoon spell to trap your power beneath his. Then he released it without warning because he's a fucking prick."

Kols snorted at the summary from somewhere farther away. The kitchen, maybe? I couldn't tell because my vision was clouded by a sea of enchantment dust. At least, it looked like magic dust. Whatever it was, it made me sneeze and fire off another bolt of electricity.

I shivered from the sudden coolness flooding my veins, the humming from before disappearing.

Shade wrapped his arm around me and pulled me to him, his hand moving up and down my arm while his opposite palm guided my face to his chest.

I melted into him on instinct, absorbing his comfort and allowing it to pull me back into the land of the living.

My father's whispers still lingered in my mind, making me tremble with memories of my past. I rarely dreamed of my parents anymore. Mostly because I trained myself not to. There were so many mornings I'd wake up with the hope that that day might be the day they returned to me, only for it never to happen.

They were dead.

I felt it in my soul the moment the earth source became mine. That only occurred when the former anchor perished.

So it'd all been in my head. Because of Emelyn and her

cruel—

"Here." A bottle of water appeared in front of me, courtesy of Kols.

Shade took it from him, removed the cap, and brought the rim to my lips. "Drink, little rose. It'll make you feel better."

For whatever reason, I listened to him, and the second the cool liquid touched my tongue, I was glad I did. Because, mmm, that felt nice. So nice that I closed my eyes and just let him hold me while I accepted the refreshment down my throat.

He chuckled against me. "I think this is the most agreeable you've ever been in my presence."

He wasn't wrong.

But I didn't have it in me to comment on it. I was too tired of everything. The bickering. The feelings. This whole experience. I just wanted it all to go away and leave me alone.

Shade took the bottle away from my lips, the liquid gone.

Silence followed, the noiseless activity blissfully welcome. I inhaled his peppermint scent, allowed it to cling to my lungs and fill me with comfort.

It was wrong. I should push him away and tell him not to touch me.

Instead, I leaned into him more, seeking his strength.

The death fields always drained me; just the notion of their threat hurt my heart. They were gone now, thanks to Queen Claire and her mates defeating the abomination who'd created the vacuum of trapped souls.

That didn't stop me from remembering its existence.

Shade's lips met my forehead, his strong arms holding me tightly in the foyer of Kols's suite. The reality of the moment should have drawn a disbelieving laugh from me, but I felt too dead inside to utter such an amused sound.

Footsteps echoed around us as someone stepped through the threshold, the woodsy aroma warning me of

Zeph's presence. I snuggled deeper into Shade's chest, longing to disappear.

I felt weak.

Alone.

Just so *done* with it all.

This helplessness would pass, the emotion residual from the illusions Emelyn had created. I hated her in that moment, despised her ability to make me feel so worthless and meek. She'd gotten off easy because Kols had stopped me.

Why? Because she was his betrothed?

My jaw clenched with the thought. How ridiculous that he would stand up for his *fiancée* after spending days in the human world bedding mortals.

A growl threatened my chest, my annoyance mounting by the minute.

He was a horrible mate.

He denied me after our bond snapped into place, accusing me of planting the seed on purpose. Like I could control an Earth Fae connection on my own. A level-three placement meant he wanted it, too. But he burned all my things in response, sent me running into the LethaForest, and filled our bond with such exquisite power that I felt as if I were about to burst.

Then he claimed not to hate me and, less than a day later, had me imprisoned.

Well, technically Shade had me imprisoned with that recording.

Kols and Zeph had just orchestrated the arrest and the collar around my neck.

I frowned, touching the leather now with the tip of my index finger.

It'd done nothing to stop me from blasting Emelyn's power today. Or had it tried to thwart me and I'd just moved around it?

A consideration for later.

What was I even doing here, allowing Shade to hold me

like this? The three males were conversing around me, their words slowly trickling into my ears.

"…dismantled Emelyn's spell," Kols was saying. "Then she put the bitch on her ass."

"It was beautiful," Shade put in helpfully.

"She used her Quandary Blood abilities."

Shade shrugged, his hand still rubbing my arm gently. "No one noticed. She didn't utter a single spell out loud. From what they could tell, she just sent Emelyn into a vision, which was today's exercise, right? Not Aflora's fault that Emelyn couldn't handle a dose of her own medicine."

"Is Emelyn all right?" Zeph asked, his voice low.

"She'll be fine," Shade replied. "Our mate will be, too, by the way. In case you were wondering." The hint of annoyance in his tone created a tense atmosphere that caused the hairs along my arms to stand.

"Are you trying to imply that I can't see, Shadow?"

"No, I'm suggesting you redirect your concern to the right female, Zephyrus. You know, the one who is our *mate*."

"Say that a little louder," Kols snapped.

"Is that a dare?" Shade countered. "Because you know I will. Unlike you two idiots, I've embraced my destiny. Perhaps you should try it."

"Or I could undo it," I muttered, more to myself than to them.

Shade froze against me, the air chilling in the room. "What did you just say?"

Right. Time to tell the boys my thoughts on this whole mating business. As we were all together, why not now? It'd already been one heck of a day. Might as well end it with a bang.

I pulled away from Shade so I could see all three of the males bound to my life and cleared my throat.

"I said that I could just undo it." They all gaped at me as if I'd lost my mind. "What? I'm a Quandary Blood, right? Redirecting power is apparently my thing. Why not apply that logic to the bonds and sever them?"

CHAPTER TWELVE

ZEPH

ICE DRILLED THROUGH MY VEINS. "Absolutely fucking not."

Aflora blinked up at me in surprise. "Excuse me?"

"No. The answer is *no*." I'd claimed her. Planned or not, she was fucking mine, and I wouldn't allow her to undo it now.

She bristled at my tone, some of her inner fire climbing into her gaze. "No?" she repeated. "*No?* I'm pretty sure that's not your call to make."

"I'll just bite you again," Shade interjected, sounding bored already by the discussion. But I caught the hint of hurt in his icy gaze. He very much disliked this line of thought. For once, I agreed with him.

Kols, however, remained quiet.

I glanced at him, expecting to see rage but catching a glimmer of intrigue instead. "You can't possibly be considering this," I told him.

"It'd solve a lot of problems," he admitted with a shrug.

"Yes, it would solve several problems," Aflora agreed as

she stood on shaking legs.

"And create a thousand more," I inserted, folding my arms.

Kols gave me a look I knew well. The one that told me he was up to something. Then he returned his focus to Aflora. "Can you undo the Earth Fae bond?" he asked, the question making me realize his intent.

He wanted to test her resolve and see how far she'd go.

Which meant he didn't actually want to dismantle the bond.

Thank fuck for that.

We didn't go through all this bullshit just to undo it.

The bonds existed for a reason. If Aflora fractured our ties, she'd implode, and none of us would allow that to happen to her. She belonged to us. End of discussion.

"Um." She winced, causing me to narrow my gaze. *That*, right there, told me she didn't actually want to do this. Something else was driving her to suggest this insanity. "I'm not sure, but I'm going to try."

"No, you're not," I replied, done with this conversation. "You're not going to do anything."

"Again, that's not for you to decide," she bit back.

I grabbed the back of her neck and tugged her to me. "You're upset. I get it. You don't trust us. Fine. But those are not reasons to break a blood vow. Relationships require work. And I'll be damned if I let you just Quandary-magic your way out of this, pixie flower."

She pressed her palms against my chest and tried to shove me away. "Don't touch me."

"Too late." I clamped my opposite arm around her lower back. "You're angry. You think we betrayed you, but everything we've done is to protect you."

She huffed a laugh, her nails digging into my button-down shirt. "Right."

"Do you think I liked seeing them take you away?" I asked her. "It wasn't my recording that landed you behind bars, Aflora. I did what I could to protect you."

"You mean you did what you could to protect you and Kols," she corrected. "Without the collar, the Council would have sensed our connection. So don't lie to me and pretend it had anything to do with me, because I know it didn't. You will always look out for Kols first and foremost. Now I'm suggesting we find a way to free you both so you can go back to guarding him without me being in the way."

"The collar protected you as well," I pointed out.

"But it wasn't me you meant to protect," she tossed back. "Stop toying with me, Zeph. This whole thing is a big mistake. I'll figure out how to undo it, and we'll go our separate ways."

"What about your balance?" Kols asked, confirming my earlier assessment. He wanted to test her resolve and see if she'd truly thought this through. "Our biting you is what helped you stop imploding the other night. If you remove the bonds, you risk imploding again."

"Exactly," I agreed.

"So put me out in the middle of the LethaForest and let me explode," she retorted. "I mean, really, it's not like you care, right?" She tried to extract herself from my hold again, but I didn't budge.

"Stop telling us how we feel, Aflora," I chastised her, annoyed by her inaccurate assessments.

Her blue eyes rolled in response, causing me to tighten my grip on her neck. "Let. Go." She uttered the words through her clenched jaw.

So I uttered one back at her. "No."

Power flickered through her, and I welcomed the fight, but Kols chose that moment to speak again. "I would care." The soft words had me glancing at him. "I would care a great deal, actually."

Aflora snorted. "Sure. Is that why you spent the last few days humping your way around the Human Realm?"

Ah. There it is—the real reason she's suggesting this.

She was hurt, not just by our perceived betrayal but also by Kols's notorious behavior. He realized it at the same

91

moment, his nostrils flaring as his golden irises pulsated.

I released her, knowing he would grab her in turn, and he did, his palms going to her hips as he walked her into the wall.

"What are you doing?" she demanded, her hands flying up to his shoulders as if to force him back.

"There's a problem with your theory, *mate*," he said, his thigh sliding between her legs as his palms slipped up her sides to slowly memorize her curves.

Her scent began to change as interest darkened her blue eyes. "What problem?"

"Midnight Fae bonds occur when a male bites another Midnight Fae." One of his hands shifted back down to her hip while the other lifted to cup her neck, his thumb brushing the underside of her jaw to ensure she held his gaze.

"I'm aware," she replied.

"Yes, and it's a permanent claim that your Quandary abilities might be able to unravel," he conceded. "But you can't unweave our Elemental Fae mating, princess. We're already mated on the third level, which required agreement from both of our souls. Do you understand what I'm telling you?"

"You don't think my magic can dismantle Elemental Fae bonds."

"No, sweetheart," he murmured. "I'm saying I know it can't."

She shook her head, the movement stilted thanks to his grip on her neck. "I haven't even tried yet, so you can't know that."

"But I do, Aflora." He pressed his nose to her cheekbone and drew his lips across her cheek to her ear. "You would need my cooperation to even attempt it, and you don't have it. Because my soul wanted yours, just as yours desired mine. Our spirits won't allow us to break the vow now. It's too late. Which makes you mine, *mate*."

Her lips parted on a quick breath, her pupils dilating. "I

want to break it."

"No, you don't," he replied softly, pulling away from her ear to meet her gaze once more. "As Zeph said, you're upset. I'm sorry. He's sorry. Fuck, I think even Shade's sorry. None of us meant to hurt you. And before you accuse me of not caring again, why do you think the three of us went to the LethaForest, Aflora? Why did we bite you?"

"To hide my growing powers," she answered without hesitation. "Everything you've done is to protect yourselves."

He shook his head. "How did forming an Elemental mating bond protect me?"

"That was an accident. You blamed me for tricking you, remember?"

"Because I was shocked," he admitted. "But that doesn't change the fact that I wanted you and still do."

"Is that what you told the humans this week? The ones you played with and fed from?" She narrowed her gaze at him. "Do they all get false promises, Kols? Or just me?"

"Just you," he murmured, his lips going to her ear. "But they're not false, princess. My vows to you are every bit true."

She snorted, not buying it at all. "Right." Those blue eyes met mine over Kols's shoulder. "And what about you, Zeph?"

I arched a brow. "What about me?"

"I saw you last night, looking refreshed from blood consumption. Did you give her false promises, too? Or do you just tie up your playmates and gag them?"

A vision of her tied up in my bed entered my mind, intriguing me. "Do you want to be tied up, Aflora?"

"Is that really all you heard?" She shook her head and searched out Shade.

He'd hopped up off the ground some time ago to lean against the wall and observe. His expression now dared her to taunt him with her exquisite mouth.

"I don't even want to know where you've been the last

few days," she muttered.

"Miss me in your dreams, little rose?" he asked, amused.

"No."

"Liar," he murmured.

She growled, then went back to trying to shove Kols away from her. "Let me go."

"Never," he promised, his hand gliding to her throat to force her attention back to him. "Our souls are engaged, Aflora. You can't change that."

"Watch me," she snapped.

His lips curled. "It's not possible, sweetheart. Your soul claimed mine and vice versa. Even Sol saw it, despite the glamour tied to my wristband. He about killed me for it."

Aflora stopped fighting, her eyes widening. "Sol?"

"Yeah, big guy with rocks for fists," Kols drawled. "He introduced one to my face. Thankfully, I heal quickly." He released Aflora and took a step back. "He gave me a few things for you. They're in a bag in my room."

"What? Why didn't you give them to me when you returned?"

"Because you stormed through the room last night, slammed your door, and refused to come out afterward," he replied, crossing his arms over his chest. "You haven't exactly been all that chatty lately, Aflora."

"Because you were off playing in the Human Realm."

"If by 'playing,' you mean meeting with Exos, Cyrus, and Sol, then sure. And before you ask, yes, I fed. Something I can do without fucking, by the way. But I'm really glad we're having the exclusivity discussion because if you so much as touch another male, I'll kill him."

"Same," I agreed.

Shade merely shrugged. "You two have it covered."

Aflora gaped between the three of us, acting as though we'd all grown multiple heads. "How...? How did this conversation become about *exclusivity*? I just told you all that I want to undo the mating."

"And we told you that's not happening, pixie flower." I

cocked my head to the side. "Three votes against one."

"Hardly seems fair," she muttered.

"Welcome to Midnight Fae society," Shade drawled. "Where men make the rules and women are expected to follow them. Isn't that right, Prince Kolstov?"

Kols ignored his commentary, his focus on Aflora. "You chose me."

"Yeah, and you rejected me," she countered. "And then, to add insult to injury, you set all my things on fire. Which, I guess, didn't matter since none of them belonged to me anyway." She shook her head, her exasperation palpable. "Why are we even debating this? None of us want to be in this situation."

"You're right," I agreed. "None of us want to be in this situation."

She flinched, the movement slight but visible. And then she waved her hand at me. "See? Zeph admits it."

"I admit to not enjoying our current situation," I clarified. "The one where you're mad at all three of us and punishing us with hurtful comments about breaking our ties to you. I strongly dislike this situation and would like it to cease. Now."

She gaped at me, her mouth working without sound.

"Much better," I praised, stepping toward her and brushing her dark hair behind her ear. "How about we go sit in the living room and try to discuss this like adults, hmm?"

"I-I don't understand." She seemed to be talking to herself more than to me, but I answered her anyway.

"We don't want to break our quad, Aflora. Well, I might be okay with removing Shadow, but something tells me he's staying."

"I am," he put in, seemingly unperturbed by my comment. If anything, he appeared amused.

I'd evaluate that later.

"You're upset, and I know we hurt your ability to trust us. But we can't change the past, Aflora. We can only fix the future." Shade coughed, causing me to level a glare at him. "Is this entertaining to you, Shadow?"

He cleared his throat. "I can't even begin to explain that reaction. Just. Yeah, continue." He still appeared to be fighting a grin.

I sent a question to Kols with my eyes, and he just shrugged as if to say, *It's Shade. What do you expect?* Which, yeah, what did I expect?

Rolling my eyes, I refocused on the female before me. "I'm sorry for not telling you what was about to happen. There wasn't time, and I worked the situation to the best of my ability to ensure *your* safety, in addition to mine and Kols's." I cupped her cheek and tilted her head back as I stepped into her personal space. "I'll prove to you over time that your best interests are important to me. But I need you to allow me the opportunity to try."

She swallowed, her pretty eyes still holding a touch of that fire I adored. "Why should I?"

"Because I'm your mate, Aflora," I replied, lowering my lips to brush a chaste kiss against the edge of her mouth. "Whether you want me or not, we're bound together. And this will be a lot easier if you just accept that our fates are intertwined."

"What if I want to undo them?" The breathless quality of her voice belied her words, yet her stubborn side refused to back down. I really did adore that about her. I just wished she'd direct that fight to another topic, one less hurtful.

"You don't," I whispered, rubbing my nose against hers. "So stop suggesting it." I nipped her lower lip hard enough to hurt without breaking the skin. A gentle reprimand for her cruel words. Maybe I deserved them, but I didn't have to like them. "You're mine, Aflora. And one day, you'll trust me again. If you allow yourself to try."

"I can't," she admitted. "I can't trust you."

"Not yet," I agreed, pressing my forehead to hers. "But soon. You'll see." With a final kiss to her cheek, I released her once more. "Let's continue this discussion over midnight lunch." I held Aflora's gaze as I added, "I'm cooking. I hope you like burning thwomp."

A muscle in her cheek twitched, one that told me I'd almost earned a smile from her. Better than nothing.

"I need to take care of something first, but I'll be back," Shade said, disappearing into a cloud of smoke before any of us could comment.

A second later, Sir Kristoff ran into the room, red eyes glowing. "Where are they?!" he demanded, spinning in a circle, his little hand holding a stone dagger. Well, I supposed it was a sword for him, considering his size.

"What are you talking about?" Kols asked the little hellspawn.

The gargoyle growled, low and menacing. "The Death Blood and his sword-wielding friend. *Where are they*?"

Kols and I shared a look. I had nothing.

Aflora seemed just as lost. "Are you talking about Shadow?"

"Yes," the stone demon hissed. "And his sword friend. The ti—"

Shade appeared once more and shot a puff of purple dust at the gargoyle, causing the little hellion to sputter and cough, its red eyes blinking repeatedly. Then he frowned and glared up at the Death Blood. "*You.*"

"Aww, did you miss me, li'l buddy? I'd be happy to tie you up again. I know how much you enjoyed that last time."

Sir Kristoff growled and stalked off, returning to his duty at the door while mumbling something about killing Shade in his sleep.

The Death Blood just watched with deep amusement and shook his head. "I think your gargoyle is broken, Kols."

The gargoyle in question raised his dagger like a middle finger and disappeared into the door.

"What the hell?" Kols snapped. "What did you blast him with?"

"A chill pill," Shade drawled. "Seems to have worked."

"Why was he going on about a sword-wielding friend?"

Aflora asked, her brow furrowed.

Shade just shrugged. "Fuck if I know."

I didn't believe him. Not for a second. But I also knew Shade wouldn't tell us unless he wanted to. Kols must have come to the same conclusion because he didn't bother to argue. Knowing Shade, it was what he wanted anyway. Maybe he'd gone out into the hall to enchant the gargoyle into acting like an idiot. A distraction to the bigger picture.

"Oh, right. Not done yet. But I promise to be back soon," Shade said, disappearing again.

"What the hell is he up to?" Kols demanded, staring at the place Shade had just vacated.

I just shook my head. "I'm going to make lunch. Then we're having a quad meeting."

"A quad meeting?" Aflora repeated.

"Yeah," I replied, locking my gaze on her. "We're a quad, pixie flower. And you had better get used to it because you're stuck with us. Now I'm going to go make you a burning thwomp sandwich. Would you like that with a side of fire gnat juice?"

Her lips twitched this time. Briefly, but I caught the little movement, and my heart gave a thump in response. "Sounds lovely," she deadpanned.

"Good." I winked at her and turned for the kitchen, leaving her to talk to Kols alone. He still had some groveling to do.

Hell, we all did.

But I'd let him go first.

I was honorable like that.

CHAPTER THIRTEEN

KOLS

AFLORA WATCHED ZEPH THROUGH WARY EYES, then shifted that look to me. She still stood against the wall, right where I'd put her, but she appeared a lot less feisty now. If anything, she reminded me of a wilted flower with her shoulders caving inward in insecurity and her arms curling around her middle.

I sighed, hating myself a little for making her feel this way. "I have a reputation for fucking around," I told her softly. "I upheld that image during our break days to deter the others from asking any questions. But I used glamour spells to do it. Exos and Cyrus were there the entire time, if you want to ask them. They were immune to my enchantment, mostly because they knew I'd bonded to you and would have killed me otherwise."

It'd been hard enough to calm them down when they sensed my new mating bond—something that had shocked the hell out of me.

Apparently, my wristband only applied to Midnight Fae links, not Elemental Fae ones. However, the Council didn't seem to have the same ability to sense my connection to Aflora. Which made sense because, according to Exos, it was a link on the spirit plane that gave me away, something only Spirit Fae could see.

And Sol, apparently.

Because he knew right away.

Although, I suspected his was earth source related.

Elemental Fae were fucking complicated.

"If they know about our mating link, then they know I'm an abomination," she whispered, her eyes filling with tears. "They're never going to let me back, are they?"

I immediately pulled her into my arms, needing to soothe her. She'd been so strong, fighting every step of the way, but the helplessness always weighed on her. I saw it peek at me whenever she second-guessed herself. Yet she always pushed it back.

Until now.

"Shh," I hushed, leading her to the couch to sit.

She didn't even try to stop me, her breaths coming in short bursts as the weight of everything seemed to crush her at once. "They shouldn't take me back," she admitted on an exhale, her shoulders trembling. "I'm… I'm…"

"One of the strongest females I've ever met," I told her as I pulled her into my lap to hold her.

That she didn't even object told me everything I needed to know about her current frame of mind.

She'd given up.

Just for a moment.

But that moment broke my heart.

I pressed my lips to her forehead and drew my fingers through her hair.

"Actually, I think you might be the strongest female I've ever met," I corrected, smiling to myself. "It's what drew me to you initially. That, and your altruistic nature. You put the safety of your people before your own needs and desires, just as a royal should. I admire you for it."

She said nothing for so long that I thought perhaps I'd

lost her to the sadness, only her eyes were shimmering with unshed tears when she pulled back to look up at me. Aflora hadn't truly broken, just been on the verge of it.

"It's my duty to protect them," she replied softly. "To do otherwise is to fail. It's why I need to talk to Sol, to officially relinquish my power. Because I can't be trusted as an abomination, something I imagine you confirmed with him, Exos, and Cyrus, yes?"

I tucked a lock of hair behind her ear, then drew my fingertips down her neck. "Not exactly."

"But they know we've exchanged a mating promise to each other."

That must have been her definition for the third level. Seemed appropriate. "Yes. They know I'm your intended mate, and they're aware of the complications involved with such a vow. Particularly as it's well known that Shade has also claimed you and that I'm betrothed to another Midnight Fae."

Her delectable mouth twisted to the side, the tears glimmering in her gaze slowly subsiding to an intelligent gleam that told me she was considering every angle of the puzzle before us. "This is why I need to break our bonds. It's one thing to sacrifice myself. Entirely another to take you all down with me."

I slid my palm to her nape, my thumb dancing along the pulse point at her neck. "Maybe I want to go down with you, Aflora." *Or on you*, I added in my mind, my lips curling at the thought.

She snorted. "You accused me of tricking you into our mating, Kolstov. I know you don't really want this."

"Then why did we connect?" I countered. "From what I understand of Elemental Fae bonds, they require mutual agreement." Very unlike Midnight Fae connections.

"We connected because we're compatible," she said matter-of-factly. "We're both royals of very strong lineages, and we got carried away."

"We did," I agreed. "Because I knew from the moment

I met you that you were a worthy female of mating potential. I tried to fight it, but I was too weak to resist you. And while the connection shocked me, thus causing me to act like a fucking idiot afterward, I don't regret it. Which is why I won't allow you to remove it."

I pressed my lips to hers, silencing whatever argument brewed inside her thoughts. Because I meant it. I refused to let her break this bond.

Would it make things easier for us all? Maybe.

Would it save me from certain punishment? Absolutely.

But somehow I just knew we'd end up right back here, with my soul tied to hers and a whole hell of a lot of bad blood between us as a result.

I didn't see the point in fighting the inevitable. "I want to find a way to make this work," I told her in a breath, my mouth brushing hers with each word. "We may not have meant to tie our souls together, Aflora, but it already happened. And rather than fight it and each other, I'd like to figure out how to move forward. Together."

She shook her head. "It's impossible, Kols. I shouldn't exist."

"But you do," I replied, kissing her again, this time with more force than before. Her lips yielded to mine, her body betraying her mind. "You exist and you're mine," I added, then fully claimed her mouth with my tongue. My grip shifted from her neck to her hair, my fingers tangling in her thick blue-black strands and holding her to me as I devoured her.

If she didn't want to acknowledge my words, then she could listen to my body.

My opposite hand went to her hip to guide her across my lap and encourage her to straddle my thighs. She followed my lead and wrapped her arms around my neck, then began to return my kiss as if to say goodbye.

I saw right through it, felt her magic humming to life to test her resolve, and tugged on her hair to expose her neck. "Try it," I dared her, my incisors already at her throbbing pulse. "I'll just bite you again and again, Aflora. And you can't break our Earth bond unless I allow it, which is never going to happen. Our souls are already welded together."

At least that was what I understood after talking to Exos and Cyrus. They said something about my essence weaving around hers, similar to how theirs always gravitated to Claire's in the Spirit Realm.

"Don't you see that it's for the best?" she whispered, her body shaking over mine with a convoluted mixture of arousal and resolve.

"You'll implode," I warned her before licking the tempting point of her neck. "I'm the one absorbing most of your magic right now, Aflora. If you release me, you'll detonate." It wasn't a lie. I'd absorbed the brunt of her power the other night, my connection to the dark source forcing me to serve as a funnel.

Her fingers threaded through my hair, her grasp tightening as if to yank me away from her neck, but I didn't budge.

"You'll have to try harder than that, sweetheart."

She growled in response. "You're being impossible."

"And you're being unreasonable," I retorted, nipping her neck. "I won't make excuses for myself, Aflora. I reacted badly and I'm sorry." I nibbled my way up her throat to her ear. "Our relationship is forbidden. It breaks all the rules. It's probably going to cost me my crown. But you know what?"

She swallowed, her nails biting into my scalp. "What?"

"That all only makes me want you more," I admitted. "And if given the opportunity to do it all over again, I would, even knowing what it would cost in return." I nuzzled her tender skin, my lips skimming her pulse once more. Her blood called to the predator within me, urging me to bite, to *claim*. But I wouldn't. Not without her permission.

Unless she tried to unweave our bonds.

In which case, I'd bite her repeatedly until she stopped.

"Why?" she whispered.

"Why what, sweetheart?"

"You're risking everything, Kolstov."

"Am I?" I replied, drawing back to meet her gaze.

"You are," she insisted. "You just praised me for being altruistic by putting my people before myself. What are you doing? You're putting an abomination before your ascension. You're going against everything you've been working for. I want to know why."

"Because it's time for change," another voice replied on my behalf.

I glanced sideways to find Shade lounging in my favorite recliner chair with his feet propped up on the coffee table. As I hadn't sensed his presence, I assumed that meant he'd just arrived. Unless he'd been lurking in smoke form.

His Death Blood abilities irked me greatly.

"Change?" Aflora repeated.

"Yep," he drawled.

"Care to elaborate?" I asked, arching a brow.

His icy blue eyes flashed with knowledge and secrets. "Do you believe all abominations are evil, Kolstov? That they should be exterminated on sight without any trial or cause aside from their mingled blood and powers?"

"Abominations have historically proven problematic," I pointed out, avoiding his direct questions like he did mine.

"Have they?" he countered, arching a dark brow. "Or is that what our Council wants us to believe?"

"It's an international directive to execute abominations," I reminded him. "Not just our Council's."

"Fair," he conceded. "But who proposed that mandate originally?"

"My grandfather," I replied, aware of the history involved. "Shortly after a certain issue a millennium ago."

He nodded. "Yes. Right around the time he also had all the Quandary Bloods executed." He cocked his head to the side. "Now, I might be overthinking this, but it seems to me your family has a history of fearing those with the potential to be more powerful than them."

I narrowed my gaze at him. "If you're trying to accuse me or my family of something, Shadow, then I suggest you stop hiding behind riddles and spit it out."

His lips curled. "I see I've struck a nerve."

"With your cryptic bullshit, sure."

"No. With my concise recollection of just why all this started in the first place. Your grandfather didn't want to risk the source being realigned again, so he exterminated the Quandary Bloods—or at least those he could find—and also strongly encouraged the fae community to execute all abominations. Which, when you think about it, is a very strange choice indeed when Midnight Fae males can become Fortune Fae Alphas by just refusing to ingest human blood. Thereby suggesting fae are actually somewhat related across the species. But I digress."

He kicked his feet off the table and leaned forward, all signs of amusement leaving his features.

"Our Council requires change," he continued, his blue irises landing on Aflora. "So you want a reason, little rose? That's your reason. Our quad is going to change everything, including rebalancing a power source that has long been abused by the Nacht family. With, or without, Kols's knowledge."

"All right." My hands went to Aflora's hips to remove her from my lap, but her thighs clamped down around mine.

"Hold on," she said.

"No. He's just insulted—"

Her palm covered my mouth, shocking the hell out of me. "Why do you feel it's been abused?" she asked Shade.

"Because the Quandary Bloods were removed from the equation, thereby dismantling the balance and allowing the Elite Bloods unfettered access to the source via the Nacht family line. Kolstov's grandfather destroyed the Midnight Fae who were meant to protect the balance, all because he feared the source would be redirected to another line."

LEXI C. FOSS

I moved my mouth away from Aflora's hand. "Is that the bullshit your father tells you?" I demanded with a humorless laugh. "Un-fucking-believable."

"Yes, he's told me this version of events, and he's also droned on and on about how the source was stolen from our family." Shade lifted his hand, palm up, in a version of an odd shrug, then let it fall back to his lap. "He wants it back for all the wrong reasons. As do all the members of the Council. Which brings me back to the need for change."

Zeph chose that moment to enter with a tray of food. He set it down on the coffee table and fixed his gaze on Shade. "You have my attention, Shade. Elaborate on your suggestions for change."

Of course Zeph would want to entertain this nonsense.

This time Aflora allowed me to lift her off my lap and into the space beside me. Zeph took the spot on her opposite side, his forearms going to his sprawled thighs as he leaned forward to focus on Shade.

"Well?" my Guardian prompted.

Shade studied him for a long moment. "Did you enjoy being demoted to headmaster as a result of your sexual shenanigans?"

Zeph merely smirked. "Nice try at evasion. Tell me your ideas for change."

"It's not my ideas that will matter," he replied cryptically. "It's our mate's."

Aflora had been staring intently at the tray of food, but Shade's words pulled her gaze sideways. I stretched my arm out across the back of the couch so my fingertips could lightly brush her shoulder. It was a natural move, similar to Zeph widening his legs to ensure his thigh touched hers.

Shade noticed but didn't comment. Nor did he seem bothered by it. Actually, he appeared almost content with the possessive display, as if it satisfied some part of him.

"I will never understand you," I decided out loud.

Mischief danced in his features. "You will. One day. Just not today." He looked at Aflora. "I'll see you in your dreams later, little rose." And then he disappeared into smoke once more.

"I hate when he does that," I said, irritated as hell.

"Which part?" Zeph asked. "Accusing your family of hoarding magic, or the vanishing act?"

"Both," I admitted on a huff. "He's infur—"

"Is that dragon steak?" Aflora's attention was on the tray again, her blue eyes wide.

I followed her gaze to the dark gray meat surrounded by leaves. The other two plates just had sandwiches. I assumed one of those was meant for me, the other for Zeph. Shade was definitely not on our guest list, despite being able to get past my gargoyle. Which was a discussion I'd need to have with Sir Kristoff later because I hadn't given approval for the Death Blood to enter at will.

"Yeah, with salad patty," Zeph replied, palming the back of his neck. "Kols asked Sol for some meal suggestions since you're not fond of our meals. This was what he recommended."

"He also told us to get you some scurbuttle snacks," I added. "After he left, Cyrus informed me that would be a bad idea and suggested I stick to dragon steak. He also recommended I not give you bacon."

"Bacon?" she repeated.

"Yeah. I guess it's like troll fat?"

Her eyes rounded in horror. "Why would you eat troll fat?"

"I wouldn't."

"Then why eat bacon?"

I shook my head. "It's not the same, it's just… Never mind. He recommended dragon steak. So." I waved to the plate as if to say, *There it is*.

"I hope I cooked it right," Zeph mused. "Reminded me of beef, so I grilled it the same way."

That explained why it took him so long to prepare the food. "What kind of sandwiches did you make us?"

"Turkey and cheese," he replied. "I added mayo to

yours since you like it." He grimaced with the comment, causing me to grin.

I covered my heart with my hand, my other arm still draped over Aflora's shoulder. "You do love me, Z."

He snorted but didn't deny it.

"You made me dragon steak," Aflora said, still focused on her plate. "Because Sol suggested it."

Zeph glanced uneasily at her. "Yeah, he suggested it to Kols. Did I make it wrong?"

"And you added salad patty."

"Yeah, that part just seemed appropriate based on what I know of Elemental Fae cuisine. Seems like a popular side? But I had to use magic because we don't have a lot of those root vegetables here. So, uh, I hope it's okay."

She finally looked at him. "I thought we agreed on burning thwomp and fire gnat juice."

My lips twitched at the mock condescension in her tone. Teasing had to be a good sign, right? Maybe it meant she was past the idea of rewiring our connection, or had at least put it on hold. Regardless, I'd take it.

"Yeah, sorry, all out of burning thwomps, I'm afraid," Zeph replied, his tone contrite. "But if you don't want the dragon steak, I'll eat it, and you can have my turkey sandwich."

He made to reach for her plate, and she batted his hand away. "Don't you dare."

Zeph smirked at her. "Oh, you want it now?"

"Did you poison it?" she countered.

He nodded. "Yep. Laced it with an agreeable charm so you'll do everything I say for at least a week."

"I actually think you might mean that," she replied.

He grunted, grabbed her plate, and set it in her lap. "Eat, Aflora. Or I really will enchant you."

Rather than snipe something back at him, she plucked a leaf off her plate and used it to rip a piece off her dragon steak, then made a show of putting it in her mouth.

Suddenly, food was the last thing on my mind.

And her lips were all I could see.

"Fuck," I muttered.

"No," she replied without missing a beat. She finished chewing and swallowed before looking at me. "I'm not ready to do that again yet."

Zeph met my gaze over her head, then we both gazed down at her. "All right, sweetheart," I conceded. "That's fine."

My Guardian nodded in agreement. "I'm not ready to fuck yet either."

She glanced at him. "You're not?"

"No." He leaned in to whisper in her ear just loud enough for me to hear as well. "I won't fuck you until you beg, pixie flower. And even then, I still might not fuck you. Do you want to know why?"

"Why?" she asked as if hypnotized by his voice. And maybe she was.

"Because you haven't earned it yet." He kissed her on the cheek, then reached for his plate and began to eat.

"He's a dick," I told her conversationally as I grabbed my own sandwich. "And, unfortunately, he means it."

When Zeph set his mind to something, there would be no changing it. He was a stubborn ass like that. But on this, I sort of agreed with him. Until we were in a better place with Aflora, sex was off the table.

However, that didn't mean we couldn't play in other ways.

Such as in her dreams.

I smiled at the memories of all the times I joined her in her mind. Mmm, that was fun. Maybe we'd do it again later. After Shade finished toying with her.

Or perhaps I'd kick him out and take over.

Zeph caught my gaze again, the knowing flicker in his green irises telling me he agreed with my plan. We didn't even need to talk about it; he just knew.

Poor Aflora. Now she had three mates hungry for her dreams.

I pressed my lips against her temple, showing affection because I wanted to, then returned to my midnight lunch. "I'm glad to see you eating a healthy meal, Aflora," I told her. "You're going to need that energy later."

"What?" she asked, her mouth full of dragon steak.

"For your dreams," Zeph replied. He lifted his hand to draw his knuckles down her cheek. "And for your independent training tomorrow."

She groaned, the sound going right to my cock. "Stay out of my head."

"Never," Zeph and I replied at the same time.

"Willow stumps," she muttered to herself. Then she dug back into her meal, the argument forgotten.

Well, one thing was clear—I needed to order more dragon steak.

CHAPTER FOURTEEN

AFLORA

SEVEN NIGHTS OF SEXUAL TORMENT.

With no orgasms.

To say I hated my mates right now would be an understatement.

And they knew it, too, the three of them all watching from different corners of the yard with matching expressions of amusement. Even Zephyrus smirked, his lips reminding me of the way he'd held me down last night and devoured me to within an inch of my life.

Just to stop and wake me up seconds before I exploded.

I glared at him, not caring at all that he was in headmaster mode today.

Physical Training with No Magic. Yeah, I'd show him some *physical training,* all right.

That Shade and Kols had chosen to go shirtless for today's sparring activities only added insult to injury. Because yeah, they looked good and they knew it. And while Zephyrus's torso was covered, his arms were fully exposed in his sleeveless shirt. He made a show of stretching, his muscles bulging and inviting me to lick him.

I preferred it when I thought they all had betrayed me.

This was worse.

Much, much worse.

I was even starting to dream of some random guy with long white hair and silver-blue eyes. He at least let me come in those fantasies, which was how I knew I'd made him up. Because it hadn't escaped my notice that his traits were the opposite of my mates'—clearly, my mind's way of retaliating.

Tulip-burning willow stumps, I thought, glaring at the males in question. *I hope you all fall into a burning thwomp.*

"You okay?" Ella asked, appearing out of nowhere at my side. Or maybe she'd been there the entire time. As my focus was entirely on the eye candy across the yard, I couldn't be sure.

"I'm fine," I replied, my voice sharper than I intended.

"You sure? Because it sounded like you just growled at Zeph."

"I probably did." I'd been growling at him a lot lately.

"I thought you were getting along better," Ella murmured. "You've all been studying a lot."

"Yeah, they're helping me with control," I muttered. *And then tormenting me in my dreams afterward.*

"Come spar with me, little rose." Shade's voice came from my left, drawing my focus to his toned physique. The moon played off his tan skin, making me wonder what he'd look like under the heat of the sun. Gorgeous, obviously. And wicked.

I almost refused, but then a better idea entered my mind. I couldn't be alone in my agony here because the guys hadn't orgasmed either. Which meant they'd been teasing themselves, too. Maybe it was time I returned the favor a little.

"Okay," I replied.

"Hey, I thought we were sparring together," Ella cut in. Tray scooped her up into his arms before I could comment, his lips brushing hers as he murmured, "I guess you're all mine, El."

She sighed. "I'm already yours, Nacht."

"I know." He waggled his brows at her. "How about we ditch sparring and do a little of our own physical activity back at the suite?"

"How about you do the exercises I gave you and stop trying to get laid in my class, Trayton," Zeph deadpanned.

Tray just smiled. "I prefer my plan."

Zeph did not share his amusement. "Put her down and start running. Ten laps."

Ella groaned and Tray cursed.

"Okay, fifteen," Zeph amended.

"Put me down," Ella snapped.

Tray did reluctantly and gave Zeph a look that spoke volumes. "You're a cockblocking dick, Zeph."

"Shall I make it twenty?" he countered, that famous eyebrow of his inching upward into his hairline.

"I'm only listening to you right now for Ella because twenty laps would piss her off," Tray replied before taking off after his mate.

"Goading my brother?" Kols asked as he jogged up to join us, his abs flexing seductively with the movement. And now I wanted to lick him.

"He just makes it so easy," Zeph drawled.

Shade wrapped his arm around me, pulling me back into his hot form. "I thought we were sparring?" he whispered against my ear.

"You all are killing me," I muttered, more to myself than to them.

"Ready to beg already?" Zeph pitched his voice low so the others couldn't overhear. "That's a shame, Aflora. I expected to have to try harder."

Kols chuckled, but Shade just pressed his nose to my neck and inhaled softly.

My blood was on fire.

And I wanted to choke all of them.

"Stop stalling and come play with me," Shade breathed, causing goose bumps to trail down my exposed arms.

He pulled me backward by several feet, drawing me into one of the sparring rings. His flirtation captured the attention of several students in our class, including the two standing in the circle beside ours.

"Well, aren't you two cute," Emelyn drawled, her tone holding a touch of derision.

"Someone's jealous," her partner replied, smirking at Shade and giving him a friendly nod. Yeah, these two were definitely friends. Which had me wondering how Emelyn had found herself partnered with Ajax for today's assignment. Elite Bloods didn't tend to mix with Death Bloods.

"I'm not jealous," Emelyn snapped back.

"Yeah? Could have fooled me, Your Majesty," Ajax replied, executing a mock bow.

"Ugh, why am I partnered with you again?" she demanded.

"Because your friends didn't want to fight you today. You're too moody for them." He folded his arms. "So are you going to try to hit me or what? I'm getting bored over here."

Emelyn charged him with a roar that made me wince.

Moody was an understatement.

She had Ajax flat on his back in less than a second, his expression registering shock, which quickly morphed into determination as he wrestled her across the ground in several skilled maneuvers.

"I don't know how to do that," I admitted, watching him twist and pin her. But Emelyn wasn't one to be outdone. She had him in a headlock two moves later, causing my eyebrows to shoot up.

Shade yanked me backward, away from their violent game, and drew me around to face him. "Then show me what you know how to do."

"Earth Fae don't fight," I told him. "There's no need."

He gave me a look that said he wasn't impressed. "I know Zeph's been training you."

"Yeah, mostly with magic."

"And I've seen you and Ella spar, so I know you're learning how to fight," he added, undeterred.

"Okay, she's shown me a few things, but—"

"Show me what you've learned," he interjected. "No excuses. I need to know what I'm dealing with here."

"Why did you want to spar?" I asked him, deflecting. "You rarely talk to me during class. I mean, you barely even acknowledge me in Death Class, and we're partners in that one. Why today? Why now?"

He cocked his head to the side. "I'm tired of giving you space. You're mine and I want to play. Now stop deflecting and give me a preview of your abilities. Then we'll go from there."

"I gave you a preview that first time you bit me."

"Yeah, and you played with your elements and still lost," he replied, unimpressed. "Now you have that collar around your neck hampering your abilities. Which makes this class a lot more important than you seem to realize."

"Why? Because you're anticipating I may need to fight you off again soon?" I countered.

He swept his leg across my knees, sending me to the ground on a whoosh of air. I coughed and sputtered as he landed on top of me, his hands easily capturing my wrists to bring them above my head as his hips pinned mine to the black grass below.

Not green, but black.

Like all the other vegetation in this realm.

"I'm anticipating that you're going to need to fight others," he whispered against my ear. "And soon. So I need you to stop flirting with me and actually pay attention, Aflora."

"I'm not flirting with you," I managed to say on a harsh exhale, my back throbbing from his unexpected attack. "I think... I think I hate you."

He chuckled and pressed a kiss to my jaw, then drew his lips to my ear. "Best me and I'll make you come later."

I snorted at the offer. "Did that when I woke up, so I'm good, thank you."

Only after I uttered the words did I realize what I'd just admitted out loud. My cheeks heated as Shade went to his elbows on either side of my head, his lips curled in amusement. "Yeah? And did you scream my name?"

"Get off of me."

"Not until you detail the experience for me," he replied, his wicked gaze falling to my mouth. "Did you think of me?"

"I'm not talking about this."

"Then I guess we'll be lying here all night. Works for me, as I find this position to be rather comfortable for all parties involved." He gave a little thrust, allowing me to feel his growing arousal against my heated center.

My thighs clenched, my insides doing all sorts of weird somersaults in response to his small action. I'd told him the truth about my earlier release, but it hadn't done anything to cool the flames burning inside me.

All because my mates wouldn't leave my dreams alone.

And now this!

"Off," I snapped.

He merely smiled. "Make me."

I growled and tried to shove him off me, which did absolutely nothing. Well, no, that wasn't true. Pressing my palms to his bare shoulders sent a zap of electricity through me, making me that much hotter for him.

Because he was shirtless and on top of me.

A fae could only take so much skin-to-skin contact after all these nights of sensual torture.

Or, at least, that was what I told myself. It had absolutely nothing to do with the fact that my three mates were irresistible males with the bodies of gods. And it definitely wasn't because of their skills in the bedroom.

"Your squirming is only turning me on more," Shade

whispered, his lips brushing the shell of my ear as he trailed his mouth down my neck to my thundering pulse.

"Why are you doing this?" I asked him, desperate for a way to *remove* him. I also wanted to ask him to shadow us somewhere more private so I could join him in the shirtless department.

Not voicing that desire. Nope. Nope. Nope.

"You're not the only one amped up from all the dreams, love," he said softly, his mouth teasing the sensitive spot behind my ear now. "I've waited for you to come to me all week, and you've stubbornly remained in your room. So I'm increasing the stakes in the game."

"Wh-what?" I stammered. "You never—"

"Stop making out and get to work," Zeph snapped. "Unless you need a more thorough demonstration of today's sparring activities?"

"Seems to me you need a lesson on what making out means," Shade drawled, rolling off of me and popping up to his feet. "Shall I go fetch Kols for you?"

"Cute," Zeph replied.

I pushed off the ground and brushed the strands of grass—if it could even really be called that—from my pants. The razor-like edges sliced across my fingers, making me grimace. *Definitely not grass.*

"All right, Aflora. Let's try again," Shade suggested.

"No. You're out. Go spar with Kols. I'm up."

"You mean, you want me to make out with Kols?" Shade sounded surprised. "All right."

Zeph snorted and shook his head. "Fuck off, Shadow."

"You're an amazing headmaster, Zeph. It's a real wonder that you didn't go into this profession right after finishing up at the Academy."

"Now," Zeph said through his teeth.

"I'll see you later, little rose." Shade winked at me and wandered off in the direction of Kols and one of the other Elite Bloods. Tray and Ella were training beside them, their cheeks pink from exertion. Or maybe something else.

Because I'd woken up with a similar look this—

"Aflora," Zeph snapped, his broad chest suddenly blocking my view as he stepped in front of me. "What the hell is wrong with you?"

"I've not been sleeping very well," I replied primly.

He coughed to hide a smile, but I caught the twitch of his lips. "Well, that's not an excuse to slack off in my class. We fight even when exhausted."

"Oh? Are you also having difficulty sleeping?" I asked him with false innocence.

His green eyes narrowed. "Stop flirting with me and get to work."

"I'm not flirting with you."

"You are," he insisted, taking a step closer to crowd my personal space. His lips went to my ear as he whispered, "And if you continue down this path, I will punish you later."

I shivered, my damn body thrilled by the notion.

Why was it so damn hard to control my reactions to these males? I hated them. Well, not really. Maybe. I wasn't sure. I *wanted* to hate them, but they'd been wearing down my defenses over the last week with their soft touches and—

Zeph grabbed my ponytail and tugged it sharply to expose my neck. "Are you purposely being disobedient?"

I considered that. "Well, no. But sparring is still new to me. Elemental Fae don't really fight unless it's in the Powerless Champion arena."

"Maybe ask her to go pick some flowers instead, Zeph," Emelyn suggested. "She's not really cut out for athletics."

I frowned. "Fighting is only one form of physical activity."

"Yeah, and it's a crucial one that you're terrible at," she spat back. "Just like everything else in this realm. When are you going home?"

"Enough," Zeph cut in, shooting her a bored expression. "Go back to your assignment. I'll deal with this."

Emelyn heaved a dramatic sigh. "She's like a full-time job, constantly requiring a babysitter to hold her hand through even the simplest of tasks."

I bristled at her condescending tone. "I'd like to see you try to perform with a collar around your neck." I pointed to the thin leather choker sitting against my throat. It probably had Shade's lip prints all over it from his date with my pulse a few minutes ago, but I didn't care. "Maybe I should take it off and let you wear it for a day," I suggested.

She laughed, the sound lacking proper humor. "I don't need a leash, because I already know how to control my powers. But the same can't be said about *abominations*."

"Emelyn!" Zeph barked, his tone harsh.

"Oh, did I accidentally admit out loud what we're all really thinking about her?" She pressed a hand to her heart and gave me a mock-apologetic look. "My bad."

My teeth ground together, mostly because I didn't know how to reply. Since everything she said was true.

I was an abomination.

A powerful one.

And I didn't know how to control my abilities. Not completely, anyway.

My heart squeezed at the knowledge, a part of me feeling helpless all over again. But I couldn't let her beat me.

I'm stronger than this.
I can learn.
I don't want to hurt people.
I have anchors to ground me.
I—

A ripple of energy danced over my skin, causing the hairs along my neck to rise. I frowned down at my arms, noting the static electricity humming across my being. It wasn't visible, but I *felt* it. The warmth familiar in a strange way, reminding me of my own magic.

Yet it wasn't coming from me.

"That's enough, Emelyn," Zeph bit out, oblivious to the sensations swirling around me. "You're excused for—"

An explosion rocked the ground, sending us all to our knees. Another boom shook the surface, causing shouts to sound throughout the yard. Zeph yanked me to him, his stance protective, his gaze sharp as he glanced around seeking the source.

Ravens screamed through the air, followed by a cloud of smoke as the burning thwomps around campus unleashed fire into the sky.

And then came the gargoyles, their screeches reminding me of nails against a sharp stone.

I pressed my palms to my ears as Zeph pushed me flat onto the ground, his larger body covering mine.

Shrieks, heat, and a flutter of wind whipped through the Academy. "What's happening?" I shouted at Zeph.

"The Academy is protecting itself," he shouted back.

My eyes widened. "It does that?" But my words were lost to the new wave of chaos swimming around us. The hisses on the wind sent chills down my spine.

Snake vines, I realized, horrified. Those things didn't like me on a good day. This wouldn't go over well.

Zeph's grip tightened around me, his warmth bleeding into me, wrapping me in a cocoon of safety. *Literally.*

I blinked, realizing his magic poured out of him in a defensive shield, covering not just me but all the students in the field. I peeked around him to find Kols at the other end, his own power connecting to Zeph's to bolster him in his effort in protecting the entire class from the debris and insanity flying overhead.

It rippled around us like a tornado, reminding me of an Air Fae activity gone bad.

More of that familiar power buzzed through me, then fled, as if kissing my soul goodbye on its way out. The sirens above grew louder, the slithering snake creatures heading right for me. I cringed, waiting for their impact, only they slid over Zeph's shield and took off into the wind to chase some menacing figment.

My blood ran cold, my heart stopping in my chest. The creatures had sensed the dark energy running through me.

What would happen when Zeph lifted his protection? Would the Academy attack me with the same brutal force?

I shivered and felt Zeph's lips ghost across my temple, the touch brief but there. "I've got you," he vowed, the words meant for my ears alone.

How would I explain to him what I felt? Had it even been real?

He slowly started to sit up, his palm against my breastbone keeping me down on the ground as he glanced around. After several moments of searching, his touch eased, and he moved his hand to my shoulder to pull me upward.

"It's done," he said gruffly, the words carrying across the now silent field.

"The source is calm," Kols replied, his statement clear despite the distance.

No one uttered a sound, everyone gaping at the rocks and ash littering the grounds.

Then someone screamed in the distance, causing Zeph to jump to his feet.

"Go," Shade said, appearing beside me. The statement must have been meant for Zeph, because he took off at a sprint, Kols hot on his tail, along with several other students.

Cries pelted the air, all coming from the same direction. Shade practically yanked me to my feet, his palm finding my lower back as he guided me through the wreckage toward the commotion rising ahead. It didn't take long for us to find the cause.

The Death Blood Education Building had been reduced to a pile of rubble, the once proud spire a cascade of obsidian rocks without any structure.

And above the destruction was a single word written in red flames, the smoke spiraling up into the sky in lethal ropes that resembled chains.

It was a word I knew well.

Because I'd sung it many times before, as had my mother.

"*Alqisian*," I whispered.

"Yes," Shade replied just as softly. "Do you know what it means?"

"Not the translation of it, no."

He swallowed, his focus shifting from the rubble to me. "Retribution."

"Retribution," I repeated, my voice just as low as his. "Meaning what?"

Shade gave me a grim look, his icy blue eyes holding a myriad of secrets underlined in pain. "It means the future is officially now."

CHAPTER FIFTEEN

AFLORA

S<small>ILENCE</small>.

It started after Shade's revelation and continued long after he left with Kols and Tray to attend an emergency Council meeting. I sat on the couch between Zeph and Ella.

None of us knew what to say.

Ella glanced at me, her lips twisting like she wanted to say something, only she kept deciding not to speak. I understood why.

She'd recognized the word because of my song. It was one of the primary phrases repeated throughout the ballad. And it'd been written in fire above the destroyed Death Blood Education Building.

I couldn't explain that. Just as I couldn't explain how I'd recognized the magic. It wasn't mine but felt so familiar. Like I knew the fae who cast the spell.

Impossible, I thought for the millionth time. *It's just not possible.*

Who could it be? My parents? I nearly laughed at the thought. They were dead. I felt their souls depart when the earth source moved to me. And why would they attack the Academy?

However, I'd sensed something ancestral about the magic, like it was somehow connected to me, yet not.

I didn't know how to articulate it, so I kept the knowledge to myself while we waited.

And waited.

And waited some more.

Ella picked up her phone for the millionth time to check for any updates, then set it down again. Zeph did the same. I just sat with my hands clasped together on my lap, useless. Elemental Fae didn't really do technology. We preferred more natural methods of communication.

I pinched my mouth to the side and glanced around for the thousandth time. Zeph looked at me, his dark green eyes sheltered and not giving anything away. I wanted to ask him if this had ever happened before. I also wanted to tell him what Shade had said about the future being now. And I sort of wanted to confide in him about what I felt out on that field.

What if he betrays me again?

Can I really trust him?

A few nights of sexual torment didn't really mean much, and while he'd been against me unweaving the bond, there still wasn't a lot of evidence that he cared about me.

Except he'd guarded me on the field today.

No, he'd shielded the whole class.

Hmm, however, he'd yanked me beneath him in a protective gesture, and I'd felt his concern for my safety. Unless that had all been in my head.

His gaze narrowed at me now, my emotions probably running across my face with reckless abandon, making it obvious what I thought about.

Because I was still staring at him while I ran through all my considerations about trusting him or not.

I swallowed and looked away just as a cawing sound echoed through the suite. Clove swooped in through the threshold, her black and white feathers splayed in a manner that showed off all her falcon glory. My lips curled at the sight of her, my heart warming from the nearness of my familiar.

"Hello, Clove," I welcomed her.

She cooed in response, then dropped something in my lap from her long talons. I glanced down at it, curious, then froze at the sight of blood on my blouse and skirt.

"Oh," I breathed, my eyes widening.

"It seems your familiar brought you a present," Zeph said, his amusement palpable.

"What the hell is it?" Ella asked, clearly horrified by the dead, uh, *thing* in my lap. It was definitely an animal of some kind, but it seemed to be a cross between a rodent and a bird.

Zeph reached over to pick up the item by its long, wiry tail and held up the grotesque sight before us. "It's a stonepecker," he marveled, his tone suggesting we should be impressed.

"A *what*?" Ella gaped at it. "It looks like a possum mated with a… a…" She squinted at the sharp-looking beak. "A woodpecker?"

Zeph considered and nodded slowly. "I can see the resemblance, yeah. They're a bit of a nuisance, yet incredibly powerful. And they're known to absorb enchantments from whatever rock or stone they choose to destroy by pecking, hence the name *stonepecker*."

He set the dead little guy on the coffee table, then glanced at Clove. She'd perched on the back of the recliner chair and was busy preening her feathers.

"Seems someone's been playing in the LethaForest," he mused.

"The LethaForest?" I repeated.

He nodded. "Stonepeckers are nearly extinct as a result of them being a nuisance to Midnight Fae housing structures. Their ability to absorb enchantments also enables them to be used for nefarious purposes, such as circumventing wards or runes."

"What do you mean?" I asked, not understanding.

Zeph brought his ankle up to rest on his opposite knee and stared thoughtfully at the animal, his brow furrowing. "Many important Midnight Fae establishments are protected by wards. You've seen the Academy walls; they're riddled with protection charms."

"The snake vines," I said, nodding.

"And many others," he replied, his expression darkening. "They're controlled by a variety of spelled runes to ward off any evil intentions. But if a stonepecker were to peck at some of the surrounding walls, it could absorb the magic, which could then be used by a Midnight Fae to create a counterspell."

"A counterspell," I repeated. "Like to dismantle the protection spells?"

He nodded, his focus still on the stonepecker. "Yes. It would essentially create a safe portal for the fae to enter and exit through. It may also allow the fae to craft a shield of sorts to deflect any and all counterattacks that may be incurred after harming someone or something inside of the protected structure."

"Such as blowing up a building and writing *Alqisian* in flames above the destruction," I suggested, following his train of thought.

"Yeah. Just like that." He looked at Clove, then at me. "Your familiar just brought us evidence."

"That can't be good," Ella interjected. "I mean, especially after Aflora sang about…" She trailed off, her hands twisting in her lap.

"I didn't do this," I promised.

"Oh, I know you didn't," she replied without missing a beat. "I'm just…" She cleared her throat and looked past me at Zeph. "Is someone setting her up?"

My eyes widened as I glanced back at Zeph.

His expression turned grim. "That's certainly what it seems like. Why else—"

"We have a problem," Shade announced as he materialized across the room. He started toward us, then paused at the sight on the table. "Why the fuck is there a dead stonepecker in the living room?" Then his gaze widened. "Oh, shit. You need to dispose of that. Right fucking now. Before the Warrior Bloods arrive."

"She didn't do it!" Ella blurted out, jumping up to her feet in a defensive stance. "She was with us the whole damn time. I will go in front of those Council idiots myself if I have to. And fuck their male chauvinist bullshit; I will bang down their damn doors and scream at the top of my lungs."

Shade blinked at her, then glanced at me and Zeph. "What is she going on about?"

"Clove brought the stonepecker to Aflora," Zeph explained, gesturing at the blood residue on my uniform. "We believe someone is trying to set her up for this."

Shade huffed a laugh. "Close, but no. The attack has Elite magic all over it, and my father is blaming Kols."

My jaw dropped. "*What?*"

"There's no time to explain. The Warrior Bloods are on their way to conduct a thorough search of the premises, and *that* cannot be here." He pointed at the stonepecker.

"That's ridiculous," Zeph scoffed. "Kols was in my class during the explosion. There's no way he did this."

"While I agree, the scene reeks of source power. And Kols—"

"Is the one closest to the source," Zeph finished for him, cursing under his breath.

Shade dipped his chin once in confirmation, his icy gaze holding a touch of unease. "He looks good for the setup, Zeph. Which means someone is trying to take down the future king."

"Where's Tray?" Zeph asked.

"With Kols. He's the second potential suspect for obvious reasons." Shade ran his fingers through his dark hair and blew out a breath. "I need to get back before they notice I'm gone. I came to warn you that the Warrior

Bloods are on their way to conduct a search, authorized by the king himself. So I suggest you hide anything incriminating." His expression flashed with meaning.

Then he vanished into a puff of smoke.

Zeph immediately pulled out his wand and uttered a spell that incinerated the evidence on the table. Then he uttered another one after it that caused the surface to shimmer. He spoke so quickly and efficiently that I couldn't even decipher his words. When he focused on me next, I opened my mouth to stop him, but the magic was already working its way over my outfit and destroying all evidence of the creature from my lap.

I gaped at my pristine uniform.

"Well, that's one way to do laundry," Ella muttered, then shook her head. "Okay, there's something I don't understand."

"Only one thing?" I asked, completely taken aback by the last few minutes of conversation and the revelations Shade had dropped on us.

"Well, many things. But what I really want to know is, why did Shade just come here to warn us? He hates Kols. I'd expect him to be gloating and celebrating the accusation, not"—she waved her hand around the space he'd just vacated—"you know."

Zeph cleared his throat. "Well—"

A commotion at the door interrupted his ability to reply as three Warrior Bloods entered the suite with an irritated Sir Kristoff right behind them. "Fucking royals overriding royals," the stone creature muttered. He waved at them and looked at Zeph. "I'm taking the night off." His stone wings bristled and crunched, then he disappeared into a cloud of white chalk.

"They can do that?" I asked, shocked.

"Unfortunately," Zeph muttered, standing up. At some point, he'd put his wand away, but I sensed his magic lingering in the air. "What the hell are you doing here?" he demanded, his attention on the three male fae in the foyer.

"We're here on order of the king to search Prince Kolstov's suite for anything related to the attack today," the one with white-blond hair to his shoulders replied, his tone devoid of emotion.

"You can't be fucking serious." Zeph folded his arms. "What the hell could Kols have to do with any of this?"

"That's Council business," another of them replied, his chin notching upward in clear dismissal. "You're no longer privy to that information, *Headmaster*."

"Oh, fuck you, Danqris. I'm Guardian-bonded to Kolstov, which makes me your superior by default. A temporary demotion will never change that."

Danqris's lips pulled back into a snarl. "It will if I find anything that incriminates his ass."

Zeph scoffed at that. "Yeah, be my guest, asshole. But when you don't find anything, and Kols returns to see that you've destroyed all his shit, I'll be sure to tell him who to thank."

The Warrior Blood seemed to take that as more of a challenge than a threat and proceeded to rip apart the suite. When he reached my room, he demanded I unlock it.

And then began to destroy everything inside.

Including my new plant.

Zeph vibrated with anger by the end, but it was nothing compared to Ella. She actually slapped two of the Warrior Bloods after they rummaged through her personal items. Then she kicked the one called Danqris when he went for her underwear drawer.

I watched in amazement as they actually backed off, the blond one even looking a tad contrite as he sidestepped her to exit the bedroom.

After what felt like hours of unnecessary damage, the three Warrior Bloods left without a shred of evidence.

Clove hadn't moved from the recliner, having chosen to nap there while they rummaged through the suite. But I sensed her alertness, as if waiting for me to call her to my aid should I need it.

I wondered why she brought me the stonepecker, if it was something she found outside the walls or if she was trying to tell me something.

My suspicions told me it was the latter, but I couldn't figure out what she wanted me to know aside from the obvious—the perpetrator had used a stonepecker to breach the Academy walls.

"I'm going to fucking kill those assholes," Ella seethed as soon as they left, her eyes flashing with blue fire as she took in the mess they left behind.

"Kols will take care of them," Zeph promised. "But in the interim, we should probably clean this shit up."

Ella muttered a few more choice words before pulling out her wand. "I'll be in my bedroom."

Zeph nodded, his gaze catching mine. "Come on. I'll help with your room."

"Oh, you don't have to do that. I can, uh, well, I can pick up everything," I finished lamely, my lips twisting to the side.

I totally had this. I would just put everything away by hand. How hard could it be?

CHAPTER SIXTEEN

ZEPH

"I TOTALLY DO NOT HAVE THIS," I heard Aflora mutter to herself on the threshold of her room.

My lips twitched as I took out my wand and created a pair of figments. "Put everything back where it was two hours ago." They would be able to sense the history of objects to know where each item went.

The two invisible entities started immediately, causing items to essentially float across the room as they followed my edict.

"When you're done in here, work on the kitchen, then the study area and the other guest room."

They didn't reply, but I felt their agreement through my magical bond to them.

I left them to it and followed Aflora's scent down the hallway to her room, where I found her standing in the center of a disaster zone with her hands on her hips. "You sure you don't want my help?" I asked her softly.

She studied the shattered pot in the corner, her brow furrowing. "Why did they destroy the fairy plant? I mean, what could it possibly have been hiding?"

"They were being assholes," I told her from the entrance of her room, my hands in my pockets. "Want me to teach you a spell that can fix it?"

She glanced over her shoulder at me. "We can fix it?"

I smiled. "Magic can fix almost anything, Aflora." I pushed off the door frame and walked toward her. "Here, take out your wand and face the plant."

Surprisingly, she did exactly what I requested, her focus intense as she surveyed the corner. "Okay. Now what?"

I lightly pressed my chest to her back, then drew my fingers down her arm to the hand holding her wand. "Lift it up to about here," I explained, guiding her wrist upward. "You want to aim at the plant and draw a U just like this." I demonstrated while I spoke by moving her hand subtly into the shape I described before leading her back to the beginning point and releasing her. "Now repeat that action while saying, '*Illa'shala.*'"

She cleared her throat, then followed my instructions to the letter. Excitement hummed through her as the object adhered to her command to repair itself.

"Try it again on your closet door," I suggested.

"But the plant isn't done."

"Don't worry. The spell will continue until it's finished or until you tell it to stop. Trust me."

She shot me a look over her shoulder, one that said she didn't trust me in the slightest, then grimaced upon realizing what she'd just done.

I didn't comment, allowing the moment to pass, and waited for her to try the spell again.

After a few seconds, she conceded, her shoulders tense as if expecting the enchantment to backfire. When it didn't, she visibly relaxed.

"Now say, '*Badan clothes,*' and do a zigzag motion over the closet," I murmured.

"Zigzag, like this?" She drew her wand through the air in a Z pattern.

"Yes, but don't exaggerate your wrist that much." I reached for her again, this time placing a hand on her hip while my opposite reached for her hand. She didn't tense, so I took it as an invitation to press my chest to her back again, then brought my lips to her ear. "Like this." I guided her through a much smaller Z, then drew my fingers up her arm to rest on her shoulder. "Try it."

She did and grinned as her wardrobe pieced itself back together. I was about to tell her to repeat the command for her shoes when she beat me to it, her boots and other articles lining themselves up in the same place they'd been before Danqris had sent a tornado through her things.

Aflora focused on her dresser next, using the same command, then looked at her books. "Do I restack those manually?"

"You could, or try the same spell and see what happens." I still had my hands on her with my chest pressed to her back, so I felt her hesitation once more. But rather than look at me questioningly, she chose to utter the incantation.

All her school supplies returned to her nightstand and to her spot in the corner where she seemed to keep her books.

"You need a desk," I realized, frowning at the space.

"There's not enough room for it," she replied.

She was right. "Okay." I considered for a moment. "I want you to draw a square in the air and say, '*Kala'key bookcase.*' And when you do it, picture the kind of bookshelf you'd like in the corner."

"I thought *Tareero* was the spell for wanting something?"

"Only food. *Kala'key* is how you create something, but you have to be very specific in your mind and make sure to push that knowledge to your wand. Otherwise, nothing will happen. Or you'll get something you don't want. Depends on how it's done."

"That's… promising."

"Do as I said and you'll be fine." And if she didn't, I'd

help her fix it.

"Right." She took a steadying breath, then muttered something about tulips under her breath.

My lips twitched in amusement. "Not flowers, a bookshelf."

"I'm concentrating," she chastised.

I released her shoulder to grab her hips with both hands. "Okay. I'll be right here."

She didn't seem to hear me, or perhaps didn't care, because she continued to stare at the corner like she could will the bookcase to appear without a spell. Which would be a neat trick and entirely possible for an older Midnight Fae, but she wasn't quite there yet.

After a few moments, she nodded, lifted her wand, and spoke the enchantment out loud while drawing her box. Then she added, "*Badan books.*"

A floor-to-ceiling shelving unit appeared, the wooden poles on the sides decorated with vines of gorgeous blue blossoms that reminded me of her eyes. And on the shelves sat all her books, including the ones from her nightstand.

"Beautiful," I praised.

She gave a little clap and spun around to face me. "I did it."

"You did," I replied, smiling at her. Then I gestured with my chin to the ceramic pot in the opposite corner. "Looks like your plant is appreciative as well."

Aflora twisted toward it, her eyes widening. "Oh! How pretty!"

Hmm, I'd have to mention to Kols later that she'd finally figured out how to access her earth magic through the collar, which implied our earlier enchantment that diminished her power had finally worn off. We'd discuss it right after I told him how Clove delivered a stonepecker moments before the Warrior Bloods arrived.

My jaw ticked as I considered the situation. "When you're done in here, we need to talk about your familiar." I realized the mistake of my comment the minute I said it because Aflora froze, her excitement over the plant dying in an instant.

Fuck.

We still hadn't discussed that day in class when Raph killed Clove. I'd been in a mood, and it seemed right at the time to teach her a lesson about familiars and etiquette.

And yeah, that hadn't gone as planned.

She practically hated me after that.

"I mean in regard to the present she brought you," I amended quickly. "I want to make sure she's not enchanted or under the influence of another fae."

Aflora frowned at me. "You think someone cast a spell on her?"

"Why else would she bring you the stonepecker?" I countered.

My little mate didn't speak for a moment, her expression going from confused to wary. "What do you have to do to her to determine if she's been enchanted?"

I sighed. "I'm not going to hurt her, Aflora."

Her eyes told me she didn't believe me. "Okay."

Right. I'd have to prove it to her, then. "Are you done in here, or do you have other things to straighten up?"

"It's mostly good, I guess," she replied, noting the rumpled bedding, skewed rugs, and ripped blinds.

I called forth a third figment and told her to tidy up the mess.

Aflora's eyebrows lifted. "Why didn't you just show me how to do that?"

"Because the other spells provided a teaching moment."

"Since when do you like to teach?" she asked, her gaze holding a touch of humor that lightened the atmosphere a little between us.

"Never," I admitted. "But I don't mind teaching you." It was the truth, but I didn't expect her to accept it. Rather than wait around for another of those distrusting looks, I said, "Come on. Let's go have a chat with Clove."

"A chat," she repeated with notable sarcasm. "Sure."

"I've been an ass and you don't trust me. That's fine." I wrapped my arm around her shoulders and hugged her to me, my lips going to her ear. "But keep it up and I'll torment you for the rest of the evening and day with my tongue."

"You do that in my dreams already," she pointed out even while her cheeks blossomed into a beautiful shade of pink. "Nothing new there."

"Mmm." I drew my nose across her pretty flush until my lips hovered a scant breath away from hers. "Who said anything about dreams?" I pressed a chaste kiss to the corner of her mouth—the only place I'd allowed myself to truly kiss her outside of her mind. "I'm in your room, Aflora. Right now. Right here. None of this is a dream, and I will absolutely tease you with my tongue on that freshly made bed. Just say the word, pixie flower."

She shivered, her arousal scenting the air in a sultry aroma I longed to taste.

But I wanted to prove myself first.

And for that, I needed Clove.

With a lingering kiss to the same place as before, I released her, grabbed her hand, and tugged her into the hallway without another word.

If we stayed in her room for a second longer, I'd forget all about my task and make undressing Aflora my sole priority. But she wasn't ready yet, and I refused to push her more than I already had.

"You still have your wand, right?" I asked her.

She waved it in response, her knuckles white from clasping the end of it so harshly.

I smirked, understanding why. She'd been teased all week and desired a climax, one I would give her if things went well later.

Clove hadn't moved from her perch on the recliner, her feathers smoothed back and her eyes alert. She watched me with a similar wariness to her master's, confirming everything I already knew about Aflora's confidence in me.

"Raph isn't here," I assured both of them. "Last I saw

him, he was sleeping in my closet on a bed of shirts he'd taken off the racks." He was a dick like that and enjoyed creating nests out of my clean clothes.

Clove bristled at our approach, her dark eyes narrowing at me.

I let go of Aflora's hand and stepped away from her slowly before holding out my palm for the falcon to sniff. She didn't budge, her displeasure evident.

"You're going to have to get used to me," I murmured. "I'm one of Aflora's mates."

This didn't seem to placate Aflora's familiar. If anything, she appeared even more anxious.

I tried for a different tactic and kneeled before her, making myself appear inferior, then held out my palm again. "I'm sorry for our first introduction. I promise not to harm you again."

If Kols saw me right now, apologizing to a bird, he'd lose his shit. But this wasn't about the falcon. It was about Aflora.

I had hurt her.

For us to move forward, she needed to see that I knew how to apologize properly. Which required me to get this falcon to essentially forgive me.

Clove tilted her head slightly, her intelligent gaze on my hand.

She shifted forward and snagged my fingers with her beak, biting down hard enough to warn without breaking the skin.

I didn't move.

I didn't even flinch.

Instead, I continued to stare at her. "If you need to exact blood, then fine. I'll give it." Mostly because one taste would tell her who I was to her master and she'd immediately release me.

"Don't," Aflora said, talking to Clove. "Zeph is… a friend."

Just a friend? I nearly asked her, amused. But I kept quiet, allowing her to run the show. It was what the situation necessitated.

Clove slowly released my hand, her gaze flicking affectionately to Aflora.

"Yeah, I like her, too," I admitted softly.

The falcon let out a gentle caw that I interpreted to mean she approved, so I slowly reached out to touch one of her plumes. She didn't react or try to bite me again, which was a good sign. She even leaned into my touch a little, allowing me to win her over with a few gentle strokes down her wings.

I glanced at Aflora to see her staring at me in surprise. "What?"

"You… you…" She shook her head. "Never mind."

"Surprised your falcon forgave me?" I asked her.

"No. I'm surprised you said you liked me. I'm pretty sure you implied the opposite just a few weeks ago."

I frowned. "I never said I disliked you."

"No, you're right," she said, her blue eyes flickering with fire. "You called me pitiful, like Clove."

I flinched. "I was trying to teach you a lesson."

"That you have to kill to protect yourself. I remember."

We were never going to move past this if she wouldn't allow it. And I could only apologize so much.

I sat back on my heels and stared at her. "The Midnight Fae world isn't like your Elemental Fae one, Aflora. I'm only trying to prepare you for survival, something I'm going to take even more seriously now that our souls are tied together."

"I already said I could try unbinding us."

"And I already told you no," I snapped, irritated that she'd even think to bring it up again. "If you release us, you'll implode."

"That's not really your concern, is it?" she retorted.

"That's where you're wrong, Aflora. It *is* my concern. I'm a Warrior Blood. It's literally my job to guard and protect." I ran my fingers through my hair and sighed. "At some point, I vowed to keep you safe. I can't say when it happened, but I suspect it was shortly after we met. I claimed you before I allowed myself to realize it."

I really didn't know what else to say to convince this female that all I ever wanted was to help her survive. Maybe I'd been hard on her, but I didn't know any other way. Warrior Bloods weren't exactly known for their gentle touch.

She stared at me for another long, hard moment. Then looked at Clove. "What was it you needed to check?"

Part of me admired her for yanking us back to the important topic at hand. The other part was disappointed because it left our conversation unfinished, and I was really tired of her holding the past against me. We couldn't move forward if she continued to hate me for what I'd allowed Raph to do to Clove.

Rather than harp on it, I followed her lead, knowing full well we'd return to this topic again soon.

"We need to see if she has any energy strands circling her," I replied. "If someone enchanted her, their signature would be left behind for a few hours."

"And if someone didn't?" she asked.

I shifted my focus to Clove. "There really aren't many options. It could be a coincidence, which I doubt. Or someone asked her to take it to you as a message."

"Fae can do that?"

"Fae that are close to you in some way, like a mate." I almost wanted to suggest that Shade could have done it, but I knew that was impossible considering he was at the Council meeting and had been clearly shocked by the stonepecker on the table. He also wouldn't have popped in to warn us if he wanted to set up Kols.

"Close to me," she repeated. "Like a mate… or family?"

I lifted a shoulder. "Yeah, I think a family member could call a familiar." I studied Clove, searching for any traces of magic. Most fae wouldn't be stupid enough to leave visible evidence, but it was worth checking.

Unfortunately, I saw nothing.

"You'll need to do a tracing spell," I told her. "Or I can do it, if you prefer." I glanced at her, expecting her to agree to the former.

However, she surprised me by saying, "You do it. I'll watch and learn." My face must have registered some shock, because she added, "If you hurt her, I'll make you eat a burning thwomp."

"You seem really fond of the notion of eating burnt wood," I replied. "It's making me question Elemental Fae diets."

"Ha. Ha." She rolled her eyes, but I caught the hint of amusement teasing her lips. "Go on and test her for energy strands."

I grinned. "Then afterward, I'll make you some fire gnat juice."

"Or another dragon steak," she offered.

"Or that," I agreed, winking. Then I took out my wand and gave Clove my undivided attention. "Let's see who sent you, shall we?"

CHAPTER SEVENTEEN

KOLS

WHAT A FUCKING NIGHT.

I blew out a disgruntled breath as I entered my suite, expecting to see the whole thing shredded to hell and pausing upon discovering the pristine interior awaiting my entry.

"They cleaned," Tray explained from the couch, catching my confusion. He had a content Ella snuggled up against him, her head pillowed against his shoulder. "Zeph and Aflora are actually in your room finishing up, and there are some leftovers on the stove, if you want any."

He had an empty plate on the table, suggesting he'd just finished eating. As he'd only left about thirty minutes ahead of me, that timing made sense.

"I'm not hungry," I admitted, still riled up and pissed off from the bullshit the Council had thrown at me.

The only reason they hadn't locked me up for observation was because of Aflora. My father had argued that I needed to be on campus with her to continue her monitoring. Others had suggested she be locked up with me. Then he'd reminded them of my role as future king and the importance of completing this task for my upcoming ascension.

It was all a fucking mess.

And I really just wanted to take a damn nap.

Tray nodded in understanding, then kissed Ella on the forehead, holding her close. "I'll put the leftovers in the fridge for you," he said.

"Thanks," I muttered, meaning it despite my gruff tone. "I'm going to go make sure Zeph hasn't rearranged my room."

"Good idea." He returned his focus to the blonde in his arms, his palm cupping her cheek as he angled her face upward to receive his kiss.

I had spent the last three and a half years envying him and his ability to choose. Not that I'd ever admitted it out loud. My destiny was to serve the crown, a future I'd taken seriously and devoted my entire life to fulfill.

However, tonight the Council rewarded my fealty with an unwarranted accusation followed by a search of my private quarters, all to hunt for evidence that didn't exist.

No one had believed my innocence.

Not even my father.

After everything I'd given up for those assholes, they'd refused to take me at my word.

And that fucking burned.

I yanked on the knotted tie at my throat and started down the hallway to my room, only to pause on the threshold at the sight of Aflora giggling. She sat cross-legged on my rug with a plate in her lap, while Zeph stood over her with his hands on his hips.

"Seriously, I'm going to start feeding you bark," he was saying. "Maybe topped with some charcoal blades."

"Is that what it's called?" she asked. "The black grass in the fields?"

He snorted. "Yeah, that's not grass, pixie flower."

"Well, I know. It's sharp and brittle and... charcoal-y."

His lips twitched. "Hence the name—charcoal blades."

Her nose scrunched upward. "I'm not eating that."

"Yet you'll eat a leafy salad patty monstrosity with mussleberries."

"They're mouseberries," she corrected him. "And yes, I would eat that." She held up her plate. "Please."

"I've already fed you dragon steak and the other version of salad patty. If you want more, you can make it yourself."

I leaned against the doorjamb, entertained by this entire exchange. But my movement drew both their eyes to me and caused Aflora to jump up off my rug and onto her feet. "Oh! You're back."

"I am." I tucked my hands into my pockets and glanced around my room. "Seems like you did a good job cleaning."

"Figments," Aflora said quickly. "Zeph made figments. We were just making sure it's all sorted. So, uh, looks good. I'll leave you two to it, then." She started toward the door, and I moved to block her exit.

"I'm nearly arrested for an explosion at the Academy, and you're going to leave me with a 'looks good'?" I arched an eyebrow at her. "Seriously?"

Zeph came up behind her, effectively caging her between us. She lifted the plate to her chest like that would be able to protect her.

"Um." She bit her lip, considering. "I'm glad you're okay. We know you didn't do it. Oh, and Clove had no magical ties that Zeph could find. So we're not sure who gave her the stonepecker or where she found it, but we're pretty sure it was done on purpose to set you up. It's a good thing Shade stopped by to warn us about the search."

That was a hell of a lot of information in a handful of seconds. I gaped at Zeph. "Stonepecker?"

"Yeah. Aflora's familiar brought it to her as a gift and dropped it in her lap. We're guessing it's how the culprit entered the Academy grounds, but I had to destroy it because of the Warrior Bloods."

Of course. "What about my other things?" I asked him,

knowing he'd interpret my question.

He jerked his chin at the closet. "Sir Kristoff did his job."

I nodded. "Good."

Aflora's brow creased. "I thought Sir Kristoff took the night off?"

I grunted and put my hands on her hips to walk her backward into my Guardian's chest, then kicked my door closed behind me. "Sir Kristoff doesn't take time off," I said, releasing her to Zeph. He promptly wrapped his arms around her, knowing I didn't want her to leave. The two of them watched as I walked over to my closet. As soon as I opened it, the gargoyle in question came strolling out with my box.

"Here you go, My Prince," he drawled, holding it up for me.

"Thank you, Sir Kristoff," I murmured. "You're excused."

He bowed and disappeared into a white cloud of dust, his trademark exit.

"Now he's taking the night off?" Aflora guessed.

"No, he's gone back to the front door," I replied, my focus on the box in my hands. I opened it to check the contents inside and nodded. "All here."

"Then the gargoyle did his job," Zeph murmured.

I nodded. "He did."

"What's in the box?" Aflora asked, unusually bold tonight. Or maybe she was just getting more comfortable with us, in which case, I approved.

"Your real collar and a few other items I don't want the Council to know about." Such as the photo of her parents from Sol.

I went to my closet to return the container to the rightful place, one Sir Kristoff knew about so he could hide it again should the need arise.

While my father commanded the kingdom, the gargoyle's allegiance belonged to me. I'd seen to that minor detail the day I started attending the Academy. It was an easy task, mostly because I treated Sir Kristoff with respect and listened to his requests. A few negotiations later and his loyalty was mine.

"My real collar?" Aflora asked, touching the thin leather around her throat. "I thought that's what Zeph put on me before the guards came for me last week."

I met his gaze over her head, wondering if he wanted to explain it or if I should. He gave a subtle nod for me to go ahead.

"This isn't the collar from the Council," I said softly, stepping in front of her again. I lifted my finger to the leather encircling her neck and traced it along her throat. "Remember how there were two before?"

She nodded. "I destroyed one in the LethaForest."

"Yes. So Zeph and I created a new one to replace it, but we had to make it match the one from the Council. We added a temporary enchantment to mask your powers—specifically, your Quandary Blood abilities—and also created a concealment charm to hide our bonds to you. It was done hastily, but it worked."

I pressed my thumb to the side, near her pulse, and unsnapped the leather to bring it away from her neck to see it.

"The spells have slowly worn off over the last week, bringing the concealment to a dull thrum that should only be protecting our bonds, not diminishing your power. Have you felt it weakening?" I asked her softly.

She frowned at the item in my hand. "I hadn't thought much of it after that initial zing."

"I imagine that hurt," I replied, regretful. "But we didn't know what else to do, and there wasn't time to explain."

"So you never put the real collar on me."

I shook my head. "No. Just touching it zaps all the energy right out of me. I can't imagine what it would do around your neck." Which was precisely why I'd never make her wear it.

Zeph bent down to kiss her freshly exposed skin, his eyes holding mine the entire time. I read the message in his depths, just as I noted her sharp inhale.

"Oh," she breathed, her lashes fluttering a little. "I... I didn't realize they were... different."

I set her collar off to the side and returned to brush my knuckles down her flushed cheek. "The primary purpose of that collar is to hide your connection to me and Zeph." I showed her the band around my wrist. "Zeph and I have to wear these, or others will sense the mating claim. Shade doesn't need one since everyone already knows he bit you."

"I think we can remove them for a bit," Zeph mused, his lips still at her neck. "Assuming we're all staying here for the next few hours."

My lips curled. "I think we're staying here for a while."

Aflora swallowed, her pupils darkening. "Are you going to bite me again?"

"Do you want us to?" I countered, removing the cuff around my wrist and setting it beside her collar. Zeph held out his for me to add to the pile, then grabbed her hips to hold her between us as I returned to my position in front of her.

"Do you, uh, need blood again?" she asked.

"Not really, no. I had a shake just yesterday."

"A shake?" Her brow furrowed. "You call humans 'shakes'?"

I smirked. "No. I mean a literal milkshake. Tray and Ella make them all the time instead of feeding on mortals."

"They do?"

"You've never noticed?" I countered, arching a brow. "Ella has a protein shake flavored with blood every evening."

"I thought it was just a human food."

"It is, mostly. With the added nutrients Midnight Fae need to remain connected to the source. Zeph's been ordering blood-laced food as well."

"Not my favorite, but I need to get used to it," he said,

lifting a shoulder.

"Why?" Aflora asked.

She tried to glance back at him, but he pressed his mouth to her ear to murmur, "Because Midnight Fae with mates typically don't feed on humans. It complicates matters, as you found out last week with your reaction to Kols feeding in the mortal realm. We're territorial and we don't like to share."

"So no more drinking blood from the vein, unless it's from your vein," I said, closing the space between us. "And I won't bite you again until you ask me to." Or if I needed to suck power out of her, but I didn't add that part, because it would be implied consent like it was the first time.

"Yes," Zeph agreed softly. "We heard you loud and clear last week, pixie flower. No more sharing."

"I-I didn't say that," she stuttered, her chest rising and falling in fast pants against mine.

"It was implied by your reaction," I informed her. "And we did discuss exclusivity, if I remember correctly."

"We never agreed to it," she pointed out.

"Again, it was implied." I drew my finger down the center of her torso, fondling the buttons of her blouse along the way. "I've had one hell of a night, Aflora. There's really only one thing I want to do right now, and that's to make you come with my mouth. May I?"

Aflora's eyes widened. "Like, really come? Or just tease me more?"

"There will definitely be teasing involved," I promised her, unfastening the top button of her shirt. "But it will lead to a climax that will blow your mind."

An arrogant assessment, but that didn't make it any less true.

The glimmer in her flaring pupils told me she knew it, too.

"Okay," she whispered, leaning back into Zeph. "But if this turns into a dream where you leave me unfulfilled, I really will break our bonds."

"Then I guess we'll need to bite you again, too," Zeph replied, his tongue tracing the shell of her ear. "Can't risk having you force us out."

"Please me and you won't have to worry," she countered, causing my lips to curl.

"Mmm, I rather like this bolder side of you," I mused, popping another button to expose her lacy bra. "Take off your panties for us, baby. Then give them to Zeph."

She shivered, her irises smoldering with intensity. "Yes, My Prince," she whispered, the title going straight to my cock. Zeph had told her to call me that the other night in one of our fantasies, and hearing her use it now made me want to kiss the ever-living fuck out of her.

But instead, I focused on the next button while she lifted her skirt to take hold of the lace between her thighs. She slowly drew it down her legs. I stepped back to allow her to bend while Zeph watched from behind, his green eyes glimmering with anticipation.

Aflora pulled the soft white material over her bare feet, then straightened and held it over her shoulder for Zeph. He took them and nodded at me to finish removing her blouse.

Each button revealed more and more of her creamy skin, drawing my focus downward to admire her subtle curves and flat abdomen. She really was beautiful. It almost hurt to look at her.

Her shirt fell to the floor, leaving her in a bra and skirt, the picture of "naughty schoolgirl." My mouth twitched at the thought of all the ways I could make that title come true, but instead I allowed Zeph to walk her backward to the bed.

"Remove your bra," I told her. "Zeph wants it."

I didn't move from my spot, my hands going to my tie instead to finish unknotting the silk and remove it from my neck.

"On the bed," Zeph said, taking over as soon as her gorgeous tits spilled into view.

She handed him her lacy bra without an ounce of

nervousness and hopped up onto the mattress.

"Lie on your back and grab the bars of the headboard," Zeph instructed her.

Aflora frowned but did as she was told. He'd slowly introduced her to his tastes over the last week, exerting his dominance at every turn. This experience would be similar, his methods mostly gentle as a result of not wanting to frighten her.

And this would be the first time he truly touched her.

To my knowledge, the two of them hadn't even kissed yet. Because the dreams didn't really count. They were just erotic fantasies driven by playing minds.

I walked forward to lay my tie over her abdomen as Zeph secured her wrists above her head with the lace of her panties and bra. She watched him with surprise in her gaze, then flickered her focus to the silk on her stomach, her brow pinched.

But she wasn't entirely concerned.

No, she was equally turned on. Her nipples had stiffened to taut little peaks that begged for a man's mouth. Goose bumps stampeded an alluring path down her arms. And her arousal sweetened the air, forcing me to inhale her aromatic scent with every breath.

She liked this.

She wanted this.

Something she confirmed by clenching her thighs and fighting a moan as Zeph drew his fingers down her arm and over her breast to the tie waiting for him near her belly button.

"We're going to play a game, Aflora," he informed her softly.

"What kind of game?" she asked, her voice holding a sultry quality to it that made my blood pump a little faster.

"One where you guess who is touching you," he murmured, trailing my silk tie up her neck. "If you're right, we'll reward you." The garment met her cheek. "And if you're wrong, we'll teach you."

"Teach me?" she repeated, her tongue sneaking out to lick her bottom lip. "Teach me what?"

"You'll see," he replied, draping the fabric over her forehead, preparing to slide it down. "Now close your eyes. We're about to begin."

CHAPTER EIGHTEEN

AFLORA

MY HEART THUMPED WILDLY IN MY CHEST, my breathing escalating with each passing second. My mates had gone quiet after Zeph had slid the silk over my eyes. I could hear their clothes shifting, the sounds of zippers unfastening, and fabric dropping to the floor. But I didn't know who was where or what they intended to do.

Heat warmed my insides, the intensity mounting with each inhale and subsequent exhale.

What did they plan to do?

What if they left me like this?

In my dreams, they often teased for hours and hours. They might do the same now and deny—

I jolted as a palm gently wrapped around my ankle, then slipped slowly upward, tracing my leg all the way up to my inner thigh where a single finger brushed my slit. A moan escaped my mouth, only to be swallowed by one of their mouths.

Oh…

The tickle of hair against my chin told me who this was.

Zeph.

My assumption was confirmed in the next breath as his tongue parted my lips and demanded control inside my mouth. His woodsy scent poured over me, claiming me, overpowering me, *devouring* me. I'd thought he was dominant in my dreams, but the reality was so much *more.*

His strength became mine, emboldening me and making me long to free my hands to thread my fingers through his hair.

My thighs squeezed together, drawing my focus back to the hand between them. That had to be Kols, or I'd feel the heat of Zeph's arm across my torso, but all I could sense was his mouth on mine.

Dear Fae, he was a good kisser. He led me every step of the way, his lips a confident presence against my own, teaching and taunting and hypnotizing me with every move.

I groaned as Kols's finger slid inside me, drawing my focus back to him.

Then someone grabbed my breast, his thumb flicking over my nipple and drawing a gasp from my throat.

Their hands were suddenly everywhere, confusing my senses and overwhelming my instincts. My veins burned with need, my lungs forgetting how to work, my throat raspy and dry.

Zeph's lips left mine, moving downward to my breast as Kols sealed his mouth around my clit. They sucked in unison, just like in my dreams, only the scrape of teeth against my core reminded me of Zeph more than Kols, leaving me confused.

Had they switched places? Zeph's mouth hadn't skimmed my neck on his way to my chest; he'd left me completely but only for a brief second. Or that was how it felt before sensation overloaded my—

"Oh!" I cried out, arching off the mattress.

That was *definitely* Zeph between my thighs. I recognized that rasp of his beard, teasing my sensitive lips. However, Kols had left his finger inside me.

No, not one.

Two.

He scissored them back and forth, enticing me closer to the edge with each twist. I lost myself to the heat and longing induced by their touch, their intimate kisses, and their licks and bites and nibbles.

A week of sensual torment created a maelstrom in my lower abdomen, shooting flames through my veins and forcing moans to tickle my throat.

I couldn't focus.

Forgot how to breathe.

Let go of all my thoughts and feelings and fears.

And allowed them to pull me into an oblivion that literally stole my consciousness for a brief moment, introducing me to the afterlife and beyond before pulling me back to the reality of their presence. One of them was chuckling. *Zeph.* The other had slipped down to feast on my arousal.

They were everywhere at once, driving me close to the edge again. "Not yet," Zeph said, pulling back. "We need to play our game first."

I growled in response to his idea of *playing a game.* I wanted to come again. *Right now.*

"Don't be greedy, little mate," he murmured, stretching out alongside me. Kols took my other side, the heat of their bodies bathing me in a lust-induced ecstasy that I longed to swim in forever.

They were naked.

I couldn't see them, but I could *feel* them. Zeph's impressive length met my hip, his cock pulsating with a desire I knew too well. He'd remained clothed in all our shared fantasies, never once allowing me to *see* him. And oh, how I yearned to see him now.

Then Kols pressed his groin to my opposite side, his arousal more familiar, yet not. We'd only been truly intimate once, and it hadn't ended well.

Now I had them both.

In reality.

Naked.

And I couldn't see either of them. Or touch them.

I must have growled again, because Zeph tsked. "None of that, Aflora. We let you come once—without my permission, mind you—so now we'll play a game."

I bit my lip, recalling all the times he'd demanded I ask for permission to orgasm. He had to be in control at all times, his dominance written into everything he did. And I'd broken one of his rules.

Which meant he intended to punish me for it, probably by denying more orgasms—another of his favorite activities. Or so I assumed, given everything he'd done to me over the last week.

"I'm sorry, Zeph. I forgot," I admitted.

He leaned in and pressed his mouth to mine in a tender kiss. "You're forgiven, pixie flower," he whispered, nuzzling my nose. "I loved watching you come in your dreams, but this..." He ground himself against my hip, then palmed my breast and gave it a sensual squeeze. "Mmm, this was so much sweeter and *real*."

His mouth captured mine, forcing me to taste my own arousal from his tongue. I moaned, my grip on the headboard tightening as I fought the urge to rip free from the lacy bondage around my wrists. His knots were loose— something I suspected was done for my benefit—but I didn't want to displease him by pulling away from the bonds too soon.

Something about Zeph made me want to obey him.

And so I did, kissing him as he kissed me and allowing him to guide me into the intimacy he craved.

However, I couldn't stop the sound of protest that left my lips as he pulled away, his mouth my new favorite addiction. He chuckled in response, his teeth nipping my chin. "Don't worry, pixie flower. I enjoy kissing you, too. But you need to answer a few questions for us first."

"Okay," I agreed, my cheeks warming.

Kols leaned in to kiss my neck, his lips finding my pulse as he hummed his approval against my skin. "I hope you answer correctly, sweetheart."

"Who kissed you first tonight?" Zeph asked, beginning the game.

"You," I answered without hesitation.

"Good girl," he replied, leaning down to take my mouth again, this time as a reward.

Kols continued to lick a path up and down my neck while Zeph possessed me with his tongue, the combined intensity forcing me to squeeze my legs together in search of necessary friction.

"Whose fingers slid inside you first, princess?" Kols asked against my ear. "Were they mine? Or did they belong to Zeph?"

I swallowed, this one not as clear. But I felt pretty sure it was Kols. "Yours," I said. "You touched my ankle and slid up my leg and beneath my skirt, then Zeph kissed me."

He pressed his palm to my stomach before gliding down to repeat the action beneath my skirt, his two fingers sliding into me with ease to scissor once more, confirming I was right because it felt the same. "Who sucked your clit?" he asked. "Me or Zeph?"

"Zeph," I whispered, recalling the way his stubble felt against my flesh.

"And who brought you to orgasm?" Zeph asked, his lips still hovering over mine.

"Both of you," I replied on a moan as Kols hooked his fingers to stroke a spot inside me that caused stars to blink behind my eyes.

"You're amazing at this game," Zeph praised, his lips sliding to my ear. "Now we're going to feed you our cocks, and you're going to guess which one of us is inside you based on taste alone."

Kols removed his touch from below and brought his hand to my mouth. "Suck," he instructed, dipping his fingers into my mouth.

The wantonness of tasting myself on his skin had me groaning in approval, my heart hammering inside my chest. Then they were moving again, rearranging themselves on the bed and pulling my wrists free of the restraints.

I allowed them to guide me to where they wanted me, aware of who held me based on their scents alone. First, Kols guided me up onto my knees. Then Zeph twisted me around and urged me to bend forward until my palms met the mattress.

Neither male released me until they were sure I was steady, their palms tracking over every inch of me and lighting my skin on fire along the way. They shifted again, one of them moving behind me while the other positioned himself at my head. I recognized Kols's spicy scent as he nudged my chin upward to the angle he preferred.

Then the head of his cock kissed my lips.

I opened for him on instinct, allowing him to enter and indulging in his familiar flavor.

Cinnamon, spice, and man.

I groaned, swallowing him as deep as my throat allowed. His fingers twined in my hair, stilling me when I started to pull back for air. He seemed to be trying to catch his breath, perhaps even not make a sound, but I already knew it was him, something I would have told him if I could.

After a beat, he allowed me to move, my nostrils flaring to inhale much-needed oxygen, but he didn't let me pop him out of my mouth. Instead, he drove back in, his grip tightening as he forced me to take more of him.

I relaxed my throat, allowing him to drive while a hand slipped between my thighs to test my arousal. The kiss against the base of my spine told me Zeph approved of what he found.

That little gesture gave the game away, confirming what I already knew about their positions—Kols being in my mouth with Zeph behind me.

Zeph always guarded me in my dreams, his gaze ever watchful as if needing to reassure himself that I was enjoying the act. And he frequently touched me to gauge my interest in certain things, like he did now by sliding his finger through my damp folds.

It made me trust him, even when he took me outside of my comfort zone.

Kols left my lips slowly, drawing me back to him and eliciting a complaint from my throat. He caressed my cheek in response, then moved to switch places with Zeph.

I considered telling them I already knew who was where, but the velvety kiss of Zeph's arousal against the edge of my mouth distracted me.

Oh, yes, please. I wanted to taste him. To learn his likes and dislikes. To please him. To swallow his pleasure just as he did mine.

My lips parted for him, my tongue already moving to greet him as he slid inside far gentler than I expected. I could feel the tension in him, the way he held himself back, and for some reason, that made me want to push him. To see if I could dismantle some of his control and set him free.

Because I wanted to experience *him*, the man behind the dominance, the one who craved me without remorse. I'd seen that male lurking in his gaze, had felt him rising in my dreams, but had yet to experience him in the flesh.

I needed to devour him, to know him, to feel him inside me.

I wanted him to *come*.

I hollowed my cheeks, my throat working to take him deeper, only his palm gripped the back of my neck to pull me away from him instead. Kols's palms burned against my hips as he held me in place, the tip of Zeph's cock whispering against my lips.

I leaned forward to lick him, only to be held back by his hand around my neck. "You already knew it was me, didn't you, pixie flower?"

"Yes," I admitted. "Kols went first, but I wanted to taste you, so I didn't say anything."

He released my nape and drew his knuckles across my cheekbone in a tender manner. They both seemed keen on that little motion.

Actually, there were a lot of similarities between Zeph and Kols.

I knew they shared women, the rumors were rampant about it, but now I understood why. They worked well as a team. Even now with how Zeph gently stroked my face while Kols's thumbs drew hypnotic patterns against my hips.

Always touching and ensuring my comfort. Minus the orgasm denial bit.

Zeph slipped his thumb beneath the makeshift blindfold, slowly guiding it upward and over my head to allow me to see.

I blinked a few times, my eyes unadjusted to the light.

He pressed his palm to my cheek when I swayed a little, his strength providing me with the stability I needed to find my bearings once more. Meanwhile, Kols's thumbs continued that delirious pattern against my skin, the heat of his groin a firm presence at my backside and exciting my nerves.

I wanted them both inside me.

Now.

I looked up at Zeph, my lips parting on a demand. Only, whatever I'd been about to say died in my throat, my gaze hypnotized by the marvelous display of muscles and sinewy skin before me.

Oh, Fae… Removing the blindfold had been a really bad idea. I couldn't think, let alone speak.

Because wow.

Zeph was all man, every inch of him perfectly proportioned and sculpted from stone.

No wonder he could move so fast. He was solid muscle in warrior form. I felt small in comparison, almost inadequate, but equally intrigued.

What would he feel like inside me?

He drew his thumb over my bottom lip, which served as a notification that I was gaping at him with my mouth open. Not my proudest moment, but I was beyond caring at this point.

"I want to properly taste you," I told him. He'd barely been in my mouth at all.

"Do you?" he mused, his fingers gliding back into my hair to knock the blindfold the rest of the way off and onto the bed beside us. His gaze left mine to focus on Kols behind me. "She played our game very well. I think she deserves a reward."

CHAPTER NINETEEN

AFLORA

"I AGREE," Kols said, one of his palms moving to smooth over my back. "What did you have in mind?"

"A choice," he replied.

"Yeah?" He paused to consider, his finger gliding down my spine to rest at the bottom. "Hmm, yes. Give her the options, let her decide which way to go."

I shivered, intrigued by whatever they weren't saying out loud.

Kols's touch returned to my hips as he pulled me back to sit on my heels, his arms wrapping around me from behind in a cocoon of comforting warmth. Zeph reached forward to widen my legs, his gaze dropping to my core before slowly tracing up my torso to my breasts and eventually to my face.

My palms rested on my thighs in a natural position, something he seemed to approve of.

"She's perfect," he marveled.

"Yes," Kols murmured, his lips going to my neck to trail kisses up to my ear. "Gorgeous, too."

"A bit stubborn," Zeph added.

"Mmm, true, but also regal and intelligent and loyal," Kols whispered.

"And ours," Zeph said, his palm finding my cheek again as he leaned down to kiss me. "Fuck, I love your mouth, Aflora."

He didn't give me a chance to reply, his tongue dueling with mine in the next breath as he lost a fraction of his steadfast control. I reveled in it, excited that I held this mystical power over him, if only for a brief moment.

And then he snapped back, his green eyes blazing with lustful fire.

"You have two options," he said, finally addressing me again.

I would have commented on their penchant for talking about me like I wasn't in the room, but a darker part of me had enjoyed that a little. Almost like they'd provided me with a voyeuristic glimpse into their minds and what they truly thought about me.

"The first option is for you to stay just like this while Kols and I jack off onto your pretty pussy. Then Kols will lick you clean afterward and make you come until you can't speak anymore."

My heart kick-started at the visual his crass words created in my mind, and a fresh surge of warmth tickled the sensitive space between my thighs. *Yes. Yes, I want that.*

"Or," he continued, his gaze twinkling with dark secrets, "you can suck me off while Kols fucks you, then I'll go down on you and make you come so hard you'll lose consciousness for the night."

I stopped breathing.

The second option.

Definitely the second option.

He arched a brow. "Aflora?" he prompted, clearly unable to read my mind.

"Second," I managed to force out, my throat suddenly dry.

"Full sentences, pixie flower. Tell me what you want, or I'll decide for you."

Kols tugged on my earlobe before whispering, "Zeph has a thing for communication. Tell him explicitly what you want, and he'll give it to you."

Which meant I had to repeat the option I desired. Out loud. My legs clenched, the urge to touch myself hitting me hard in the chest. *Need. So much need.*

All driven by my mates teasing for nights on end.

And now I had the ability to soothe some of that aching fire. I just had to *speak.*

Zeph didn't push, his expression patient as he waited for me to gather my courage. I peeked down at his impressive length before allowing myself another thorough perusal of his sexy form.

Mine.

All mine.

I cleared my throat and met his smoldering gaze, my pulse pounding in my ears. "The second option," I said, my voice husky and nearly unrecognizable. "I want Kols to fuck me while I suck you off, then I want you to lick me clean."

His nostrils flared at hearing his words repeated back to him, and Kols's arms tensed, his breath shuddering out against my ear.

"I love hearing you say the word *fuck*," Kols admitted softly. "So damn hot."

"Get back on all fours," Zeph said, his dominance taking over once more.

Kols kissed my neck before helping me into the position. I trembled with need, my thighs quivering as he parted them to accommodate his larger form. The heat of his groin seared my insides as he aligned himself with my entrance, his hands smoothing down my sides.

I only had a second to ready myself before Zeph grabbed my jaw and drew my focus forward to the precum lingering on his tip in welcome invitation. "Lick," he ordered. Not that he needed to. I was already moving forward to taste him.

The second his essence met my tongue, I groaned, yearning for more, and took him into my mouth with an eagerness I didn't know I possessed.

Kols pushed inside me at the same time, his girth stretching me and forcing me to accept him as he slid home in a single thrust.

Zeph seemed to like the idea, because he replicated it in my mouth, forcing himself deeper than before and giving me my first real introduction to his strength and preferences.

I'd been right about him going easy on me before, and I suspected this was still his version of gentle, but his fingers knotted in my hair to guide me into his preferred rhythm. Kols must have known, because he matched the pace between my legs, both of them going long and deep and thorough, their groans aphrodisiacs to my senses.

"Make her come," Zeph demanded, his voice deeper and causing my thighs to spasm.

Kols kept one hand on my hip while smoothing his other along my side to my belly and lower to the place that burned for his touch. I jolted at the first stroke of his thumb, my body far more primed than I realized.

"I want to feel you moan around my cock," Zeph murmured, his thumb ghosting over my jaw as his opposite hand continued to drive the tempo. "Open your throat a little more, baby." He tilted my head to a new angle, his touch coaxing me to submit.

My body bent to his will, allowing him deeper access just as Kols pressed down on my clit. I screamed at the sensation, rapture shaking my limbs and lighting my soul on fire.

"Fuck," Zeph groaned, his movements increasing in time with Kols's. "That feels amazing."

"So damn tight," Kols breathed, his grip on my hip gentle while his opposite hand continued to strum out my pleasure below. "Fucking wet, too. *Shit.*"

"Not yet," Zeph breathed.

"Fuck you," Kols bit out.

"I will do exactly that if you come before I'm ready."

Kols convulsed behind me, his body stilling against mine. "*Fuck.*" He throbbed deep inside me, hitting a point that had me crying out in pain-induced pleasure. I wanted more of that.

So. Much. More.

Zeph pistoned between my lips, his green gaze capturing mine as my own eyes began to water from his harsh thrusts. I didn't dare tell him to stop, my throat parched and ready to accept his warmth.

"Your irises are alive with power," he whispered, his own irises flaring with wonder. "I've never seen anything so beautiful in my entire existence." His movements slowed, as if he were drawing out the moment, lost to the sensations of our embrace. Color flushed his cheeks, his abdominal muscles tensing. "Now, Kols."

"Thank fuck," Kols breathed, his hips picking up the pace and hitting me in that delicious place that made my legs go weak.

"She's going to come again," Zeph marveled, his voice strained.

Kols responded with his magical touch, his fingers and cock working me in tandem to draw me closer and closer to that edge of oblivion.

I felt drunk on their lust, their masculine growls, their mounting ecstasy, and their sensual knowledge. They knew exactly how to move and where to stroke me, their bodies working mine toward a realm of rapture only they had the keys to open.

Zeph groaned my name, followed by Kols, the two of them dragging me into a sea of sensation with them. Their hot essences bathed my insides, Zeph erupting down my throat at the same time Kols released deep in my channel, their joint exaltation yanking me into a world of bliss I'd never recover from.

They'd destroyed me.

Claimed me.

Made me theirs without having to bite me again.

Because I'd never be the same after this experience.

These two males had ruined me for anyone else.

No, not two.

Three.

Because I felt Shade inside me, too, his essence a shadowy kiss against my spirit. He wasn't here, yet he was at the same time.

I sighed in contentment, my eyes flickering open only to realize I'd been moved to the center of the bed, naked and warm and fully sated. Kols's palm rested on my belly, his opposite one propping up his head as he stared down at me.

"There you are," he murmured, leaning down to run his tongue over my mouth. "Zeph was worried we'd already exhausted you."

"I'm not one for incomplete promises," Zeph added from between my splayed thighs.

My eyes widened, my legs immediately threatening to close, but he held me open with ease, his body much larger than mine. Kols eased backward to allow me to better see the view and kept his palm firmly on my abdomen as if to hold me in place.

"I promised to knock you out with my tongue, Aflora," Zeph said softly. "I meant it." He leaned in to kiss my mound while his gaze held mine, then his mouth slid lower, forcing my back to come up and off the bed.

Kols pushed me back down, his chuckle a breath against my ear. "You're the one who wanted orgasms, love," he whispered, then drew his lips down to my throat and lower to my breasts.

"I can't... I'm not... Oh, Fae..." I couldn't form a single thought, let alone speak. The two of them were driving me insane, their mouths everywhere at once, their tongues wicked instruments of torture that they knew how to use all too well.

And before I knew it, I was flying once more, utterly captivated by them both and falling into an oblivion of insanity underlined with rapturous quakes.

My body hummed.

I screamed.

Their names resembled curses and prayers as they left my mouth.

Darkness consumed me, followed by light, and still I trembled, my world shattering over and over again. I lost track, unsure of who touched me where. All I knew was that I felt owned by them both.

And Shade, whose presence lingered in my mind.

What am I going to do? I wondered, overwhelmed.

A firm lick between my folds drew my attention downward, a plea on my lips for him to stop and grant me a reprieve. Only, the head between my thighs wasn't the one I anticipated.

Long white-blond hair.

Sinful silver-blue eyes.

I jolted, scooting backward until I hit the headboard of an unknown bed behind me, then brought my knees upward to my chest. Kols and Zeph were gone, and the sheets were a silky black very unlike the dark red ones I'd been in moments before.

"What are you doing here?" I breathed, gaping at the figment of my imagination.

"You called for me," he replied, prowling forward like a predatory cat, his upper body fitted muscular perfection. He even had those little muscles by his hips. I knew because I'd created them in my dreams. Just as I'd ensured he was well-endowed to round out the package. Yet tonight he wore black pants.

I cocked my head to the side. "You shouldn't be here."

"Why not?" he asked.

"Because I don't need pleasure right now." I frowned.

"And... well, it's sort of wrong, I think. I mean, it wasn't before because my mates were being dicks. But now..." I trailed off, thinking. "It sort of feels like cheating."

His lips curled, amusement shining in his hypnotic gaze. "Cheating, hmm?"

I nodded. "I created you to avoid them."

"Did you?" He paused right before me on the bed, his chest pressing against my shins as he planted his palms on either side of my hips.

So big, I marveled. Even more muscular than Zeph, his shoulders broad and taking up my view of the room. "You shouldn't be here," I repeated on a whisper.

"Probably not," he agreed.

My brow furrowed. "So why are you here?"

"You tell me, little star." His voice dropped to a dark whisper that teased my senses. "Why do you think I'm here?"

"Because I've dreamt of you every day this week," I thought out loud. "So it was only natural to call you to me again."

"Definitely natural," he agreed, his face a few inches away from mine. "Did you think of me when they made you come?"

I shook my head and bit my lips. "No." But now I felt like I should have, which was ridiculous considering I made this guy up for my own personal satisfaction.

He didn't appear disappointed, just curious. "Did they bite you again?"

Shouldn't a figment of my own imagination already know the answer to that? "No."

Now he seemed pleased. "Good."

Odd. "You don't want them to bite me?"

"Not particularly, no," he admitted. "Do you want them to bite you?"

His words gave me pause. *Is this my subconscious's way of telling me I don't want them to mate me?* I wondered, the thought making me uneasy. "I... I don't know," I whispered. "Do

I?"

"That's not for me to tell you," he replied, easing backward just a bit before moving to sit beside me with his long legs stretched out and crossed at the ankles.

He reminded me of sex. Dangerous, hot, sweaty sex. Not that we'd indulged in any of that in my fantasies. It'd always been him pleasing me, never the other way around.

Hence, fantasy.

I glanced at him. "Why are you here?"

"You already asked me that," he replied, amused.

"You never answered me."

"No, I didn't." He smiled. "Then again, I rarely do."

"Because it's all in my head," I muttered, understanding. "Are you supposed to be my conscious? Because that'd be kind of weird."

"Why is that?"

"Because I'm not sure what it would say about my mental state if, uh…" I shook my head, the consideration making me dizzy. "Never mind. You're just too attractive to be my mind."

"Oh, I don't know. I find your mind rather fascinating," he replied.

"You would say that as a figment of my imagination," I drawled back at him.

He chuckled. "And is that what I am?"

"What else could you be?"

"Maybe I'm one of your mates," he suggested.

I giggled. "Oh, what fun that would be. Zeph would just love you. Kols, too." They already wanted to kill Shade. Why not add Fantasy Guy to the mix? I giggled again. "That'd be entertaining."

"Wouldn't it?" He smiled, a pair of dimples appearing at the edges that made me giddy. He really was an attractive figment.

"I suppose you can stay around, but no more, uh"—I waved to my naked body—"no more of this. No more sex."

His silver-blue eyes lazily ran over my nudity, his palm reaching out to push my knees away to reveal my breasts to his view. "What if I want sex?"

"That can't happen."

"Why not?"

"Because it's cheating," I decided out loud. "I... I don't want to be unfaithful, even if it's just in my mind."

"What if it's me you are cheating on?" he asked, arching an ash-blond brow.

I snorted. "Cheating on my own mind. There's a riddle for you."

"Maybe it's true."

"You know it's not," I replied, amused. "I can't cheat on someone who isn't real."

"Then, by that definition, playing with me isn't cheating at all. Since you don't see me as real."

I considered that for a moment before saying, "No sex."

His lips curled again. "All right, little star. We'll play by your rules. For now." He reached for me and leaned in to kiss my forehead, his touch warm and tender and kind of perfect.

A sigh escaped me, something about his presence familiar and calming.

Maybe that was the real reason I called him to me—I needed some normalcy after being destroyed so completely by my mates.

Funny that a figment could make me feel *normal*.

"Sweet dreams, darling star," he whispered against my ear.

"Sweet dreams," I mumbled back to him, falling back into my delirious state.

An oceanic kiss met my senses, drowning me in a sea of bliss.

One that reminded me of my childhood and a memory just out of my reach.

Then, finally, I slept.

CHAPTER TWENTY

SHADE

I HID IN THE SHADOWS, watching Aflora's lips curl as she slept. Kols and Zeph were passed out on either side of her, oblivious to her dreams.

But I knew.

I sensed his presence inside her, the dark power thriving through her veins. It'd been growing all week, culminating in tonight's events, and would continue to seduce her until fate forced her to make a choice.

It was only a matter of time before he came for her. I'd just hoped to have a better hold on her heart before it happened. However, her song had called for him in the village, the haunting melody carrying a spell with it that she hadn't understood.

Tray and Kols had been just as oblivious.

Similar to how Kols and Zeph were now.

I wanted to tell them, to shake them awake and point at the magical essence hovering over Aflora. But they wouldn't even be able to see it, let alone believe me.

Hell, they'd probably lose themselves to a fit of rage at

realizing I was in the Royal Prince's bedroom without permission. But this entire situation went beyond the formalities of our society.

If we weren't careful, Zakkai would win.

My fists curled, failure a nagging sensation that churned in my abdomen.

This wasn't over.

Not yet.

She could still choose us.

I just hoped that when she did, it wouldn't be too late.

The darkness eventually lifted, the powerful fae releasing his hold on Aflora's dreams and dissolving into nothingness. I watched her for a beat, debating on entertaining a date in her mind, but her sigh of contentment had me stepping away from her, not forward.

She needed rest.

We'd play another day.

And I had business to tend to.

I cloaked myself in smoke, using it to pull me through time and space to the LethaForest where Kyros stood waiting for me in his trademark leather jacket and jeans.

"Huh. I timed you to arrive thirty seconds from now," he drawled in welcome. "I guess you were a bit less preoccupied with your pretty flower than I anticipated."

I rolled my eyes. "Let's just get this over with."

"So eager," he taunted, pushing away from the tree, the sword against his hip flaring with violet flames. "All right, my shadowy friend. We'll start in New Orleans, as I have a few idiots to question there first. Then we'll move on to Dallas."

I narrowed my gaze. "How long is this going to take?"

"How many times did we work through that whole bonds-realignment discussion with you and your mates?" he countered, tapping his chin thoughtfully. "Five? Six? No, seven times. So I think seven days' payment is more than kind on my part, really."

"Yeah, minus me having to go in and wipe the gargoyle's

memory after the fact," I retorted, still irritated by that not-so-minor mishap in our arrangement.

Kyros's head tipped back on a laugh, his amusement at my expense evident. He sort of reminded me of Ajax a little in muscular size and angular features. They also both had the same thick black hair that always fell into their eyes no matter what they did. However, Kyros had tattoos from his neck all the way to his fingertips, covering every inch of his torso, while Ajax just had the lip ring.

That was the difference between Paradox Fae and Midnight Fae—our bodies healed all wounds, including those inflicted by colorful needles. Meanwhile, Paradox Fae could be injured and remain injured. Although, they carried around magical time-wielding swords that allowed them to fix themselves by falling into the past, so it evened out in the end. Mostly.

"That little bastard was so pissed," Kyros mused, wiping tears away from his near-black eyes.

"Yeah. Ha." I folded my arms. "New Orleans?"

He grinned. "Yep."

"Then hold on. It's going to be a smoky ride."

He latched onto my forearm, and I began my journey to the Human Realm to raise the dead.

* * *

KYROS MADE ME HELP HIM for all seven fucking days, the bastard only allowing me to sneak back to campus a handful of times to check on Aflora and her other mates. Fortunately, they seemed to be getting along just fine.

Although, I sensed her distress at my continued absence—a fact she made evident now with her expression upon seeing me in my seat in our Advanced Conjuring class.

Her eyes widened in surprise, then narrowed in annoyance.

Yeah, I was in trouble.

Luckily, I had an excuse. "Hi, little rose," I murmured as she slid into the seat beside me. "How was your week?"

"Fine," she replied, then grimaced at the word she'd used to describe a week of intense sexual activity. Because that was how she'd spent her time outside of class and during her free days—exploring with Zeph and Kols. From what I could tell, they hadn't bitten her again; they were just playing and introducing her to their preferences, which were a bit darker than mine.

Zeph, specifically.

He had a penchant for bondage. Fortunately for him, Aflora didn't mind. She also didn't seem to mind that Zeph and Kols enjoyed sexual activities with each other—something they'd demonstrated for her thoroughly last night.

Her cheeks flushed as if she was recalling the memory now, her tongue slipping out to dampen her lips. "Where have you been all week?" she blurted out, her face darkening to a pretty red shade. "Sorry, I mean, uh…"

"You're allowed to ask me where I've been," I told her softly. "I'm your mate, Aflora."

"Then why didn't you tell me you'd be gone?"

"Would you like me to let you know in the future if I intend to leave the Academy?" I asked her, genuinely curious.

"Um, only if you want to."

"There are a lot of things I want," I admitted, catching her gaze.

"Ain't that the truth," Ajax muttered as he arrived to claim the chair on the other side of me.

I held out my fist for him to bump, the way we usually greeted each other. His knock was a bit harder today, telling me what kind of mood he was in.

No doubt a result of his latest rendezvous with a certain female who was deemed off-limits to him. It seemed we both had a proclivity for picking women we shouldn't want.

"You and Kyros have fun this week?" he asked me, not

at all concerned by Aflora listening on my other side.

"*Fun* is not the word I'd choose," I said, cringing at the number of ghosts I'd spoken to this week on the Paradox Fae's behalf. "But I'm out of his debt again."

Ajax grunted. "Maybe you should stop asking him for favors."

"I wish that were possible," I replied, knowing full well I'd need to use him again, and soon. "But he's a useful ally to have."

"Most Paradox Fae are," he agreed, causing Aflora's eyebrows to shoot upward.

"You've been dealing with a time-dweller?" She seemed both impressed and mortified. "They're tricksters."

"I'm very aware," I drawled, shifting my attention to Headmaster Irwin as he arrived. He ignored the class in favor of taking in the freshly renovated surroundings. The Council had restored the Death Blood building with an abundance of power shortly after its destruction, but the magical kinks were still working themselves out.

The gargoyles were having a field day trying to keep order within the building. Students continued to find themselves lost or in the wrong place, snake vines were uprooted and trapped, and a horde of fire gnats had been released from Headmaster Jericho's lab.

I would have been entertained by the chaos if I hadn't known *who* had caused it.

My mood soured at the thought of Zakkai, mostly because I knew Aflora had dreamt of him every day this week again. Was that what caused the hint of guilt in her eyes now? Or was it related to her bedroom gymnastics with Zeph and Kols?

"What did you do all week?" I asked her, curious to see how she'd reply.

"I, uh, studied a lot," she offered, her cheeks revealing that was a lie.

Well, not entirely.

"Zeph is a thorough headmaster, hmm?" I couldn't help

teasing her, and the horrified expression she gave me in return said it was worth it.

"I… I mean… I don't…" She cleared her throat, her beautiful eyes conveying an intoxicating mixture of apology and annoyance that made me smile.

"Yes, very thorough indeed," I murmured, winking at her.

Headmaster Irwin chose that moment to begin class, leaving Aflora blushing beside me and unable to reply.

I smirked, amused.

"Today, we are going to practice psychometry," Headmaster Irwin announced. "As you all know, objects have histories, just like souls. But sometimes, calling up the past of an item is harder than that of a person." He used his wand to produce a box with a slit on the top. "Everyone will pick something from this box at random, then work with your partner to decipher the story behind the item."

The container floated to his desk at the center of the room, landing with a flourish amid a stack of papers and spreading them everywhere like confetti.

"I'll go first," he continued, sauntering up to his creation and sticking his hand inside. The older Midnight Fae pulled out a watch that belonged in the Human Realm more than in this one and held it up for all of us to see.

Ajax snorted beside me.

I agreed with his sentiments completely.

What a colossal waste of time, truly. Our building was attacked a week ago, and Headmaster Irwin wanted to teach us all how to look at objects. We should be focused on defensive spells, such as calling up former warrior spirits to help protect our school. But everyone was too busy acting as though we hadn't been attacked last week.

Ridiculous.

At least Kols seemed to be favored as innocent by those on campus. If only the Council had the same faith in him as all the younger Midnight Fae had.

Prats, I thought, not at all impressed by our governing

structure—a fact my father very well knew. As did my mother.

"Guess I need to go partner with Janice," Ajax muttered, drawing my attention to the shifting chairs. "Wish me luck."

"You don't need it," I replied. "She does." It was no secret that the Death Blood female had the hots for my best friend. Unfortunately for her, he preferred another fae—one he shouldn't.

Ajax twirled his lip ring with his tongue, then heaved a sigh. "You're a dick."

"I know." I smiled at him. "Yet you hang out with me anyway. What does that say about you?"

"I prefer bad company," he drawled, his amusement palpable as he gathered his things and headed for the petite, dark-haired female waiting for him with stars in her eyes.

Aflora cleared her throat beside me. "Are you going to get the item, or am I?" she asked.

As I'd totally blanked out on the demonstration, I suggested she go first so I could see what spell we were supposed to utter. There were several related to psychometry, and I had no idea which one Headmaster Irwin had chosen for us to explore today.

My mate left her chair, her skirt distracting me as she moved.

Such a fine ass.

Long legs.

Mmm, I liked the little boots she chose today, too. Yeah, I'd let her leave those on while I took her against the wall.

But the blouse could stand to lose a few buttons. And I much preferred her in this outfit without the undergarments. I had nothing against silk and lace; I just wanted to see her tits through the thin white fabric.

A crass consideration, but it'd been a long fucking week of watching without touching.

And I really wanted to touch her.

"Why are you looking at me like that?" she asked,

standing in front of me with a rock in her hand.

I glanced down at it. "That's what you picked from the box?"

She shrugged. "It was the first thing that fit in my hand."

My lips twitched. I'd happily give her something else for her hand, but it might not *fit*, as she put it.

"Seriously, why are you looking at me like that?" she demanded.

I stood so I could step into her personal space. Then I leaned down to whisper in her ear. "Because I'm thinking about all the things I'd like to teach you with my tongue."

She stopped breathing.

I kissed her throat—right above her collar—and lifted my head to gaze down at her. "Now let's get this assignment done so I can play with you properly."

She shivered, her pupils flaring. Her lips formed an O without sound, then she swallowed.

Seconds passed.

Then our moment was destroyed by Headmaster Irwin clearing his throat. The entire room had emptied around us. "Get to work," he snapped.

I frowned. "Where did everyone go?"

Aflora sighed. "Did you listen at all when he gave instructions?"

"No, I had other things on my mind." I allowed her to hear the innuendo in my tone and enjoyed her resulting blush.

Then she shook her head, grabbed her things, and said, "Follow me."

"Happily," I agreed, picking up my only notebook and trailing after her into the hallway. "Please tell me we're going to find a dark corner to make out in."

She scoffed at me, leading me out of the building and into the night rather than to a quiet room without windows where I could devour her. "Headmaster Irwin told us to spread out and find a safe place to practice so our spells don't overlap. Then we're supposed to report back with our findings."

"Well, that's much more boring than the idea I had in my head," I admitted, disappointed.

"I bet," she replied, but I caught the flicker of amusement in her features. "How about over there?" She pointed to a bench beside the building, directly across from a new dragon statue guarded by two gargoyles. One of the Death Bloods had probably put them there to protect the building from another attack. It wouldn't help, but they wouldn't know that.

"Shade?" Aflora prompted.

Right. She wanted to know if we could sit there.

So I heaved a shoulder. "Sure. Why not?"

"Good." She plopped down on the charcoal blades decorating the paved path rather than on the bench, then set the rock on the ground.

I glanced between her and the bench but decided to join her on the ground, because why not? She was an Earth Fae, after all. She probably preferred the grasslike substance more than a metal seat. So I indulged my little rose by sitting beside her with my legs stretched out and crossed at the ankles.

"What spell did Headmaster Irwin tell us to use?" I asked her.

"You really weren't paying attention at all," she muttered.

"Nope." I stared at her mouth. "As I said, I had other things on my mind." I couldn't remember what those things were now, but I was reasonably certain they had something to do with her delectable assets. Zeph and Kols had played with her all week, while I'd barely touched her since the night she'd slept in my bed.

"Focus, Shade."

"I'm very focused, Aflora."

She huffed out a breath, but I caught the lingering amusement in her expression. She liked my teasing, which was good because I intended to tease her a hell of a lot more.

I reached out to brush her long black strands over her shoulder. Kols had been allowing her to sleep without her collar in his room, just as he removed his own band. I'd studied how he removed the mechanism the other night, just in case I needed to replicate the action. It was tempting to do so now, simply to expose her pretty throat, but I didn't want to risk anyone sensing her bonds to Kols and Zeph.

They weren't gifted enough to hide their links.

Unlike certain other fae.

"All right, princess. Show me what we're doing," I said, dropping my gaze from her mouth to the rock on the ground. Aflora already had her wand out, her lips moving over the spell without saying it out loud. When she seemed confident in her words, she waved her wand over the rock and uttered the incantation aloud.

Perfect form. Perfect spell. Perfect female.

The way her eyes fluttered closed confirmed she'd executed the assignment accurately and was now deep in the history of the rock. I went back onto my elbows to wait. Depending on how much that little stone had to say, we could be here for a while.

I dipped my head back to admire the moon overhead, my thoughts starting to drift to more intriguing topics, when Aflora began to shake beside me. Frowning, I sat up. "Aflora?"

She didn't reply, her teeth beginning to chatter as if she were freezing. I touched her arm and cursed at the droplets of ice water covering her skin.

"Aflora!" I snapped at her.

Nothing.

Just more shaking.

And then she collapsed.

CHAPTER TWENTY-ONE

AFLORA

Several Minutes Earlier

"*ARIE ANNI TARIKH NUK*," I said, drawing a star in the air over the rock.

Energy hummed around me as the spell activated, drawing me into a world of heat and despair. I flinched at the sudden change, my lips parting on a scream that didn't escape.

Where am I? I wondered, spinning in a circle and frowning as the Academy unfolded around me.

A raven clucked overhead.

Students giggled as they gossiped in the corner beside the Death Blood Education Building entrance.

"How did I...?" I trailed off, whirling around once more and searching for Shade.

He was gone.

I blinked.

Had he left me in the middle of our assignment? It would be just like him, as he seemed to have a penchant for

180

disappearing. What business did he have with a Paradox Fae, anyway?

I blew out a breath and shook my head.

Oh well. Now, where did my books go?

I took a step forward, only to be snapped backward by some invisible force. My brow furrowed. "What…?"

Then my feet began to walk, as if I were possessed by someone else.

"What's happening?" I demanded. Only then did I realize my voice wasn't resonating and my lips weren't actually moving.

My body continued to operate on its own, my hand drawing out a wand—one I recognized, yet didn't—and waved it over the gargoyle outside of the Death Blood Education Building.

"*Nahni Haki Aldukhi,*" a deep voice said.

Everything inside me froze at the sound because it came from *my throat*. But it wasn't my voice at all. However, I recognized it. Sort of. From long ago, a song—

The doors opened with a flourish, distracting me from my thoughts as I stepped unwillingly into the building. I ducked immediately into the shadows, creeping along the walls and pausing with every shift of magic around me.

A glimpse of a mirror caught my eye, but my head refused to turn toward it.

Wait…

I caught a glimmer of a shoulder that was far too wide to be my own.

Then I heard the voice speaking again, this time in a low hum of musical energy I recognized. It reminded me of my mother's ballad, only different. Darker. Deeper. *Hypnotic.* I swooned a little, the power warming my veins, the sound a reverberation against my throat.

It's me.
I'm humming.
No.
Not me.

Him.

My eyebrows shot upward. *I'm trapped in someone else's body!*

How? How did this happen? And what were we doing here?

Had I uttered the spell wrong? It'd been a rock, not a person, so why…?

Oh… Oh, Fae… No!

Fire ignited around me, my wand the source of the power. I paused to listen, then more of that ballad hummed from my lips as I whispered enchantments to urge the students to flee. *There will be no casualties today. Just a warning. A message. To let the Council know it's time.*

I tried to shake my head to clear it, confused by the thoughts taking over my own. They were much deeper, masculine in nature, and not at all mine.

This isn't me.

It will be, a deep voice replied, shocking the hell out of me.

Who are you?

You know me, he vowed. *You'll see.*

I didn't understand, but an inferno blazed all around me, making me hot and cold at the same time. Shivers racked me from head to toe, my lips parting on another one of those silent screams.

And then we were outside, our hand rising into the sky to script out a word I already knew was meant to be written.

"*Alqisian,*" I whispered at the same time as the male, our voices commingling into a beautiful song I couldn't help but hum.

My heart began to break, memories of a past long buried tickling my mind with glimpses of my parents.

"*Sweet darling flower, we love you so much,*" my mother breathed, her arms tight around me. "*We're doing this for you, to ensure you survive.*"

"*It's the only way,*" my father agreed, his palm against my lower back. "*…take care of you, baby.*"

"Who?" I wanted to ask them. "Who will take care of me?"

But they were already gone, the aftermath of destruction blazing before me in a furious wave of devastating power.

A rock tumbled out of the debris, bumping my boot. I bent to retrieve it, then brought it to my lips.

"I'll come for you soon, Aflora," a gruff voice whispered to it. "I vow it."

I couldn't stop trembling, confusion mounting with each passing second as a cloud of thick smoke surrounded me from the wreckage. The rock fell to the ground and I took to the air, swirling in a cloud that reminded me of Shade.

"I've got you," I heard him say. "It's going to be okay."

"Shade?" I couldn't see him, but I *felt* him, our shared bond yanking at my essence. "Shade!" I tugged on that strand, our frail, initial link, following him through the sea of darkness to a place where his peppermint scent surrounded me in a fog of familiarity.

Tears tracked down my cheeks, my heart hammering in my ribs, my consciousness lost somewhere in the abyss, but his voice carried me to the present.

"Wake up," he demanded. "Show me your eyes, beautiful."

I wanted to.

But I didn't know where to look, or which way to go, until I felt another tug, his intoxicating essence swimming all around me. I breathed him in, my mind working through the trickery and blackness left behind by the other entity, my heart racing against my ribs.

"That's it," Shade coaxed. "I'm right here, little rose. Come get me."

"Shade," I whispered, my voice sounding hoarse but finally coming through my own body. *I'm me again.* Only, I couldn't see.

"Hi, sweetheart," he replied, his lips brushing mine.

Mmm, I felt that.

I yearned for more.

But I needed to see him, to know this was real and not another game or spell gone awry.

"I'm right here," Shade promised, his warmth seeping into me and drawing me out of the stillness of my mind and into his arms. "There you are, gorgeous." His thumb drifted across my cheek. "You had me worried for a moment."

I stared up at the sun, then at him, and finally at the tree behind him. "Our meadow," I breathed, my throat sore and scratchy. "How?" *Am I dreaming? Am I still trapped inside that man?*

"I shadowed us here to get you away from that rock," he replied, his lips curling down. "What happened, Aflora? What did you see?"

"Destruction," I told him, shuddering at the images flashing behind my eyes. "He destroyed the education building after making sure everyone got out alive. Then he kissed the rock. He… I was him and he was me. And then I destroyed the building. But I didn't. He did. Except it was me, Shade. I was… I was *him*."

I sat up abruptly, only then realizing Shade had been cradling me in his lap. But he let me move, his gaze guarded as I jumped to my feet and spun around the familiar field. "Is this real?" I demanded.

"Yes," he replied, standing up as well. "This is the meadow I took you to a few weeks ago, after the recording incident."

"And it's real?" I asked again, needing to know if I was somehow trapped in my mind.

He grabbed me by the waist, yanked me to him, and pressed his mouth to mine.

A zing of energy zapped through my system, my eyes widening at the unexpected power.

Then his tongue parted my lips, forcing me to *feel* him. To see him. To be with him.

I wrapped my arms around his neck to better align our bodies and allowed him to ravage me with his mouth.

This, I thought. *This is real. So, so, so real.*

"Mate," I whispered, recognizing the fervor burning between us. "I need you."

He walked me backward *into* the tree. I glanced around, shocked by our new surroundings of wood and leaves. A secret house with windows that overlooked our meadow.

"What is this?"

"Our place," he whispered, continuing to walk me backward. "I enchanted it just for you."

His lips met mine once more, drowning me in sensation and lust and yearning. I moaned, needing this more than I needed to breathe.

We'd yet to truly explore each other, all the dreams leading to a few orgasms that he usually inspired without even really touching me. At least not with his hands or mouth.

Well, sometimes with his hands and mouth.

But it didn't count. They were fantasies of the mind.

This was real.

Our bodies touching, the mattress meeting my back as he pushed me onto the bed, his groin settling between my splayed thighs.

Yes, yes. *This* was my ultimate craving, the forbidden yearning I hated to admit. He was the one who tricked me into this entire mess, the one to bite me without permission, and while I should hate him, deep down I couldn't.

Because I felt connected to him.

That connection was what drew me out of my nightmare and into our dream meadow. Then he'd pulled me into this house. Oh, how I adored this house! Flowers scented the air. Fresh cypress trees, too. And, mmm, something very sweet like chocolate.

"Cookies," he whispered against my neck, his hands roaming up my sides. "They're cookies."

I must have spoken that out loud, and I couldn't bring myself to care. "I need you."

"I know," he said, his lips tracing a path up to my ear.

"I need you, too."

"Will you bite me?" I asked, arching my neck backward in invitation. I barely even recognized myself, this wanton energy flowing through me and captivating my every move. Yet, it felt entirely right. I wanted him inside me in all ways. "I missed you," I realized out loud. "Please don't leave without telling me again."

Who am I? Who is speaking these words?

Oh, who cares!

I felt high on life, our bond thriving inside me and pulsating with an intense craving.

Shade kissed me instead of answering, his tongue sparring beautifully with mine. My blouse fell apart, his hand ripping it from me in an eagerness to expose my breasts. I followed his unspoken suggestion and tried to tear his own shirt off, but I lacked the finesse required to mimic the movement.

He chuckled against my throat, then went up to his knees and began the tedious task of unbuttoning his dress shirt. I went up onto my elbows to enjoy the show as he displayed his tanned torso one slow inch at a time.

He truly was a work of art, his lithe form lean and strong, his muscles flexing as he removed the fabric from his shoulders and arms. I admired his alluring display and eyed the trail of dark hair that led to the button of his dress pants. He flicked it open and drew down the zipper while I watched, his intentions clear.

You have a choice, he was telling me with his unhurried movements. He wanted me to be sure, to not rush into my decision, but we both knew I'd end up here with or without today's events.

"I want you," I told him earnestly. "I have for a while."

"I know," he replied, a wickedness in his gaze that lit my blood on fire. "But I need you to be sure, Aflora."

"I am." I meant it. Maybe it was the insanity of the moment or the very real power I felt thriving between us, but I was done fighting the inevitable. He'd bitten me for reasons I still didn't understand, but one thing was abundantly clear to me.

Everything Shade did, he did for me.

To others, it may seem like he had ulterior motives that were self-serving, and maybe some of them were. But somehow, I knew in my gut that all his decisions revolved around me.

He considered me important.

And it was time for me to show him I felt similarly.

"I should hate you," I admitted out loud. "And part of me does."

"Yes," he agreed.

"But another part of me..." I trailed off, my heart beating rapidly in my chest, my mouth suddenly dry. "Another part of me needs to finish this." And he'd ignited that part of me when he'd used our bond to draw me back to him, to save me from whatever hellish ride I'd been on through the Death Blood Education Building tour. "I want you, Shade."

CHAPTER TWENTY-TWO

SHADE

AFLORA WAS HIGH ON OUR BOND, her pupils blown wide with lust.

It took every ounce of willpower I possessed not to take advantage of the situation and fuck her the way her body begged me to.

I needed her mind to catch up with the emotions, for her to realize *what* she demanded of me.

"Will you bite me again?"

Those words were music to my ears when she uttered them, but I couldn't be sure she actually meant them. Not in her current state.

I leaned down to kiss her again, my muscles tensing with restraint as she rubbed her hot center against my groin.

Shit, I thought, my heart threatening to burst out of my chest from beating so hard. I really shouldn't have unfastened my pants, but fuck, I needed to *breathe*. She was killing me.

"Aflora," I whispered, fighting for control. She bucked against me in response, her skirt pooling around her hips.

"Take me," she breathed.

"I want to," I assured her, my lips trailing down her neck to her breasts. "You have no idea how much I want to."

It physically hurt not to bite her, to not finish our bond, but everything else had been forced upon her. I wanted this final step to be because she truly desired it, not because she was lost in our connection.

The only way to ground her was to give her an outlet for the power mounting inside her.

And I knew just the way to do that.

Her bra disappeared with a snap of my fingers, revealing her pert tits to my mouth. I took a nipple between my teeth while I palmed the other one.

She hissed, her arousal perfuming the air in a luscious scent of *need*. I'd only ever tasted her in our dreams, not in reality. And I longed to rectify that now.

My palms slid down her sides to her skirt, my fingers finding the zipper and dragging it down. When it hit the end, I ripped the rest of the fabric away from her, earning me a moan from my little mate.

Her fingers threaded through my hair, holding me against her breast. I responded by taking her other stiff peak into my mouth and twirling my tongue around the tip.

"Shade…" She uttered my name like a plea, her skin heating beneath my touch.

She wasn't cold now, but *hot*.

Energy sizzled beneath her skin, seeking an escape. She didn't seem to notice, too lost to the sensations and drunk on the way they made her feel.

I continued my path downward with my lips, stopping to dip my tongue in her adorable belly button before situating myself between her thighs. Her lacy white panties were soaked through, leaving nothing to the imagination. I took the bands on either side of her hips and yanked on the fabric, snapping it with ease and leaving her naked on the bed.

Well, mostly naked.

She still had those adorable ankle boots on.

Her fingers tightened in my hair as she tried to guide my mouth to the place she wanted it, causing me to smile against her slick folds. "You're in a demanding mood, aren't you, pet?"

"Please, Shade," she whimpered, her limbs trembling with the electricity humming through her veins.

Whatever had happened with the rock, coupled with me yanking her out of the enchantment, had awakened her Quandary Blood with a vengeance. That paltry collar around her neck would do nothing to help her now.

But I would.

"I'm going to make you come, Aflora," I told her softly. "I want you to give me everything and let it all go, okay?"

"Yes," she groaned, her nails digging into my scalp.

My cock pulsed in response to her throaty moan, my mouth aching to taste her. I needed this almost as much as she did, but for entirely different reasons.

She was mine, and I wanted her to know what that meant.

So I showed her with my tongue, licking her deep and thoroughly and fully introducing her intimately to my mouth. She sucked in a surprised breath and released it on a sound I wanted to hear from her again and again and again.

I hummed in approval against her slick flesh, then slid two fingers inside her. She bowed off the bed on a cry of pleasure, her cerulean flames glimmering across her skin.

Beautiful, I thought, adoring this unrestrained side of her.

No concerns.

No distrust.

Just lost to the heat of the moment and allowing her mate to take care of her in every way. I fucking loved it and wanted to stay in this place with her forever, but I knew it wasn't the right thing to do. She needed her mind back, and there was only one way to return it to her.

"Come for me, Aflora," I whispered, laving her

throbbing clit.

She whimpered, her grip tightening in my hair as she chased her pleasure against my tongue. "Shade!" she cried out, her power erupting in a hot wave of energy that illuminated our bond.

I growled at the onslaught of electricity thrumming through my veins, my incisors aching to bite her and absorb as much of her as I could.

Not yet, I told myself, my muscles tensing in protest.

Our bond was on fucking fire. Her other mates had to feel it, but I couldn't think about them right now, not with her quivering with rapture beneath my mouth. I feasted on her essence and vitality, driving her to the edge again with a few clever swipes of my tongue and groaning with her as she came again.

Glorious, I thought, marveling at her display of ecstasy. She reminded me of a goddess with her blue-black hair spilling across the pillows and her creamy skin highlighted by enchanting blue flames. Aflora didn't seem to notice, too lost in her oblivion to realize she'd lit herself on fire with her outburst.

I crawled up and over her, reveling in the heat pouring off her and into me, and took her mouth in a passionate kiss underlined in possession.

She owned me as much as I owned her.

Fate put me in her path, and duty forced me to remain despite the rocky course ahead. And this moment made that all worth it.

Every secret. Every choice. Every dark doubt. All of it disappeared beneath a cloud of rightness as I parted her lips with my tongue and devoured her.

She wrapped an arm around me, her opposite hand still in my hair. "More," she whispered. "Give me more."

"Aflora," I replied, my voice harsh with my necessary restraint.

But she seemed oblivious to it, her mouth trailing along my jaw to my neck in seductive little caresses I couldn't ignore. I palmed her cheek, then slid my hand back into her hair, intending to pull her lips back to mine, when her teeth pierced my skin.

An inferno blazed across my conscious, my heart thundering in my chest.

Aflora had just *bitten* me.

Tasted my blood.

And swallowed.

Her moan of approval shattered something inside me, spurring me into motion. My fingers tightened around her dark strands, holding her to my neck as she ingested more of my essence.

It was so fucking wrong yet felt too damn good to stop.

I'd never been bitten before—the action was typically reserved for mates during sex—and damn, I was glad I'd waited for Aflora. She could sink her teeth into me anytime she wanted.

"Fuck, little rose," I groaned, my shaft aching with the desire to slip into her velvety heat.

I released her hair to work on shucking off my pants and then my boxers. There'd been a reason I wanted to wait, but hell if I could remember it now.

Her legs parted from my hips, her teeth releasing my neck as she tossed her head back on a throaty demand to take her. I lined myself up and drove inside her to the hilt, our cries of satisfaction mingling in the air.

Home, I realized. *I'm finally fucking home.*

And what a place it was because I'd never really had one. In all my years, I stuck to the shadows, lurking and playing the games set out before me. How fucking appropriate that the biggest task of all was the one writhing beneath me and welcoming me into her with open arms.

"You're everything I didn't know I needed," I breathed, completely lost to the beauty unraveling in my arms. My heart beat for this woman and this woman alone. She was mine, and I never wanted to let her go.

"Bite me," she begged. "Finish it."

"Yes," I agreed. It was time. Our vows were incomplete, and that needed to be rectified.

I pressed my mouth to her throbbing pulse and licked the cerulean magic heating her skin. Mmm, she tasted like power and sex and everything I could ever desire.

Our connection hung in the balance, a weight on both our spirits, waiting for this final thread.

And I granted it the climax of our lives by piercing her vein.

She screamed, her hips driving upward to meet mine, our pace becoming frantic as we both fought to find our release in a wave of insurmountable gratification. Time fucking stopped. Yet our hearts continued to beat, her blood pouring into my mouth as I took her with brutal thrusts that she responded to in kind.

It was animalistic.

Hot.

Ferocious.

Fucking.

No, a claiming. Her nails scraped down my back, drawing blood and causing me to hiss against her neck. I bit her again, her essence giving me the gift of life and completion and binding us on a path to insanity.

We were one.

Together.

Forever.

We were destined to overcome the agony of our existence, to fight in a war neither of us had signed up for, or to die trying.

Every thought, emotion, concern, sacrifice, and sensation traveled from my mind to hers, igniting a marathon of information for my mate to access.

She trembled beneath the onslaught, her eyes widening in shock as her pussy spasmed around me on an incredible climax that I *felt* through my own spirit.

I tumbled into oblivion after her, the orgasm ripping a hole through my chest and damning me to hell in the space of a breath. Everything burned in the best way, our powers dancing on a plane we could sense without seeing.

Our mating was complete.

Done.

Embedded in our spirits for eternity.

And I'd never felt more alive.

Aflora shook beneath me, her blue embers starting to fade as the heat of the moment began to subside. I pulled away from her neck to stare down at her in wonder. None of the prophecies prepared me for this intensity or the feelings that followed.

Pride.

Adoration.

Fear.

Because I knew what lay ahead of us. I knew what we would have to face together. And I knew what decision she would eventually have to make.

What if she chose *him?*

What if she followed the path fate originally set out for her before I stepped in the way?

There were so many unforeseen consequences of altering someone's destiny, but I had to try. It was the only way for us to pursue the alternative future, the one Midnight Fae kind required of us to survive.

Her palm pressed to my cheek, her gaze searching. "There are so many secrets in your eyes right now," she breathed, her voice a rasp against my lips. "I can sense the burdens you carry."

"It's all for you," I admitted softly, my throat working to swallow. "No one should have to know what I know. And to tell you could alter everything."

"Who are you?" she asked, her tone one of fascination, not displeasure. "I feel you inside me, Shade. A mix of fae. And so much *pain.*"

I grimaced, not wanting anyone to ever experience the weight of my emotions but knowing it was the price she had to pay for our mating. "I'm sorry," I told her, pressing my forehead to hers. "I'm so sorry, Aflora."

"Don't be," she said softly, her arms wrapping around me. "Share with me instead. Let me help you."

I shook my head slowly. "I can't. Not yet." *Not until you choose*, I wanted to add but didn't. Because it was unfair to lay that burden at her feet now. She wouldn't understand it, not until Zakkai decided to reveal his true intent.

And then the future would realign again.

More prophecies would be born.

Allegiances would change.

Fae would die.

I closed my eyes and pressed my nose to her neck, inhaling the sweet scent of my female. One breath calmed my mind. A second drew me back to her and the reality around us. The cabin I'd built for her. A safe haven no one could find.

How easy it would be to just remain here, to keep her all to myself and let everyone else fend for themselves.

But that wasn't me.

Everyone thought I only cared about my personal satisfaction. Little did they realize how much I'd sacrificed to be where I was today.

Yes, I took Aflora.

However, it was done with a purpose—to protect those I loved. Including her. An impossible claim, but I'd known about her for years, been aware of our intertwined fates, and had fallen for her after seeing dozens of prophecies all revolving around her fate. *Our* fate.

I couldn't even begin to explain that to her.

All I could do was continue to guide her and allow her to make her own decisions. Like she did tonight when she bit me.

I drew my mouth to hers once more, kissing her thoroughly and thanking her with my tongue for the gift of her bond. She would never know how much it meant to me. Or maybe she'd sense it.

Regardless, it was done.

We belonged to each other.

And I intended to spend the rest of the evening thanking her for accepting me.

CHAPTER TWENTY-THREE

AFLORA

SHADE'S MOUTH MESMERIZED ME. I could kiss him for hours, and I did. We lost time in the seclusion of his cabin. He brought me berries and the cookies he'd mentioned. He gave me a fruity drink to quench my thirst. He introduced his mouth to every inch of my body. And then he took me again and again.

If this was all a dream, I no longer cared, because it was perfect. A fantasy come to life, with the most unlikely of males at my side.

Yet I felt the bruises of his past echoing in his spirit. So much agony. Selflessness. A caring man hidden beneath a perpetual shadow.

No one knew him.

And for a few brief moments of time, he allowed me to truly see the real Shade—a strong, intelligent, conniving male who put everyone above himself.

Including me.

I couldn't see everything, mostly because that wasn't how our bond worked, but I sensed his sacrifice. "Do you regret biting me?" I asked him, my palm resting against his sculpted abdomen as I snuggled into his side.

He drew his fingers through my hair, tucking the strands behind my ear. "No."

The bond confirmed he meant that. Yet... "I sense so much sadness in you."

He said nothing for a while, his fingers drifting through my hair as he studied the wood beams on the ceiling. "I'm not sad," he finally replied. "I'm just tired. There's so much I want to share and can't, not without initiating substantial risk. And if I have to choose between your safety and my comfort, I'll pick you every time."

I shifted upward to rest my head on the pillow beside him. "Is that why you won't tell me why you bit me?"

"Yes." He rotated toward me, so he lay on his side rather than his back, his icy blue eyes holding mine. "Do you hate me for it?"

"Yes," I said. "And no."

He seemed to understand that, not needing me to voice anything more. "One day you'll understand. One day soon."

"And will I hate you when the truth is revealed?" I wondered out loud.

"Possibly, yes."

I was afraid he would say that. "I don't want to hate you."

"I don't want you to hate me either," he whispered. "But I'll accept your disdain, as is my due."

"You're used to people hating you," I realized aloud.

"I am."

I pressed my palm to his cheek and drew my thumb across his lower lip. "I see you, Shade."

"Do you?"

I nodded. "Yes." I leaned in to kiss him softly, craving his touch with an abandon I couldn't ignore. "I feel you, too."

He palmed the back of my neck and allowed me to

slowly explore his mouth with my tongue. It was a lazy embrace filled with unspoken words.

The bond had opened a connection to him unlike any I'd ever felt, yet something about it was familiar, too. I suspected it had to do with the roots we'd already established inside each other with his initial two bites. Now that he'd finished our mating, our link had blossomed into a world of color and sensation.

His pain became mine.

His fears, too.

Yet I didn't fully understand them or why they existed. I just knew it had something to do with whatever he'd *seen*.

"You have Fortune Fae in you," I realized suddenly, pulling back.

"Yes," he admitted softly, sliding his hand down from my neck to rest against my hip. "On my mother's side."

My lips parted. "That makes you an…?" I couldn't finish, surprise rendering me speechless.

"An abomination," he whispered. "Of a sort, anyway. Fortune Fae Alphas are former Midnight Fae who refused to drink blood, making us all related at our origin. Yet we're not allowed to crossbreed, why?"

"Because it makes powerful kin," I breathed.

He nodded. "Yes. And those who are in power right now don't appreciate the challenge cross-species pose. But a thousand years ago, that wasn't an issue. My grandmother mated my grandfathers without much prejudice. One was a Fortune Fae Alpha, the other a Death Blood—the former king before the Nacht family took over."

I frowned. "Wait, but you said your mother's side had Fortune Fae?"

Another nod, his expression grim. "My father married into the familial line of power, then claimed it as his own because females are not allowed to lead."

"An archaic law," I muttered.

"Actually, no, it's not. The Nacht family—Kols's grandfather, specifically—enacted it. My mother would have been on the Council had it not been for his chauvinistic actions. He used my grandmother as an example of why women shouldn't lead."

"How?" I wondered out loud, captivated by his history. This was the most Shade had ever revealed about himself, and I felt through the bond how much this all meant to him. And instinct told me it all tied into our fate as well.

"She went into hiding shortly after the call for Quandary Bloods to be eradicated." A shadow touched his features, one that darkened his ice-blue irises to a dark gemstone similar to sapphires. "Constantine Nacht stated that my grandmother's emotional state forced her to choose family over duty. He said all women were born with that loyalty flaw and therefore were not fit to lead. Thus, my father was marked as the Death Blood incumbent over my mother."

"He didn't object?" I asked, shocked.

"No. Actually, he fully supported it." Shade's jaw ticked, showing how he felt about that. "And the rest, as they say, is history."

"But what happened to your grandmother and her mates?"

He studied me for a long moment. "They suffered a similar fate to the Quandary Bloods."

"They died?"

"Not exactly," he replied cryptically. "What happened with the rock, Aflora?"

His abrupt change in subject took me aback, some sort of wall going up between us. He didn't want me to know about his grandparents, which meant he was hiding something.

As much as I wanted to press him, I sensed the importance of letting it go.

His Fortune Fae relations explained so much about him, particularly his penchant for secrets. He knew things others didn't, giving him an advantage underlined in a myriad of liabilities. No wonder he kept me in the dark so often; he didn't want to influence my choices, and yet, for some reason, he'd taken some of my decisions away from me.

Such as our mating.

"You bit me that day to prevent something else from happening to me," I said, ignoring his rock comment for the moment. "Gina told me I had two paths, that I was already in your sights."

"*His* sights," Shade corrected. "Yes."

My brow furrowed. "Are you saying she wasn't talking about you?"

"She was, in regard to the paths," he replied. "But I can't tell you more. The rest you'll need to learn on your own."

"Why?"

"Because there are some choices I refuse to take from you, Aflora. This is your destiny to follow, not mine to dictate."

"Yet you stole my ability to decide when you bit me that day," I pointed out. "So you'll alter some of my paths, but not all of them."

"I alter the ones I'm destined to alter," he replied, slipping his palm upward to cup my cheek. "Our paths were meant to intertwine. I just upped the timeline."

I wanted to ask him what that meant, but I knew he wouldn't tell me.

Fortune-telling was a tricky game. If he told me too much, he risked disrupting the balance and changing our fates to an unforeseeable future. Which was why he mostly focused on facts I already knew, detailing the past decisions and how they'd already impacted our lives.

But he carefully avoided anything that could explain what tomorrow held for us both, despite the fact that I could sense he knew perfectly well what to expect. Or, at least, he had an inkling.

Because that was how Fortune Fae worked—their visions didn't often make sense, the images a cluster of thoughts that may or may not form a coherent prediction. And from what I gathered of Shade's comments, there were multiple avenues for our futures to take. He only dictated the ones he could control, like that day outside the coffee shop.

"The rock," I said slowly, returning to his question and giving him a reprieve from the fate discussion. I cleared my throat. "It, uh, showed me something devastating. The fire."

His brow came down. "The fire?"

"Yeah. At the Death Blood Education Building." I closed my eyes to consider what I'd seen and relayed the information to him. He remained silent the entire time, allowing me to tell him what I saw, how it felt, the horror of realizing I was trapped inside someone else, and the eventual kiss against the rock. "He said he'd see me soon, like he knew I'd have that vision."

I shivered at the memory, my blood running cold as I opened my eyes again after several minutes of reliving the nightmare.

"How could he know that?" I asked. "Or was it…? Did my mind change it?"

He shook his head slowly, his expression holding more mysteries that I longed to decipher. "He must have placed the memory in the rock, knowing it would fall into your hands."

"How is that possible?" It didn't make any sense. "There's no way he could have known I'd pick that rock in class or that we'd be playing with psychometry."

"Unless he planted the idea in Headmaster Irwin's head," Shade suggested grimly. "Did you pick up the rock, or did it fall into your hand?"

"I…" I paused, thinking back on how I selected the item from the box. "I told you—it was the only thing that fit…"

"Because the other items were enchanted not to," he replied, falling to his back. "Fuck." He pressed his palms to his eyes and muttered a string of curses.

"You know who he is," I said. "Don't you?"

He didn't reply.

Because of course he wouldn't.

"Shade, I need to know who he is."

"You already do," he muttered, shaking his head. "Or you should, anyway."

I frowned. "What do you mean?"

"Does he feel familiar to you?" he countered, arching a brow.

The moment he said it, my heart stopped. "The magic…" I trailed off, thinking about the day of the attack. "I… I recognized it."

Shade nodded. "Yeah. You would."

"Why?"

He just stared at me, sad. "We should get back, Aflora. I'm sure Kols and Zeph are worried about you."

"And you suddenly care how they feel?" I countered, actually curious.

"You say you see me," he replied, his eyes still holding that touch of despair that broke my heart. "But do you, Aflora? Do you really see me?"

My soul squeezed in torment, his tone and expression killing me a little. "Shade…"

"It's okay," he replied, his knuckles brushing my cheek. "But we really should go. They can't sense or find us here, which has to be driving them insane."

"They can't?" I glanced around the cabin, noting the windows revealing a dimly lit field outside. *Nightfall.* "We've been here a while."

"We have," he agreed, his hand leaving my skin.

I immediately reached for him, not wanting to separate. Not yet. "Just a few more minutes?" I asked, pleading with him through my eyes.

He seemed reluctant but finally agreed with a subtle nod. "For a kiss."

"No," I replied, causing him to frown. "For more than a kiss." I moved on top of him to straddle his hips, then leaned down to take his mouth with mine. His hands immediately found my waist, his palms gently sliding up and down my sides.

"Shade," I murmured against his mouth.

"Aflora," he whispered, one of his hands gliding up my spine to my neck and higher into my hair.

"I know you care," I informed him softly, my lips whispering against his as I pressed a palm to his heart. "I feel it here."

"Yeah?"

"Yeah."

"Well, I'll deny it if you tell anyone."

I smiled against his mouth. "Don't worry, *mate*. Your secrets are safe with me."

He returned my grin and deepened our kiss. Then I felt the trickle of smoke surrounding us, the only indication he gave me of his power enveloping me to return us to the Academy. I almost protested, but his tongue silenced my ability, his grip tightening as he whisked us away in his trademark cloud.

And then I felt the familiarity of my sheets hitting my back, my room materializing around us. I giggled in amusement, and Shade nibbled my lower lip. "We can go back anytime," he whispered.

"Promise?"

"Promise," he vowed. "I made it for you, Aflora. Only you."

"For us," I corrected. "Our own little—"

A banging against my door made me jump. "Aflora! Open this door right fucking now!"

I blinked. "Zeph?"

"Told you they would be worried," Shade drawled, rolling off of me.

"Don't you dare go anywhere," I told him as I scooted off the bed to find something to throw on. I'd left everything at the cabin, including my boots after Shade finally let me take them off. Apparently, he had a thing for heels.

I grabbed a plain white shirt from my closet, as well as

a pair of sleep shorts, and pulled them on while Shade made himself comfortable in my bed. "You could magic yourself some clothes," I suggested, then frowned. "Wait, what about—"

Our wands appeared on my nightstand while I spoke, Shade following my train of thought before I could speak. From what I understood about our new bond, we literally could communicate via telepathy but hadn't yet.

Can you hear me? I asked him.

His lips twitched. *Yes.*

Good to know.

He winked. *Answer the door before Zeph has an aneurysm.*

Right. I cleared my throat and twisted the knob. Kols and Zeph stood on the other side wearing matching expressions of annoyance. "Well, at least I know the lock works," I offered.

"Cute," Kols drawled, looking over my shoulder at the male in my bed. Because of course Shade hadn't accepted my suggestion to put on some clothes. Instead, he sat up with his back against my headboard, the sheets pooling in his lap in a very inviting manner.

He seriously looked like he belonged in my bed.

Which, yeah, as my mate, he sort of did.

Are we going to give them a show, little rose? he taunted. *Because I'm game.*

Stop.

I'm not doing anything.

You're... you're...

"Aflora?" Kols cut into our mental conversation, drawing my gaze back to the hallway. "Can we come into your room?"

I wasn't sure what shocked me more—that he actually asked for permission or that he seemed uncertain of my answer. We'd shared a bed together every day this week. Why would that suddenly change? Although, it was his bed we'd slept in, but the principle still applied.

Clearing my throat, I stepped aside. "Yeah, please."

Zeph's jaw ticked, but he entered.

Kols followed.

Then Shade narrowed his gaze. "What happened?" he asked, suddenly serious and very alert.

I shut my door and leaned back against it, nervous.

"There's been another attack," Zeph said, his tone flat. "And it has Kols's essence all over it."

CHAPTER TWENTY-FOUR

ZEPH

"WHY WASN'T I ALERTED?" Shade asked, his presence irking me immensely. Mostly because I'd been worried sick about Aflora for the last several hours, just to find out he'd been playing with her somewhere out of reach.

When we were done discussing this incident, we'd be having another conversation about not stealing our mate away without any sort of notification.

Wherever he'd taken her, we couldn't sense her at all. Or him. Which had me wondering what realm he'd taken her to, because it definitely wasn't a Midnight Fae location.

"The Council is meeting right now," Kols replied. "Without Seconds or heirs apparent. I suspect the Elders have been called in."

"Great," Shade drawled. "It's always a pleasure to hear from Constantine Nacht."

Kols bristled but didn't take the bait.

"Now isn't the time to provoke each other," I interjected. "We have a serious problem."

"There's more." Kols cleared his throat, his intense gold

eyes landing on Shade. "The attack was in the village near AcaWard at the tavern Tray took Aflora and Ella to the other week. Ajax's parents were injured."

Shade's taunting aura disappeared in a breath. "Are they all right?"

"We don't know yet," Kols admitted. "My father tried to wake them, but they appear to be in a magically induced coma. Ajax is with them now."

"And no doubt blaming you for it," Shade added, running his fingers through his dark hair.

"He's not my biggest fan," Kols agreed solemnly. "But I didn't do it."

"I know you didn't," Shade replied, surprising me.

"How do you know that?" I wondered out loud, suspicious. "Where were you and Aflora?"

He arched a brow. "Are you asking if we did it?"

"No, I'm asking how you know Kols didn't do it and also where you took Aflora."

"Sounds like an inquiry underlined in an accusation," Shade drawled. "What do you think we were doing, Zeph?" He glanced down pointedly at his bare abdomen. "Frolicking around the village?"

"He's just surprised that you'd so readily believe my innocence," Kols said, folding his arms. "And frankly, so am I."

Aflora pushed off the door, drawing Shade's focus to her. She arched her brows at him, her eyes intense, but didn't say anything. He gave her a similar look, then cocked his head to the side as if he were indulging her.

Several beats passed, the intensity between them mounting by the second.

My lips parted as understanding sliced a hole through my chest. "You finished the mating."

Kols jolted as if he'd been shot, his eyes widening. "You bit her again?"

Shade grunted, then twisted to show the opposite side of his neck and the healing mark on his throat. "She bit me first."

Aflora's cheeks reddened as Kols and I turned to gape at her. "You bit Shade?" I asked, the question stabbing me in the gut.

She chose him.

She chose him and not me.

My abdomen clenched with the realization. It was one thing to watch her with Kols, but to know she enjoyed Shade, too... I wasn't sure how to accept that.

"I... yes," she whispered, her tongue snaking out to dampen her lips. "He pulled me out of the spell, and, um, things got heated."

Shade smirked at her description, while Kols narrowed his gaze. "What spell?"

Yeah, I was still on the realization that Aflora fucking bit Shade.

And not me.

Or Kols.

After a week of playing.

She still doesn't trust me, I realized. Not that I could blame her, but the knowledge of it hurt a bit. Even if I did deserve it.

"Headmaster Irwin had us practice psychometry in class today. Aflora's object took her on a ride through the past, and not one she was particularly prepared for." He gazed at our mate, his blue eyes flickering with comments unspoken.

Because they could communicate telepathically now.

Because they were fully mated.

I palmed the back of my neck. *Get a grip,* I told myself. *This isn't the end of the world. She's still mine.*

But somehow she didn't feel very connected to me. If anything, I felt... removed. I frowned, not liking this sensation at all. It made me want to grab her and bite her again, to stake my claim and ensure she still felt me inside her.

Since when did I feel possessive over women?

Since this one stepped into my life, I thought sourly, annoyed.

"You're right," Aflora said, breaking the silence.

"I know," Shade replied.

"So modest." She rolled her eyes, but I sensed her humor. They were teasing each other, their relationship having moved to a level of intimacy that was much deeper than the one I shared with her.

I glanced at Kols to see if this bothered him as much as it did me, but he seemed more intent on whatever our mate intended to say. Was he not even the slightest bit jealous? Or was he hiding it better?

Oh, but wait, he had his elemental bond to her as well.

Because she'd chosen him as her mate.

Which meant he had nothing to fear, because she wanted him, just like she wanted Shade.

So where did that leave me? And why the hell was I spending all this time pondering such trivial bullshit? Emotions weren't my thing. I preferred actions.

Except that was precisely the problem—Aflora's actions proved her desires for Shade and Kols, while I remained third. The male who had bitten and claimed her without her reciprocation, all to save her from imploding.

It'd been a required reaction to her situation.

Perhaps that was all it meant to her.

No.

She at least desired me a little, because our passion was off-the-charts hot. That couldn't be faked. I read women well. I knew their tells. And everything Aflora's body said during our sexual interludes confirmed she wanted me.

Maybe her mind just hadn't realized it yet.

I nodded to myself. All right. A challenge. I liked challenges. If she needed me to prove myself to her, then I would.

Although, I was doing one hell of a job of that right now because she'd been talking for the last few minutes and I didn't have a fucking clue what she'd just said.

This woman is destroying me, I thought, irritated.

I wasn't a man who held conversations in my head or

thought about how to woo a female. I fucked them. End of discussion.

Yet Aflora was different.

I actually cared about what she thought of me, and I didn't quite enjoy that revelation. Not giving a damn was far easier.

And utterly impossible where she was concerned.

"Shit," Kols said, drawing me out of my head.

Because yeah, I'd missed whatever Aflora had just said since I was too lost in my feelings. *Who the fuck is this jealous fool in my head, and how the hell do I get rid of him?*

"So whoever enchanted the rock wanted you to find it," Kols continued, palming the back of his neck.

"And somehow convinced Headmaster Irwin to do a psychometry lesson," Shade added.

Okay, clearly I'd missed something important. If I kept listening, maybe I'd figure it out.

"While ensuring Aflora picked it from the items," Kols muttered, then whistled. "That's…"

"Unnerving," Aflora whispered, wrapping her arms around herself. "But that's not all."

"I'm afraid to ask," Kols said.

Aflora looked at Shade for a moment, the two of them sharing some hidden message. "I recognized the magic during the attack," she whispered as if uttering the secret out loud.

Shade didn't look surprised, which meant he already knew this or had suspected it.

Which was big fucking news to me because I had no idea, nor had I come close to sensing Aflora's connection to it. And given that I'd been the one spending time with her after the incident, I should have at least had an inkling about it.

"Why didn't you say anything?" I demanded, angry more at myself than at her. However, my tone came out scolding, causing her to flinch. Yet I couldn't apologize, because she should have said something.

"I... I wasn't sure if I should mention it," she admitted softly. "I wasn't even sure what I felt."

"A simple comment stating you recognized the magic would have sufficed," I chastised her.

"And when should I have told you?" she countered. "When the Warrior Bloods were searching the suite?"

"Oh, the two-hour wait before that would have been just fine. Or, I don't know, before you sucked my cock. That would have worked, too."

She bristled. "What? Do you think I hid it because I'm guilty?"

"I'm honestly not sure what to think, Aflora."

"This isn't helping," Kols cut in, stepping forward as if to get between us. Only then did I realize I was pretty much squaring off with Aflora in the middle of her room.

Great, Zeph. Really taking that whole "wooing the female" thing to the next level, I thought sourly.

I backed off, my hand scrubbing over my face as I forced myself to cool down. My annoyance wasn't with her but with myself. Taking it out on her wouldn't fix the situation. "You should have told us," I said, my voice softer now. Well, softer than before. It still came out sounding gruff and displeased.

"I told you now," she replied, fire flashing in her eyes. "But your reaction makes me wish I hadn't."

Ouch.

And also deserved.

"I'm glad you did," Kols interjected, stepping in front of her and forcing her to look at him and not me.

Always the hero.

He was a prince, after all.

I just served him and his entire family.

And now Aflora.

"When you say 'familiar,' do you mean it was elemental in nature?" Kols asked her. "Or maybe it felt similar to your Midnight Fae abilities?"

I couldn't see her face, but I imagined she had a

contemplative gleam in her gaze—the one that always conveyed her intelligence and ability to strategize. That look always intrigued me. But as much as I wanted to see it now, I stared at the back of Kols's head instead.

He often grounded me.

Which I unfortunately needed at the moment.

"It reminded me of my Quandary magic," she finally replied. "And I sensed it before the chaos began, almost like the being had warned me of his presence before attacking."

My brow furrowed. "How do you know it was a male?"

"Did you miss the part about her journey in his body through the Death Blood Education Building?" Shade asked, arching a brow. "She heard his voice."

Right. That'd been when I wasn't paying attention. Now I really regretted the trip through my head. "She heard him?"

"She *was* him," Shade corrected, his icy gaze turning glacial. "He imprinted the memory on the rock for her to find, even left her a message. And I'm guessing it wasn't a coincidence that today, of all days, he attacked the village. Because he set it up for her to travel back in time with that rock just before making another statement. Oh, and I'm also going to venture a guess to say the tavern was done on purpose."

"Why don't I believe those are guesses?" I countered, narrowing my eyes. He spoke with confidence, telling me he knew a lot more than he was letting on. "There's something you're not telling us."

"There's a hell of a lot I'm not telling you," he retorted. "And I can't. That's not how the future works."

"Oh, for fuck's sake, not this shit again about the future." I wanted to beat some sense into his cryptic ass, and probably would have if Aflora hadn't stepped out from behind Kols and directly into my path.

Her palm found my abdomen as she ensured that I didn't step any closer to the bed, her gaze burning into mine. "Zeph."

My inner turmoil ceased in the space of a breath, my hands grasping her hips to pull her closer as if I craved her comfort. And maybe I did. "Aflora," I murmured, utterly lost to her.

Surprise flickered through her features as if she expected more of a fight. But I didn't want to argue with her or upset her. I merely needed to protect her.

"I wish you would have told me," I admitted, my voice far less combative than earlier. Hell, I sounded downright contrite. And the shock rolling off Kols told me just how out of character this was for me, but I couldn't seem to help it. "I can't protect you if I don't know what's going on, pixie flower."

Her features softened considerably, her irises flaring with emotion. "I should have told you."

I nodded in agreement. "But at least you did now," I conceded.

She lifted up onto her toes to brush a kiss against my jaw. "I'm not used to relying on others," she whispered.

"I know," I replied just as quietly.

"Well, I think it's pretty clear what our next steps are," Shade drawled from her bed.

"Yeah? Please share because I have no idea what the hell is going on," Kols said.

Shade grinned, the cocky bastard enjoying our torment just a smidge too much. "We need to take Aflora to the village and see if she senses the same energy signature. If she does, it'll prove it's the same person who attacked the school."

"The Council is already sure of that," Kols pointed out.

"Maybe, but they also think you're responsible. So if we're going on what they believe, then…" Shade let that insinuation hang in the air.

"He's right," I said, hating that I agreed with the Death Blood but also respecting the hell out of his reasoning skills. "We need to see if Aflora can sense anything at the attack site. She might be able to give us a hint about who it is, or maybe see something the Council hasn't."

Shade nodded. "Exactly."

Aflora glanced over her shoulder at the male on her bed, and they engaged in another of those secret conversations that ended with the Death Blood smirking. She shook her head in response, clearly exasperated.

"What are we missing?" Kols asked.

"He's leading us," Aflora said in a tone that sounded both amused and irritated at the same time. "He can't tell us what he actually knows, so he's ensuring we wander down the right path instead."

Shade dipped his chin in acknowledgment, causing me to frown. "Why don't you cut the cryptic bullshit and just tell us what you actually know?" I suggested, irritated with this game.

"He can't," Aflora replied, drawing my attention back to her. "Just like he can't tell me why I recognized the magic."

I gaped at her. "That doesn't make any sense."

"It does now that I know his history," she whispered.

"History?" Kols repeated. "I don't understand."

"It's a long, drawn-out story," Shade replied. "But your grandfather knows it well."

"What the fuck are you talking about?" Kols demanded, taking the words right out of my mouth.

"Ask him," Shade encouraged. "Tell him you want to know what really happened to Zenaida, Kodiak, and Vadim all those years ago. If he tells you the truth, you'll have your answer."

"Or you could enlighten me now," Kols suggested, his tone indicating he knew Shade would never oblige.

"And what fun would that be?" the Death Blood asked, clearly amused.

"Okay, that's enough," Aflora said, turning in my arms. Rather than leave me, she pressed her back to my chest, allowing me to wrap my arms around her.

215

"We're going to need to learn to trust each other." She looked pointedly at Kols and Shade, but I knew she included me in that statement. "There's someone trying to frame Kols, and whoever that person is has an energy signature I recognize. So I agree with Shade that we should visit the village, but it'll need to be on our next free day to avoid anyone wondering why we're there."

My chest warmed at her taking charge and thinking everything through logically. Kols and Shade seemed to approve as well, their gazes reverent.

We really were royally screwed when it came to this woman.

Our only saving grace was that she didn't seem to know it yet.

"Obviously Kols can't go with us," she continued. "So it'll need to be me and Zeph. Shade, too, if he wants to go. And we can just say I wanted some spritemead and proper Elemental Fae food from the tavern. That can't be too far-fetched an excuse, right?"

"It's believable," I agreed, thinking about her obsession with dragon steak and loaves.

"I'll use my next free day to talk to my dad," Kols said. "And maybe Constantine." The latter was spoken for Shade's benefit.

"A sound plan," Shade agreed, his lips curling. "And I'll definitely tag along to the tavern. Anrika's an old family friend."

"Of course she is," Aflora deadpanned.

Shade winked at her, another secret passing between them.

Rather than let it bother me, I pressed my nose to Aflora's hair and inhaled her familiar perfume, content to have her in my arms. She might not have claimed me yet, but she would. I'd make sure of it.

And in the interim, I'd protect her as best I could.

Including on our mission to the village.

Because something told me there was a lot more to this

than just framing Kols.

It couldn't be a coincidence that Aflora arrived when she did, her Quandary Blood powers flickering to awareness right before these attacks began.

Shade met my gaze, his eyes telling me a story I longed to decipher. "I'm going to figure you out," I promised him.

"Good," he replied, welcoming the challenge. "I'm counting on it."

Aflora yawned, drawing all of our attention to her. I lifted her into my arms and set her on the bed beside Shade, deciding to offer him my own version of an olive branch.

"We'll leave you two to rest," I said, pressing my lips to Aflora's temple. "I'll be in the guest room tonight, and Kols will be right next door. Sweet dreams, pixie flower."

Shade's glimmer of surprise was worth my boon.

Yeah, I could be a good guy when I tried.

Remember that, I told him with my eyes, then turned and let Kols say his good night.

Rather than wait for him in the hall, I went to the guest room and closed the door. There would be no dream-walking tonight. Aflora deserved her time with Shade. Even if it did make me want to break something.

CHAPTER TWENTY-FIVE

AFLORA

I CLASPED MY CLOAK AROUND MY NECK, my fingers drawing over the collar beneath. Kols had taken it off me again last night, then held me while I slept in his bed. Zeph hadn't joined us, choosing to stay in the guest room for the fourth day in a row.

It sort of felt like he was avoiding me. Although, I'd seen and spoken to him several times because he'd essentially moved into Kols's guest suite. And he'd led class yesterday, as well as two days before that, so he wasn't entirely evading me. He just had this distant air about him that I didn't understand.

We also hadn't been intimate since the day I returned with Shade—an oddity only because we'd spent every day for a week prior to that getting to know each other between the sheets. Then this week, he'd barely kissed me.

Something was definitely bothering him.

Which, in turn, left me uneasy.

Shade had sent a message saying he'd meet us in the village later. He wanted to check on Ajax because he hadn't been in class since the attack on the tavern. I'd told him not to worry about me, that I'd be fine with Zeph. But as I studied myself in the mirror, I wondered if that were true.

Then the male in question knocked on my door, his voice soft as he uttered my name from the hallway. "Are you ready?" he added in that same tone.

I swallowed and nodded, more to myself than to him since he couldn't see me. "Yeah," I called back to him, then grabbed my wand from my nightstand, tucked it into my cloak, and met him at the threshold of my room.

His green eyes roamed over me with interest, his lips curling a little. "Casual looks good on you," he murmured, noting my jeans and cream-colored sweater. I had on a pair of boots as well that covered my calves up to my knees. It seemed a bit strange, but Ella showed me how to wear them on the outside of my pants. She claimed it was all the rage in the Human Realm.

Some days I really missed my Elemental Fae roots and the wardrobe that came with it. Those outfits were far simpler and nature friendly. Mostly because I used to make my clothes out of the earth.

These were... not as natural.

But Zeph seemed to approve.

He wrapped his palm around my nape, drawing me to him for a long, sensuous kiss that had me wondering if I'd just misunderstood his behavior these last few days. Because wow. His tongue really knew how to engage mine. I hummed against him in approval, my body melting into his as one of his arms cradled my lower back while his opposite remained against my neck.

Minutes passed, his warmth bleeding into me and claiming me in a sensual manner. I pressed my palms to his black sweater, the soft material gliding across his hard abdomen beneath.

He nipped my lower lip, then deepened our kiss with a groan before walking me backward into my room. It was the wrong direction, but I didn't mind. I'd missed him. I'd missed *this*.

And it was our first time doing this without any sort of audience.

Because we were finally alone.

Pleasure zipped down my spine, my heart racing with excitement.

Yes, yes. More, please.

Zeph must have read the need building inside me, because the arm around my back slid lower, his palm grabbing my ass to yank me flush against his growing arousal. I moaned in response, my fingers gliding up his sweater to his broad shoulders.

The back of my knees hit the edge of my bed, when a giggling in the hallway interrupted our moment. Zeph broke away from me so quickly I nearly fell onto the mattress, but my legs locked into place, keeping me upright.

"You think that's cute, do you?" Tray asked, sounding genuinely amused by whatever Ella had just done.

The door to their bedroom closed as Ella replied, "I do, yep. If you're nice to me, I'll consider handling that issue for you later."

"Oh, you'll be handling it all right, El. I guarantee it."

"Now who's being cocky?"

"I called you confident, not cocky."

"Uh-huh," she replied, her voice growing fainter as they walked toward the living area and away from the bedrooms. "It held the same implication."

"We should probably go," Zeph said, his voice low.

I swallowed, nodding. "Yeah."

Ella and Tray didn't know about our quad-bond, something Zeph made apparent by leaving my room ahead of me and leading the way down the hall in his usual aloof manner. His presence in the guest suite didn't seem to raise any questions. He shared a history with Kols, so Ella and Tray had just sort of accepted his staying here even though he had a place next door.

"Where are you two heading off to?" Tray asked as we

entered the living area. He had Ella's hips pressed up against the counter that divided the kitchen from the rest of the room. It was set up like a little eating nook with stools, but most of us used the dining table beside the kitchen instead.

"Aflora wants a proper loaf," Zeph replied, sounding annoyed. "Because apparently my magicked ones aren't good enough for her."

"Well, if you just figured out what mouseberries were, this wouldn't be a problem," I shot back, playing along.

He grunted and grabbed his cloak from the back of the couch. "Let's go, Earth Fae."

"Hold on," Tray said, stepping away from Ella to give us an incredulous look. "Are you going to the village?"

"Where else would we go?" Zeph asked, arching a brow. "New York? London? Oh, no, I know—we'll just go visit Elemental Fae Academy. I'm sure no one will mind at all."

"Don't be a dick," Tray snapped. "Why the hell would you go to the tavern right now?"

Zeph waved at me. "Because Aflora wants some mustard berries."

"Mouseberries," I corrected him.

He gave Tray a look that said, *Do you see what I'm dealing with here?*

Tray wasn't amused, nor was he buying the excuse. "Kols is with my father right now trying to convince him that he's innocent, and you're heading off to the scene of the crime. Don't think for one second I believe your bullshit about *mouseberries*."

"You're right," Zeph drawled. "It's the spritemead she's really after."

Ella cleared her throat. "Guys, Tray has a point. The village has to be crawling with Warrior Bloods right now, and I doubt the tavern is even open."

"It is," Zeph replied. "I already spoke to Anrika. She said it's perfectly safe for us to come in, so we're going for a midnight lunch. You can believe whatever you want, Tray.

As for the Warrior Bloods, then I guess it's a good thing I'm one of them. Now let's go, Aflora." He walked through the threshold before either of them could comment, clearly done with the conversation.

"Bastard," Tray muttered. "This is a horrible idea."

"I'll be okay," I promised him.

"I don't know what you two are up to, but be careful," Ella pressed, obviously seeing right through our excuse as well.

At least we tried. "We'll be fine," I told her, forcing a smile. "See you in a few hours."

Taking a page from Zeph's book, I slipped through the threshold before they could argue and found him waiting against the wall for me in the residential hallway. He arched a brow, then cocked his head to the side as if to say, *Let's go.*

I followed him silently past all the creepy gargoyles and continued to trail after him down the two flights of stairs. He led me outside and along the various paths to the raven field without saying a word and called up the portal for us to step through.

It wasn't until the birds began to swarm around us that he touched me, his palm a brand to my lower back as he pulled me close under the guise of keeping me safe during transport. But I felt the lingering need in his embrace, just as I sensed his lips in my hair as he gifted me a kiss where no one could see.

My mouth curled upward.

This side of Zeph—the quietly affectionate side—excited me. Mostly because he didn't let anyone else see this part of him. He sometimes revealed it in front of Kols and had sort of showed it to Shade the other night, but it all tied back to his tenderness with me. I suspected it was a foreign reaction for him, which only made it more special.

"We're here," he whispered, drawing my attention to the cloak closet around us.

I glanced up at him and went to my toes to kiss the edge

of his mouth. "They're mouseberries," I informed him softly, earning a smile in return. "And I'm going to make you try one today."

He smirked. "Can't wait." His lips captured mine unexpectedly, his tongue dominating mine in a sweep of power that left me weak in the knees.

Just as quickly, he stepped back, leaving me reeling in his wake, and opened the door to reveal the exit into the street. He winked and turned, expecting me to follow.

"Willow stump," I muttered, stepping out of the closet and onto the cobblestone streets. He was only a foot ahead, his gait intentionally slow to allow me to keep up.

The village was less busy than my last visit, most of the Midnight Fae walking with a businesslike briskness rather than meandering and socializing with one another.

My stomach twisted at the change in atmosphere and the resulting sense of unease in the air. It reminded me of why we were here, especially as we rounded the corner to see the tavern's exterior. While the stones resembled the same restaurant I'd visited a few weeks ago, I could feel the newness of it and the residual magic left behind from the restoration. Just like the Death Blood Education Building.

I swallowed, my palms dampening with each step.

Dark power lingered in the air.

Quandary magic, I recognized with a breath. That was why it felt familiar. It reminded me of a puzzle recently undone and put back together, only the strings were left behind for a Midnight Fae to tease and unwind.

A Midnight Fae like me.

I paused on the sidewalk, a few steps away from the tavern.

"He knew I'd come," I said to myself, glancing around, trying to find what other clues he left for me to unravel.

"What?" Zeph asked, coming to my side.

"I can feel him," I whispered, startled by the realization. "His energy signature is thick, like he left it for me as a clue to find. But why would he do that?"

Was it even intentional?

I frowned.

Yes. It was definitely intentional. Just like the rock.

"We should—"

"Ah, you're here!" Anrika rushed outside with a giant grin on her face that didn't quite reach her eyes, silencing what I'd been about to say. "When Guardian Zephyrus called to say you wanted to stop by, I prepped my kitchen and have quite the buffet of items for you to enjoy. Come on in and I'll get you both settled."

Zeph made a gesture with his hand. "After you, Aflora."

This was where having the mate bond in place would be really handy because I could tell him with my mind how bad an idea this was, but I had no way of communicating that without alerting Anrika. So I gave him a tight smile and followed our hostess inside to the same booth I'd sat in with Tray and Ella a few weeks prior.

The gargoyle who served us, however, was nowhere in sight.

I frowned, wondering where he'd run off to, but Anrika distracted me with a large glass of spritemead a few seconds after I sat down.

"I had this waiting for you," she explained with a twinkle in her eyes.

"Thank you," I said, uncertain of how I felt about that.

She called up some American drink for Zeph. "Your usual," she drawled. "Be back in a jiffy." She disappeared into a puff of glitter that made me sneeze.

Zeph's lips curved upward, his amusement palpable. "I think you have a fan."

"Something's not right," I rushed to say, my voice quiet. "I think he's here, Zeph." Because I still felt him. *Everywhere.*

Yet the tavern was empty—the complete opposite of my last visit here. There'd been Midnight Fae coming and going throughout our meal, everyone jovial and chatty.

Today felt like… a funeral.

I shivered at the thought, the hairs along my arms rising

on end.

What's wrong, little rose?

I jumped at Shade's mental interruption, my eyes flying around the room to search for him. *Where are you?*

With Ajax, he replied. *I can sense your panic. What's going on?*

The tavern, it feels—

"Aflora?" Zeph said, his brow creased. "Are you listening to me?"

"Shade," I replied, shaking my head as my Death Blood mate began talking again.

It feels like what?

It feels like he's here, I rushed to say to him, then focused on Zeph. "He's—Shade's—in my head. He…"

Are you sure? Or is it his energy signature you're sensing? Shade asked, his voice sounding rushed in my thoughts, like he was pacing while speaking.

It feels fresh. Too fresh. Like the day of the attack. I hadn't felt him at all at the Death Blood Education Building that day we worked on psychometry spells, yet I sensed him *everywhere* here. *This feels intentional. Like he knew I'd come.*

I'm on my way.

I opened my mouth to let Zeph know, when his phone began to ring. With a frown, he pulled it from his cloak pocket and brought it to his ear. "Zephyrus." His expression gave nothing away as whoever it was spoke on the other line, his green eyes holding mine the entire time. "I see." The masculine tones of the speaker created a deep hum.

Did you call Zeph? I asked Shade.

No reply, suggesting it was him.

"Understood. You know where we'll be." Zeph hung up the phone, sliding it into his pocket once more.

"Shade?" I guessed.

"No. Kols. He's been called into an emergency Council meeting with the Elders." His lips flattened. "It doesn't look good, Aflora. We should go."

LEXI C. FOSS

I nodded, agreeing, just as Anrika appeared with a tray of delicious-smelling loaves. My mouth practically watered for them, but my pulse thrummed a warning in my ears that I couldn't ignore.

"Can we wrap these up to go?" Zeph asked her softly. "I just received a call from Prince Kolstov, and we've been requested at Nacht Manor."

The Council is convening with the Elders, Shade informed me, his mental voice annoyed. *Get the hell out of there, Aflora. This can't be a coincidence.*

We're working on leaving, but Zeph just said we're needed at Nacht Manor? I phrased it as a question because it seemed strange to me.

He must be lying to protect you. Trust him, Aflora. He won't let you down.

Famous last words, I thought back at him. *The last time I trusted Zeph, I ended up in a dungeon.*

I won't let anything happen to you, little rose, Shade vowed. *And neither will Zeph. Trust your mates.*

It said a lot that Shade wanted me to put my faith in Zeph. They constantly bickered with one another, but it seemed, on this point, my Death Blood mate trusted my Warrior Blood mate.

Anrika had been in the middle of talking to Zeph, her excitement lost to a cloud of concern. "Of course," she was saying, picking up our untouched glasses. She disappeared without the glitter this time.

Zeph sighed and rubbed his hand over his face. "I hate doing this to her."

"Doing what?" I asked, wondering what else he had planned.

"Everyone is too unnerved by what happened here to come in for a bite, and I'd hoped to provide her with a little bit of normalcy today. Unfortunately, I've just further driven the proverbial stake through her heart." He shook his head. "Things are changing. It unsettles people."

I leaned forward, dropping my voice to a whisper. "Can

you feel the magic?" I asked him. "The lingering spells?"

He frowned. "From the restoration?"

"No, the at—"

"Here you are," Anrika announced, reappearing with a floating bag beside her and two plastic cups. She tried to smile, but it turned into more of a grimace. Her disappointment was palpable.

"Thank you, Anrika," Zeph murmured, holding out a card. "Aflora has been craving food from home, so I'm wondering if there's a way to start ordering a few meals a week. I'll talk to Kolstov to see if Sir Kristoff is open to picking it up for us."

"You don't need to do that, Zephyrus."

"Oh, but I do," he replied, grinning. "Aflora needs the sustenance and hates the Academy food."

Well, he wasn't wrong about that. But I also knew he was doing this to be supportive, and seeing that side of him warmed my heart.

He stood and kissed her on the cheek. "Thanks again," he said to her before waving his hand over the bags. "I'll be in touch soon."

Anrika nodded, tears glistening in her eyes. I stood to follow him, but she stepped into my path, her hands finding my shoulders. "Be careful," she said in a voice so soft I could barely hear her. "If they find out what you are, they'll come for you, too."

I froze as she disappeared.

Zeph turned with an arched eyebrow, having missed her words.

I opened my mouth to tell him, when a strange energy caressed my skin, causing all the hairs along my arms to stand—just like it did that day at the Academy. Right before the attack. "We need to run," I told him urgently, my eyes rounding.

Chills skated up and down my body, that familiar magic kissing my senses.

Zeph grabbed my hand and yanked me forward, the

food and drinks forgotten as he pulled me outside and into the empty street.

Not a soul in sight.

Similar to what I'd seen in the vision after the mysterious male had woven spells to vacate the building.

Zeph didn't seem to notice, his focus on getting me to the portal, but the cobblestones began to shake beneath a wave of harsh power.

I jolted to a stop, my essence reacting to the incoming attack. *No!*

Electricity hummed over my being, crafting an enchanted net of cerulean blue. I didn't allow myself a moment to consider the repercussions, my instincts roaring to life and forcing me to wrap the buzzing cloak around myself and Zeph to block the incoming meddlesome energy.

Wind soared around us, the familiar caw of alarms and stone shifting to fight.

I caught the glimpse of white, there and gone in a flash, a warm chuckle brushing my ear. I whirled around, searching for the culprit, only to find air.

Zeph was speaking, his tone insistent, but I couldn't stop hunting for the source of power.

Who are you? I demanded, the words in my mind rather than out loud.

Your destiny, a deep, sensual voice replied. *My darling Aflora, you truly have grown into a beautiful woman. Just like your mother.*

Another kiss of power touched my heart, working its way through my blood, heating all my frozen limbs beneath a ripple of authority and awareness. I tried to track him, but he lingered in the shadows, his presence there and gone in the breeze.

We'll play again soon, he promised darkly. *Retribution will be ours.*

He started to hum the song my mother taught me as a child, the haunting melody weaving an enchantment through my spirit and drawing out the memory of my past.

Only it was no longer my mother singing to me, but another—a male without a face, his voice hypnotic and empowering. I closed my eyes, lost to the sound, to the moment in my history that seemed forever changed.

I began to sing with him.

A promise.

Our futures forever intertwined.

He owned half my soul.

"I'll protect her," I heard him saying. "Always."

"Then our deal is done," another voice replied. Lighter. Feminine.

"Mom?" I asked.

But no one heard me. They were too busy enacting a blood vow, with my life at the center of the puzzle.

Something sharp bit into my neck. His teeth. He swallowed. Binding us as one in a forbidden claim.

"Aflora!"

I couldn't open my eyes, my world painted in shades of black. Of a destiny I never desired, but chosen for me by another.

"Aflora!"

The voice had begun to change, the deep quality one I recognized.

My vision wavered, someone shaking me to awareness once more.

And I opened my eyes to see bright green orbs of horror staring down at me, his beautiful lips reddened by my blood.

"Zeph?" I whispered, my voice a rasp of sound. Had his been the bite I felt?

"Fuck," he breathed. "You scared the shit out of me."

His mouth touched mine, my essence sweet on his tongue.

He'd bitten me again, tying us closer together.

Yet it wasn't his image in my mind but one of a male cloaked in white.

My other half.

Then everything went black once more, Zeph's curse the last sound to grace my thoughts.

CHAPTER TWENTYSIX

KOLS

TADMIR WAS LATE AGAIN. He sauntered in with a muttered apology to my father, then took his seat with a flourish, his white hair sprawling haphazardly against his shoulders.

None of the Seconds were invited to this emergency meeting, but Shade and I were included. I met his icy gaze across the table and noted his trademark boredom. The Death Blood really was skilled at hiding his intentions. Unlike his father, Aswad, who appeared to be brimming with annoyance beside him.

"Right, now that we're all accounted for, we can begin," my father announced, drawing the focus to the head of the table, where I sat beside him. Tray hadn't been allowed to attend, which prickled my nerves. My twin usually kept me grounded, and his absence only seemed to enhance the sense of foreboding in the air.

Something's coming.
Something I'm not going to like.

The Council rarely called upon the Elders, but this was

the second time this week they were requested to join us.

My father reached out to them in the old ways, using his magic to summon the guidance of the ancient ones who ruled before us.

It was the only time I ever saw my grandfather, as well as my great-grandfather. I'd actually only met the two men three times throughout my twenty-four years, indicating how rare it was for them to be called to our chambers.

Midnight Fae lived forever unless killed via very specific means, which was why we only ascended once in a millennium. The oldest of our kind often slept to pass the time, eternity being a long time to live. Sometimes it impacted viewpoints of morality as well, causing the ancients to go mad with sadism. Those Elders were put down if they refused to sleep.

My grandfather had yet to require the mandate, his mind still sharp, as was evidenced in his gold eyes now as he appeared in the Council doorway. My great-grandfather followed behind him, their appearances similar in that they held the forever appearance of a thirty-year-old male, but I could see their ages in their gazes and in the way they carried themselves.

So incredibly old.

Several others followed them, their presence bringing with them a coldness that drilled ice through my veins. I looked at Shade again. He just yawned, like he was ready for a nap.

Never in my wildest dreams would I have imagined a time when I considered him to be my ally, yet I felt the pull to trust him today.

Because of Aflora.

This quad-bond had affected me in ways I never could have anticipated, starting with my desire to follow a Death Blood's lead.

I did my best to feign boredom as well, all the while hoping the band around my wrist concealed my forbidden connection to my mate. There was nothing I could do about the Earth Fae bond, but as none of them could see the elemental sources of power, I assumed I was safe in that regard.

The Elders sat in the available chairs, the rest choosing to stand around us. There were two dozen of them, all varying in age up to ten thousand years old.

I fought the urge to shiver, their presence always reminding me of a necropolis with their lifeless gazes and still forms. Some of them didn't even appear to be breathing.

My father cleared his throat, taking charge of the room in his classic manner. "Per our vote earlier this week, it's time to bring Kolstov into the fold," he announced.

My heart stopped beating. *What?* He couldn't be calling forward my ascension. My trials weren't done. And the Seconds would need to be here to witness it.

I didn't dare give away my confusion. Instead, I glanced at my father with an arched eyebrow, feigning confidence and curiosity at the same time.

"As you all know, Shadow was brought in on our efforts four months ago when we provided him with an induction task that solidified his membership," my father continued. "He's proven himself at every turn, and it's time to grant Kolstov the same opportunity."

Okay, I really did not like where this was going. Particularly at the mention of Shade already being on the inside. He didn't meet my gaze now, his focus on my father. "I've done what's best for Midnight Fae kind, Your Majesty," Shade said, the words probably the most respectful ones I'd ever heard leave his mouth. "And I'd do it again in a heartbeat."

Aswad dipped his head. "You've made our bloodline proud, son."

"I know," Shade agreed.

Several members of the Council nodded in agreement, while the Elders merely observed.

"Shadow's reports have indicated that Kolstov has

behaved admirably in his handling of the Earth Fae Royal," my father said. "It serves as further proof of his acceptance of his future responsibilities, marking him as a loyal observer of our laws with the leadership qualities to carry out justice as we see fit."

"Hear, hear!" several Councilmen cheered, saluting me while I fought the urge to frown.

What the hell is going on? I wanted to demand but instead forced myself to remain silent. Something told me I was about to find out Shade's true motives. *Finally.* And I'd probably want to fucking kill him afterward.

"The recent attacks framing him as the culprit have made this even more important, which is the true purpose of today's meeting. We'll need his cooperation in bringing the revolutionaries to justice once and for all."

Fists pounded on the table, the excitement of the Councilmen stirring an ominous energy in the air. This wasn't going to end well.

"Bring him in, Warrior Danqris," my father said with a wave of his wand, sending the message to somewhere else in the building. Given the context of his words, I suspected it was the dungeon.

I swallowed and dared to meet Shade's gaze again, but he was too focused on his nails as he lounged like a king in his chair, oblivious to the growing animosity in the room.

"You see, Kolstov, we've been fighting a war for over a thousand years," my father explained. "Some centuries are quieter than others, but we caught wind of a growing revolution about fifteen years ago. Our Elders, the ultimate protectors of Midnight Fae kind, handled the disturbance for us, then advised us on what to do next."

"What kind of disturbance?" I asked, forcing a calmness in my tone that I didn't quite feel.

"One involving Quandary Bloods," my father replied.

Forcing surprise wasn't required, mostly because hearing him mention Quandary Bloods shocked the hell out of me. "Quandary Bloods?" I repeated. "How is that possible? They're dead."

"Exactly what I said a few months ago," Shade put in unhelpfully.

He and I would be having a serious discussion after this, one that would likely end in my fist meeting his arrogant face. I knew the bastard was hiding something, but never would have expected that it involved the Council and the Elders.

Fucking prat.

"The Quandary Bloods were mostly eradicated by Constantine Nacht and his Councilmen," Aswad said. "However, several escaped and went into hiding throughout the fae realms. Rather than worry Midnight Fae kind about the lingering threat, he wisely chose to safeguard the details with the Council and the Elders. And we've been working in secret ever since to eradicate the issue."

"Most of the problems have been dealt with," my grandfather added, his tone flat. "However, a stronger resistance has risen over the last two decades, and they've caused a few more issues than usual. We attempted to cut them down roughly fifteen years ago, but we weren't as successful as we would have liked. Which is why we allowed the Royal Earth Fae to live."

My father nodded. "Yes. Her parents were known loyalists, and we suspect she is, too."

"*What?*" I couldn't stop my reaction, my blood thrumming in my ears.

Known loyalists?

And did they just admit to being the ones who killed Aflora's parents?!

"Why the hell didn't you tell me that from the beginning?" I demanded. And, holy fuck, did they know about her Quandary Blood abilities?

Yes. They had to. Because Shade had been informing them the entire time.

Which meant they knew about our bonds as well.

"For what it's worth, I've yet to see any evidence to

support that theory," Shade said calmly, his gaze catching mine. "You've been living with her. Have you seen anything to suggest she supports the resistance?"

I stared at him. *Is this a trap to test my loyalty to the Council? Or is he trying to tell me something?*

"I didn't even know there was a resistance until right now," I replied through gritted teeth. Technically, that was true. It also avoided the direct question he'd just asked me, something he seemed keen on doing. Time to repay him the favor. "So how would I know what to look for?" I countered.

What the fresh hell is happening here? I wondered, my mind whirring with a multitude of ideas at once.

Did Shade play us all from the beginning? Did he never care about Aflora? I knew he'd been hiding something, as did Zeph, yet the Council didn't seem to know all the details.

Unless they were biding their time with me?

"It's true. She's shown no signs of linking to the resistance," my father said, drawing my attention back to him. "Between Kolstov's and Shadow's reports, I have seen no evidence of a connection."

"That's why you had her attend the Academy," I realized, thinking out loud. "To use her as bait."

He dipped his chin in affirmation. "Yes, we felt sure the Quandary Bloods would come for her out of loyalty to her parents. We suspect that was the point of the attack last week as well, but you and Zephyrus thwarted the attempt to collect her, which is the other reason we needed to bring you in—so that doesn't happen again."

I blinked. *Out of loyalty to her parents? Because they helped Quandary Bloods?* No, those weren't the most important questions to ask. Instead, I focused on the more prevalent issue at hand. "You want her to be taken?"

Another nod. "Shadow's bonding with her allows us greater insight into her mind, and now that they've completed their mating, he can fully track her. So if the resistance takes her, we can use her as a beacon to take them down." He glanced at my grandfather. "It was Constantine's idea, and a brilliant one at that."

"You told Shade to bite her," I said, feeling numb inside.

"Yes, we did," my father confirmed.

That doesn't make any sense. "Then why did the Council almost vote him out afterward?" I asked, unable to mask my confusion.

"It was all for show," Shade informed me. "They suspect that one of the Seconds is working with the resistance and feeding them information."

My father nodded. "Yes. So we're using them to stay one step ahead, which is why we had to make it look like Shade was being punished for his forbidden actions."

"You were really convincing," I said, looking pointedly at Tadmir.

The Malefic Fae lifted a shoulder. "We all make sacrifices for the greater good. Mine is to temporarily hold off on a powerful alignment. Shadow's will be to kill his Elemental mate and take my daughter at a later date."

My stomach twisted at the casual way he just informed me of Aflora's pending assassination. But what really bothered me was Shade's bored expression, like the thought of hurting her didn't impact him in the slightest.

Yet he hadn't said anything about our quad-bond.

Which indicated there was more at play here than I knew, unless this was all leading up to that major reveal. Maybe he intended to take my throne, and that was his trump card.

Hmm, no. If that were the case, my father would be simmering with anger toward me. Instead, he seemed pleased to be bringing me *into the fold*, as he'd called it.

A knock sounded through the chamber, drawing my father's gaze to the door. "Ah, that must be Danqris with our guest." He glanced around the room as if to determine our readiness, then called out, "Enter."

Danqris and Warlow entered with Headmaster Irwin clamped between them. The Death Blood professor's eyes were wild as he took in the audience before him, his skin paling to a sheet of white. "I-I didn't—"

"Silence," my father bellowed, his cheeks reddening with anger. "You will speak when spoken to." He shot a spell through the air, aimed at the headmaster's mouth, physically silencing the fae. "Put him in the chair," he instructed, gesturing to the lone visitor chair that no one ever wanted to find themselves in.

I swallowed and risked a glance at Shade.

He didn't give anything away, yet somehow, I sensed his unease.

Yes, something was definitely not right here. *What game are you playing?* I wanted to ask him, but the attention in the room had shifted to the sweating headmaster. He appeared ready to pass out.

"Shadow, enlighten everyone with the information you provided me," my father instructed.

I already knew what story he intended to share with the room—the one Aflora had given us the other day about her psychometry experience.

Only, as Shade spoke, I noticed he left out key details of her encounter. Such as how the power felt familiar and how she sensed the energy during the initial attack. He did include the bit about the fae sending her a message, but he changed the message slightly, making it less personal and more of a warning.

"He informed her that they would be coming for her soon but didn't say when" was Shade's summary. "I'm monitoring the situation."

My father nodded at that last sentence, pleased with Shade's supposed acquiescence.

Yet I knew the real story and saw how he morphed the truth to give the Council just what they wanted to know, without revealing the crucial points.

Just like he frequently did with me.

I took that as a sign to not write him off just yet. He seemed to be playing a role here, as he did with everything.

All right, I thought. *I'll play along. For now.*

"Do you believe Headmaster Irwin knowingly provided her with the item, or was he enchanted?" Chern asked, speaking up for the first time today. The intricate patterns woven into his bald scalp seemed to thrive with power as he engaged his Sangré magic to determine the various logical avenues of this situation.

"I believe he was enchanted," Shade admitted. "He seemed rather out of it that day in class, like he was speaking without really being there."

Headmaster Irwin started to nod, but a look from my father froze the male in place.

"There are ways to determine what he knew and what he didn't," Chern murmured. "I would need a few hours with him."

"Would you mind allowing Kolstov to join you for the interrogation? I feel it would be a good learning experience," my father said. "It'll also provide a reasonable introduction into what we know about the resistance, too."

Chern nodded. "I would be happy to bestow my experience upon him."

I suspected that would include a magical transfer of knowledge, given that was what Sangré Bloods were most well-known for doing.

"May I join as well?" Shade asked. "As the key witness, I may have some additional suggestions for your line of questioning."

"Of course," my father replied, glancing at Chern. "Assuming you agree?"

The Sangré Councilman bobbed his head in confirmation once more. "It would be a wise move, yes."

"Then it's settled," my father said, clapping me on the back. "Welcome to the inner circle, Kolstov. There's not a grand ceremony for this, I'm afraid. But you'll get that when you ascend." He winked.

I forced a smile, my heart in my stomach. "Understood. Does Tray know any of this?"

My father shook his head. "He doesn't."

"You don't suspect him of feeding information to the resistance, do you?" I asked him, incredulous. "Because I can assure you, he's not."

My father chuckled. "No. We know it's not Tray, or you. We only kept you in the dark because this is usually considered an ascension privilege, and you have enough to worry about with your ascension trials. However, the recent attacks framing you required us to move up our time frame. And you also did too good a job protecting the bait, leaving us no choice but to bring you in so it doesn't happen again."

"Yes, the next time there's an attempt to collect her, we need you to allow it to happen," my grandfather added, his gold irises whirling with uncanny power. "It's our best lead to tracking them."

"Right," I replied. "Because of her mating bond to Shade."

"Exactly," my father murmured. "The Elders had originally wanted it to be you, but we feared no one would believe you'd disregard such a fundamental law on a whim."

"So they tapped the one known for rule-breaking," Shade drawled. "Me."

My grandfather grunted. "You didn't even balk at the request."

"Of course I didn't. You gave me permission to taste an Elemental Fae, and a gorgeous one at that. Why the hell would I refuse?" Shade sounded so flippant, as if we were discussing the damn weather. But I was starting to recognize his tactics for avoidance. He made jokes to deflect, and in this case, he wanted everyone to believe Aflora meant nothing to him.

However, if that were true, then he would have told them all about our united bonds, and he hadn't.

"Yeah, yeah," Tadmir replied. "Enjoy it while it lasts, Death Blood. You're still promised to my daughter."

Shade smiled. "I'm aware of my obligations, Malefic Blood. Just enjoying my freedom while I can."

"Shall we give Chern the room?" my grandfather suggested, gesturing to the patiently waiting Sangré Councilman. "Or do you prefer the dungeon for your interrogation?"

"The room is fine," Chern replied.

"Then we'll reconvene in three hours," my father announced, standing and squeezing my shoulder. "Try to learn what you can. We'll talk more over dinner later."

That wasn't a request but a demand. "Of course, sir. Thank you."

He smiled, pleased, and led the others from the room, leaving me alone with Shade, Chern, and Headmaster Irwin.

"Shall we begin?" Chern asked.

Shade kicked his feet up on top of the table and crossed his legs at the ankles, the picture of uncaring. "Sure. Have at it."

I didn't mimic his pose but instead laced my fingers on top of the wood and gave Chern my undivided attention. "Teach me."

CHAPTER TWENTY-SEVEN

ZEPH

IT WAS A TESTAMENT TO HUMANITY that no one seemed to notice or care that I carried an unconscious female through the streets of New York City. There were a few glances here and there, but not a single human tried to stop me or raise questions.

Which was precisely why I chose Manhattan to lie low.

"Good evening, sir," the doorman greeted me as I approached the familiar residential building. I'd spent a good portion of the last year here before returning to the Academy. No one really knew about this place, aside from Kols. He knew I enjoyed hiding here, mostly because of the added convenience of available blood walking around everywhere.

"Is everything all right?" the doorman asked, eyeing Aflora in my arms.

Of all the mortals, of course this one would ask. "She's fine, just had a bit too much to drink. Bringing her back here to sleep it off."

He nodded solemnly. "Ah, yes. I understand. Good

luck, sir."

"Thank you," I replied, heading toward the stairwell. My flat was on the third floor, making it easy enough to reach by foot, even with the precious cargo in my arms.

She didn't stir or make a sound as I walked, her head pillowed against my shoulder as she slept off whatever magic she'd tapped into back at the village. I'd felt the burn of it, the imminent danger surrounding us both, and her mental defensive measures.

It'd all happened so quickly that I hadn't been prepared to fight, and the next thing I knew, power exploded out of her. My only option was to bite her, to try to ground her. It'd resembled an electrical wire hitting my bloodstream, spiraling me into a dark-magic whirlpool that nearly drowned me alive. Then she surfaced, bringing me up with her, and we were back in the village again.

The whole thing had felt like a dream. But I knew it was real because of the energy humming through the cobblestone street and dancing along the wood beams of the surrounding light-colored buildings. Flares of magic had lit up the night like lanterns, drawing a straight path to Aflora.

I hadn't waited around to see if anyone else felt the disruption, and instead headed right for the portal to bring her to the Human Realm. We'd stay here until I heard back from Kols—who'd been silent since going into the Council meeting.

Balancing Aflora with one arm, I reached for my wand and muttered an unlocking spell at my door. It opened with a slight creak to reveal my one-bedroom home.

The interior didn't boast elegance or wealth, the kitchen being sorely outdated compared to the Academy accommodations, but I rather preferred this place to my Elite Residence suite. Mostly because it was mine.

I'd purchased it using my credits as a Guardian to the Nacht family. The credits could be traded in for human cash at an exorbitant amount—a good thing because owning a place in New York City required a lot of mortal money.

I kicked my door closed behind me with the heel of my boot, then took Aflora into my bedroom to lay her on the bed. Her blue-black hair sprawled beautifully across my dark green pillows, her face holding a pale glow that reminded me of the Midnight Fae moon.

Gorgeous, I thought, smiling down at her. Then I carefully removed her knee-high boots and set them in the corner of my walk-in closet. Her cloak was next—which I hung beside mine. They weren't normal accessories in the Human Realm, but no one had seemed to notice. I slipped off my own shoes, placed them beside hers, and returned to tuck a strand of her hair behind her ear.

"Be back in a few minutes," I whispered, kissing her forehead. I could feel her slowly slipping back into consciousness and wanted to be prepared to welcome her back to reality.

Since I'd left all our food back at the village, I opted to whip up a few things for us in the kitchen. It required a bit of magic, as my fridge and shelves were pretty empty—I lived primarily on blood when I visited the city—but I managed to create some of those mouseberries Aflora kept talking about.

She was awake when I returned to the bedroom, her gaze on the windows that broadcast boring views of the residential building across the street.

I liked Upper Manhattan for the location, not so much for the scenery.

Her nose twitched as I approached, her focus shifting to the plates in my hands. "What happened?" she asked, her voice hoarse.

I set the plates down on my nightstand, then magicked a cup of water for her and held it to her lips for a sip. "I'm not sure, but I think you saved our asses in the village," I told her.

She took the glass and drank half the contents in one

go.

"Someone or something attacked us, and you fought back." Or I thought that was what had happened. "Do you remember it?"

She appeared to fall into her thoughts for a moment, her throat working as she finished the drink. A spell refilled it for her, something she seemed to appreciate given the glimmer in her blue irises. "I felt him," she finally said after finishing the second cup of water. "He... he was there." She brought her hand up to her neck, frowning as she felt the healing mark against her skin. "Did you bite me?"

"Yes," I admitted, taking her glass and setting it on the nightstand. "You were buzzing with power, like that time in the LethaForest." I sat on the edge of the bed near where she lay on her side. My knuckles whispered over her cheekbone to her throat. "I had to call you back to me, Aflora. The energy seemed like it was going to swallow you whole."

She frowned, making me wonder if I'd done the wrong thing. I was the one she hadn't yet accepted as hers, and I supposed she could see my actions as a way of forcing her hand—a common male behavior of Midnight Fae kind.

"I... I had to anchor you, Aflora," I said, uncertain of how to explain it. "I could feel you slipping away, almost as if another entity had forced the power to explode out of you. If you erupted in the village, fae would have died. It was the best way to protect you, as well as the others."

Her blue eyes flickered with confusion as she met my gaze. "Did you not want to bite me?"

"No, that's not what I mean." I palmed the back of my neck, frustrated.

Why is this so damn difficult? I wondered. Probably because I never cared what a woman truly thought of me before. Really, I rarely cared what *anyone* thought of me. But Aflora was different. I needed to win her over for reasons I didn't quite understand. They went deeper than our bond. Like my very spirit required her approval, yet I had no idea how to acquire it.

"Zeph," she said, reaching out to lay a hand on my forearm. "Do you regret mating me? Is that why you've been distant all week?"

"What? No." *Fuck, what a shit show.* "This whole situation is so far outside my comfort zone, it's… I don't know how to handle it." And that was the rub right there, the reason this mess infuriated me.

I couldn't control the outcome.

"I lead," I told her. "It's who I am. I make decisions every day. Everything I do is driven by logic. But none of my training has prepared me properly for…" *For you,* I wanted to say but wisely chose not to.

I blew out a breath, released my neck, and dropped my head into my hands. I was totally fucking this up. And I hated that I had no idea what to say.

"Talking isn't my strength," I admitted. "Neither is giving up control."

This seemed ridiculous. Fretting over the bullshit would get us nowhere. So I'd just be blunt. She might not like it, but it would be better than dancing around these asinine thoughts.

"I've never agreed with the Midnight Fae mentality associated with mating," I told her. "But I never really cared too much because I never intended to take a mate. I'm independent and I do my own thing. However, you changed that, and now I've bitten you twice without your permission. Which is technically fine by our societal laws, but that doesn't mean I feel right about it."

My logical side argued that it wasn't *convenient* at all, more of a burden. Especially considering the consequences of that action.

But that was all beside the point.

"Anyway, you chose Kols with your earth magic. You even chose Shade by biting him. Yet I essentially forced myself on you. Yeah, it was for the right reasons in the end, but that doesn't change the circumstances for biting you."

Okay. I was done rambling now. It left me feeling vulnerable and weak, two adjectives that were very much not me. And I sort of hated that Aflora drew that side out of me.

Avoiding relationships had worked well for me.

Maybe I'd go back to that.

Leave Kols and Shade to handle Aflora, protect them all from afar, and just—

"Zeph," Aflora said, her hand curling around my wrist to tug my hand away from my face. "Look at me."

I was tempted to glare at her in response but chose not to make this worse and gave her my attention instead. She studied my expression, her lips curling at whatever she saw there. Probably a scowl because this was fucking uncomfortable.

"I think that's the most emotion you've ever displayed in my presence." She sounded amused, which only made me want to glower again. But she distracted me with her tits as she sat up, her sweater stretching deliciously across her chest.

Removing her cloak had been a fantastic idea.

Actually, no. I should have just taken everything off.

"You made me mouseberries?" she asked, gaping at the plates on the nightstand.

"Don't get too excited," I cautioned her. "Pretty sure they're just mustard berries or something."

She snorted. "You know what they're called."

"Do I?" I asked innocently. "Huh. Well, I guess you'll have to taste them and find out if I did it right." I knew I had, as they were pretty much the same thing as sour green grapes, but I enjoyed teasing her anyway.

She flashed me an amused smile that made my heart race. Aflora was a gorgeous woman, but when she smiled at me like that, I forgot how to think.

Because I'd made her happy.

A rarity, it seemed. But for a brief moment, I'd pleased her, and that made me want to puff up in pride.

Kols would laugh hysterically at the sight. Fortunately, he wasn't here to witness it.

Aflora took the plate, settled it into her lap, and propped her back up against the headboard. "All right, Headmaster. Let's see if your chef skills measure up, shall we?" She waggled her brows at me playfully, then lifted the loaf to her mouth and took a sensual bite.

Well, it was sensual to me, anyway. Hell, everything she did with her lips and tongue seemed to hypnotize me.

And that moan she released after tasting the food I'd prepared?

Yeah, that was hot, too.

I adjusted myself on the bed, my jeans suddenly a little too tight, and busied myself by eating the loaf off the other plate. It was okay. Sort of like having a sour fruit salad in a soggy tortilla. Not my favorite, but I knew better than to voice an opinion out loud on the topic.

"So where are we?" she finally asked, glancing out the window again.

"New York City," I told her.

"In the Human Realm?"

While she voiced it as a rhetorical question, I responded with a nod. "Yeah. We're lying low until we know what the Council meeting was about. And, well, also until we know if anyone noticed what happened in the village." Because that could go bad quickly if anyone witnessed that explosion of power.

She visibly shivered but indulged in another bite.

A comfortable silence fell between us while we finished our meal, her gaze far away with thoughts I couldn't hear. We needed to discuss what happened, but I wouldn't push her.

Instead, I considered an alternative that might provide us both with a necessary reprieve from all the chaos surrounding our lives.

"Do you want to see Central Park? It's only a few blocks away from here and should be pretty empty because of the late hour." I checked my watch. "Actually, I think it closes to the public soon as well, or might already be closed. We'll just enchant a guard or something."

"Central Park?" she repeated, her eyes lighting up. "I've never been."

I figured as much. "I'm sure it's not the same as the Earth Fae Kingdom, but it's probably more similar to it than our version of nature in the Midnight Fae realm."

Her lips twitched. "Yours is about as opposite as you can get with black grass and burning trees."

"Charcoal blades are not grass."

"Oh, I know," she said empathetically. "They're closer to knives."

I smirked. "Not like knives either."

"Sure." She set her empty plate to the side. "Do you want to go now?"

Given the eagerness pouring off her, I suspected a negative reply would upset her. Not that I wanted to refuse her. Actually, I rather liked the idea of making her smile again. "Sure," I replied, placing my dish on top of hers. "We'll need coats instead of cloaks, just to better fit in. Let me see what I can find."

Aflora released a small chirping sound that had me glancing over my shoulder at her. She had her hands clasped in her lap like she wanted to clap them together, her eyes sparkling with excitement.

I arched a brow. "If all it takes is the mention of a park to earn your happiness, then I should do all right with this mate shit."

She snorted. "I have a feeling there will be a lot of parks in our future, Zeph. With comments like that, you'll be apologizing to me all the time."

"Probably," I admitted, but I couldn't stop the grin from spreading over my lips. "Sometimes I'll make it a little more interesting, though."

"Yeah? Like how?" she asked, genuinely curious.

"Make-up sex, Aflora," I told her. "I hear it's fun. We'll

try it sometime." I winked at her and left her gaping at me from the bed as I wandered into the living area to find some jackets.

This whole "normal activity" thing would be fun.

We'd have to try it more often.

CHAPTER TWENTY-EIGHT

SHADE

FOUR FUCKING HOURS of interrogation later, Councilman Chern ascertained the same thing I'd done in a matter of seconds the other day. "Headmaster Irwin was acting under an enchantment. My suspicion is that a Quandary Blood is to blame."

The Council members and Elders listened while Chern detailed his tactics for pulling that information from the Death Blood's mind, then the Sangré Councilman continued with his suggestions for how to handle the situation. "His psyche is vulnerable, so until we apprehend the Quandary Blood who did this, we'll need to keep Headmaster Irwin under close observation."

Meaning he wanted to jail the poor man until the matter was resolved.

Several of the Councilmen bobbed their heads in agreement, while Constantine Nacht pointed out that locking up Headmaster Irwin also served as a suitable punishment for being "so easily corrupted by enemy forces." I nearly snorted at that claim. These imbeciles had no idea whom they truly faced or how many centuries of hatred had piled up toward them.

But they'd find out, and soon.

Kols met my gaze from across the table, his golden orbs flaring with a thousand questions. Fortunately, he hadn't voiced anything that could incriminate us, but I suspected we were due for a long conversation after this was through.

He probably thought I bit Aflora because the Council told me to, which was partially true—I'd done it to maintain my cover. But I knew years ago that my fate would cross her path. This was so much bigger than the Elders or the Midnight Fae Council could possibly comprehend. They would have to see beyond their own bigotry and arrogance to realize the truth, and I wasn't about to help them with that task.

Kols's father made a few closing remarks once the sentencing was done, then looked to Constantine for any further guidance the Elders wished to bestow upon us. The retired king merely advised Kols to allow Aflora to be taken next time, something he agreed to with a mere nod, likely because he was too livid to speak. I understood that feeling all too well.

When the meeting finally adjourned, I stood and stretched my arms, ready to disappear, only a look from Kols told me he'd come after me if I did.

"Your mum is looking forward to having you over for dinner tonight, Kolstov," Malik said softly, reminding his son that he'd agreed to come home after this mess.

My father, on the other hand, left without even looking at me. There would not be a similar invite to come home for a family dinner. We didn't do that, because it would require talking and making false pleasantries, something neither of us could be arsed to do.

And my mother, well, she rarely spoke these days.

"I'm looking forward to it, too," Kols replied. "I just need to talk to Shadow about a few things before I go."

"Does it involve that little power scuffle you two got

into last month? Because he told the Council how he nearly beat you." Malik grinned at me while he spoke, clearly enjoying the rivalry between me and his son.

"I believe I said I let him win," I drawled. Because that had been a far more believable story than the one Kols had come up with.

"Let me win?" Kols repeated, his eyebrows popping upward. "Since when?"

Malik chuckled. "I'll leave you two to work that out. See you in thirty minutes or so?"

"That'll be enough time for me to remind Shadow who is closer to the source, yes." Kols sounded so serious that I wondered if he intended to deliver on that threat.

A few others showcased their amusement at our trademark bickering, then left us alone in the Council Chambers. Kols cocked his head toward a painting of Constantine on the wall, then stepped toward it with his wand. A muttered spell caused the colors to shift, revealing an entrance to a room I didn't know existed here.

Kols led the way, his shoulders rigid, and I followed him into a much darker chamber lacking in windows. He uttered a spell to silence the interior, canceling out any listening devices, then he leaned back against a table in the center of a black rug. There were only three chairs, the space about a tenth of the size of the other room.

"What is this place?" I asked him, glancing around.

"Oh, something I know that you don't?" he countered. "Fascinating."

I snorted. "Want to play a game of trading information, Elite Blood? Because I have a feeling I'll outlast you by a mile."

"What the fuck?" he demanded. "What. The. Fuck?"

"You'll need to be more specific," I drawled, then ducked as his fist came for my face. "Well, now there's a positive way to seek answers." I mockingly applauded him and jumped to the side as he tried to strike me again.

Then I shadowed to the other side of the table. "Feel

better yet?" I asked him when he heaved a furious breath.

"Hardly," he muttered, fixing his suit jacket and tie. "Start talking, Shadow, or so help me, I will kill you."

I let the false threat go because time wasn't on our side, and bickering got us nowhere. "Do you really think I bit Aflora because of some edict?" I asked him, arching a brow. "You know me better than that. I've never been one to play by the rules, and authority means shit to me."

"So why did you do it?"

"Because fate demanded it," I admitted. "Because I wanted to. Because she was always meant to be ours." There were a thousand reasons I could list, none of which would truly satisfy his quest for knowledge. "I gave them that recording as proof of being on their side, just like I bit her because they asked me to, but I never do anything without a true purpose. They don't know about her collar or her additional ties. They also have no idea who they're truly fighting in this war."

"And you do." Not a question, but a statement.

"Yes." I ran my fingers through my hair and considered what else I could tell him without risking fate. "Look, I know I've not been very forthcoming—"

"Understatement."

Ignoring his interjection, I continued, "But you can trust me to have Aflora's best interests at heart. She'll have a choice to make soon, and that choice will rely very heavily on our ability to get along."

"A choice of what?"

"Which destiny to pursue," I replied.

"Stop speaking in fucking riddles and give me something I can understand."

"I don't know how to do that without risk," I admitted.

"Then you're fucking worthless to all of us," he retorted, causing me to flinch. "How the hell am I supposed to protect our mate if I keep being blindsided by bullshit? I mean, the school gets attacked, and apparently, I was supposed to let her be taken? Fuck that. Now I find out the

Council and the Elders have known all along that Quandary Bloods are still alive, and that you've been working with them for months."

He started to laugh, the sound a bit hysterical.

"They've also been killing anyone and everyone associated with Quandary Bloods for hundreds of years," I added. "Don't forget that part, or how they casually mentioned the reason they left Aflora alive."

"Right. Because they killed her parents." He placed his palms on the wood table, his shoulders bowed as he muttered a string of curses under his breath. I would have been impressed by some of them if I wasn't sensing the pain underlining each colorful word. "How the hell are we going to tell her that? She's going to hate us."

"She won't," I promised. "We didn't do it."

"You're right. My fucking grandfather did." He shoved away from the table to begin pacing, his long legs eating up the small space of the room quickly. When he nearly hit the wall, he turned and walked back to me, then rotated again, and did several laps while continuing to shake his head.

"She won't blame you," I said softly, meaning it. "She knows it's not you."

"You say that like you've already seen the outcome," he replied, pausing to look at me. "Are you working with a Fortune Fae? Is that how you know so much?"

"Yes." No point in hiding an obvious deduction. I just wouldn't give him details, something he must have known since he didn't bother to ask me for information on my source.

Instead, he looked at me and intelligently asked, "What can you tell me, Shade?"

"There's a war coming," I said, feeling that was pretty evident now based on everything that had already happened. "And Aflora is going to be forced to pick a side. Retribution or reformation."

"And what side are we on?" he demanded.

"That remains to be seen," I admitted honestly. "I've

255

seen the potential for both avenues." I realized the mistake in my wording the second his eyebrows flew upward into his hairline.

"*Seen?*"

Yeah, that'd be the word I shouldn't have mentioned. Rather than reply, I remained silent. I'd already said too much.

"Explain," he demanded.

"I can't." Not without risking everything. "One day, I will. I promise. But for now, I need you to trust that I have Aflora's best interests at heart."

"It's hard to trust someone who is constantly hiding things and withholding important details, Shadow."

"Just as it's hard to trust someone related to the male who got us all into this mess to begin with," I tossed back, tired of this bantering act. "You've studied Fortune Fae. You know that prophecies can change depending on the actions of others. If I touch or influence the wrong strand in the web too much, it could sever and end and land us on a completely new string of fate."

He didn't reply, just watched me with a tick in his jaw.

I sighed. "I'm walking a tightrope, Kols. I'm trying to help where I can without interfering too much, and it's fucking exhausting. So rather than hold it against me, why don't you try to have some fucking respect and work *with* me? I provide hints as I go along. If you're smart, you'll catch them. If not…"

Then we all fail, I thought with a shrug. I knew I was being infuriating, but I had no choice. If I gave him all the answers, our destinies would be strongly impacted and all the predictions could change.

Fortune Fae weren't supposed to interfere too heavily in the fates of other fae, and I'd plucked Aflora's strands several times within the notorious web that dictated our destinies. My meddling had already impacted the futures for Kols and Zeph, causing their strands to cross Aflora's in the process. It was a consequence I knew about ahead of time, having chosen to go that route anyway, but that wasn't the point.

I'd already altered destiny several times. The more I told him, the stronger the risk that our current strand would end in the web.

And then fate would change. *Again*.

Which would be very bad for all of us involved.

"Tell me you care about her," Kols said after a long, tense beat.

"I more than care about Aflora," I replied. "She's my reason for everything and the driving motivator for many of my decisions. And if I could, I'd take her away from this situation, but I know that's not how any of this works. She's a pivotal element in the future with a destiny only she can choose. And I'll support her, even if she makes the wrong choice."

Because that was what I was destined to do.

And the same with Kols.

"Our futures are aligned, Midnight Prince," I told him softly. "It's time for you to accept it, just as I have, and stop looking for who to blame in all this. Because, trust me, you won't like what you find down that dark alley."

"More cryptic bullshit," he muttered.

"That's never going to change," I replied. "Now go home. I'll let Aflora know we're okay." She'd told me about an hour ago that she was in the Human Realm with Zeph, something about heading to the park. Sounded like a date to me, which had made me smile.

It was about time Zeph worked to win her over.

He'd made a lot of bad turns along the way, but he seemed to be curving the right way now.

"I'll be in touch," I told Kols, disappearing before he could demand I stay. We'd discussed enough. He knew I wasn't on the side of the Council and the Elders, which would have to satisfy his curiosity for now because I had a more important place to be.

A few minutes later, I materialized in the meadow I'd

taken Aflora to twice now.

The sun illuminated the flowers, giving the place a beautiful glow I knew she'd adore, but it was the light up on the hill beyond that captured my interest.

I wandered up the familiar path to the cottage lurking beyond the concealing mist, my magic allowing me to enter at will.

"Hello, Shadow," my grandmother called from inside, welcoming me in that eerie way of hers.

Because she'd *seen* me coming.

"Hi, G'ma," I replied, stepping through the threshold into the living area. "I think I screwed up."

Her blue eyes—the same shade as my own—glimmered with knowledge, confirming my statement.

"Come," she murmured, gesturing to the dining room. "We'll discuss it over cookies."

I sighed. Sweets weren't a good sign. They meant she had bad news to share.

And I could only imagine what that would be.

CHAPTER TWENTY-NINE

AFLORA

ZEPH'S PALM COVERED MY mouth as he held me firmly against his chest. "Shh," he whispered in my ear as I giggled against his hand.

Apparently, it was frowned upon to visit the park after hours, something I found out when a rude human barked at me for dancing across the grass. He'd then tried to blind me with a flashlight, which was really quite cruel.

Zeph had responded by grabbing my hand and forcing me to run with him down a path, then ducked into these gorgeous green bushes. I wanted to pet the leaves and branches, but he grabbed me and placed his hand over my mouth, demanding I stay quiet.

For whatever reason, that made me want to laugh, mostly because I was high on life out here. The Human Realm had so many mysterious flowers and plant life, each one uniquely beautiful with its own earthy strand that I longed to follow.

No wonder Claire introduced her earth mate, Sol, to peaches. If I ever had a chance to see the Elemental Fae

Queen again, I'd ask her about these azaleas and roses and crape myrtles. Oh, those were like trees, but with flowers, and I yearned to see them bloom. And the daffodils, too! So many beautiful histories, all underlined in color and fragrant scents.

I sighed happily, causing Zeph's arm to tighten around me.

Right. He wanted me to be quiet. But how could I be silent in such a gorgeous place? I wanted to dance around more and play with my earth magic. It'd been so easy to circumvent the collar this time, proving Kols and Zeph right about the enchantments—they'd worn off.

So all my powers were free for me to explore, yet this man with the flashlight had ruined it all.

Evil human.

His boots scuffed against the path as he searched for us, his voice gruff as he spoke into some sort of communication device. "Some crazy flower chick," he was saying. "She was stripping in the middle of the fucking park."

I scowled at him. I was not *stripping*, just removing my sweater because I wanted to roll around in the fresh green grass. Really, some people had no understanding of what it meant to be an Earth Fae.

Which, yeah, humans were oblivious to our existence.

My bad.

But who could blame me when surrounded by all this life? I just wanted to swim in the nature of this place and listen to all the tales of the flowers around me.

Zeph pressed his lips to my ear. "Stop that."

I blinked, confused, then realized the leaves were swaying around us, ready to embrace my magic. It just came to me instinctively, the urge to help them all grow and prosper a part of my base existence as the conduit for the earth source.

The light-bearing human disappeared down the path, causing Zeph to relax somewhat against me. "We should get out of here."

"Why?" I asked against his hand, my voice muffled.

"Because we've already drawn enough attention to ourselves here. There's a division of Warrior Bloods who scan incident reports to spot any signs of supernatural activity in the Human Realm. If that officer files a case about a 'crazy flower chick' dancing naked in the park, it'll raise a red flag."

I frowned. "I wasn't naked."

"Not yet," he agreed, using his wand to retrieve my sweater from the field and handing it to me. "Put this back on, Aflora. Humans don't frolic without clothes on in Central Park unless they're sunbathing, or doing other things."

"I was doing other things," I pointed out as I pulled the sweater over my head. "I wanted to feel the grass."

He nodded, his lips twitching at the sides. "Uh-huh."

"What?"

"Nothing."

"That look isn't nothing, Zeph." I folded my arms. "Tell me."

He shook his head, his mouth curling into a fond smile. "I'm just amused by your Earth Fae inclinations. It's very stereotypical."

"Stereotypical," I repeated. "In what manner?"

He pressed his palm to my lower back to guide me the opposite way down the path, purposely keeping us to the dark areas to hide our presence. "Nymphs are a popular lore in the Human Realm and commonly depicted as nature beings who frolic around naked." He glanced at me sideways. "Which, I'm pretty sure, you were about to do."

"I don't know about naked," I replied. "But maybe. There are just so many glorious scents here, and the magic coming from the ground is very alluring."

"You know what's alluring?" he asked quietly, guiding me into a darker area of the park where the moonlight was hidden by the lush branches above us. He walked me backward with his palms against my hips. This was not the path we'd entered on, and my boot-clad feet were encased in the beautiful green grass once more.

I bit my lip and stared up at him. "What's alluring?" I whispered, continuing to step in the direction he led me, trusting him not to let me fall.

His lips went to my ear. "The idea of stripping you naked right here and fucking you up against this tree."

My back hit something hard, my palms finding the bark behind me and identifying the vivacious American elm tree. So big and full of life. I gave it a little pet, pleased with its sturdy roots and overbearing size. I also rather liked how dark it was beneath the trunk-like branches.

And more specifically, I enjoyed how Zeph felt as he trapped me between his body and the hard surface behind me.

"Yes," I said softly, my hands wandering up to grasp Zeph's shoulders. "I like that plan very much."

"Do you?" he asked, his words a breath against my ear. "It won't be sweet or romantic, but hard and fast. It might hurt."

"Will you bite me?" I asked him.

"If you want me to."

"I do." I hadn't been aware the first two times he'd bitten me, and I really wanted to feel him, to make this moment just about us and our unique connection to one another.

"It'll finalize our mating bond," he warned.

"I know." I wasn't afraid of it. We were already on a wild ride together, so we might as well finalize it and see where it went. That he wanted to do it here, in the middle of my element, only made it that much more powerful and intense.

His lips drew an enticing path along my jaw, leading his mouth to feather over mine. "Be sure, Aflora."

"I am," I promised him, my nails dragging along his shoulder to his neck and then into his hair to hold his head where I wanted it. "I want you inside me, Zeph." I meant the phrase in every way it could be interpreted but decided to seal the deal with the two words I knew he truly wanted to hear. Because Zeph was all about communication and trust. "Fuck me."

He shuddered against me, any restraint he had in place dissolving in a second.

And his mouth took mine.

It wasn't a gentle kiss but a claim, his tongue dominating mine. But I held my own, refusing to bow completely, meeting him as a match, and challenging him at every turn.

If he wanted to own me, he'd have to win me.

And I wouldn't bow easily.

Not tonight.

Not while surrounded by power that fueled the energy source inside me.

This was *my* domain, not his. And queens did not kneel unless they wanted to.

He smiled against my mouth, his amusement palpable. "Oh, Aflora, you just made this that much better." His fingers dug into my hips as he captured my lips once more, his kiss savage and violent in the best way.

A warrior.

My warrior.

There were moments when I hated him, but he more than made up for it during the times when I adored him.

Times like now.

He'd brought me to this place, wooed me unintentionally with the familiarity of the earth, and now I intended to let him claim his reward.

My sweater disappeared again, followed by his own. I hissed as his bare chest met mine, my bra seeming to have vanished beneath his touch. He cupped my cheek, his tongue enchanting mine into a sensual duel I never wanted to end. I ran my palms over his bare back, loving the way his muscles flexed and moved.

He was all strength and man.

Experienced and knowing.

Velvety smooth and hard as a rock.

"Zeph," I moaned, arching into him as he unbuttoned my jeans. My zipper slid down, the sound echoing in the night, accompanied by the shuffle of fabric and boots as he fully undressed me, leaving me naked against the tree. He took a step back to admire the view, his Midnight Fae eyes allowing him to see what a human wouldn't be able to.

It made him predatory.

Cruel.

A sleek panther in the dark.

My skin prickled with goose bumps, my thighs quaking with need, my core slicking in warm welcome.

I loved the vulnerability that came with being naked while he still wore his jeans and boots. I adored the sensations of earth magic humming across my exposed skin. And I craved the masculine scent of arousal tickling my nostrils.

"I can smell you," I whispered, falling back against the tree, my hands roaming my own curves. "You want me."

"I do," he admitted, yet remained still, watching me embrace my element and touch myself in kind.

Prolonging the moment made me needy, had my knees threatening to bend, but I used the earth to keep myself upright, to be the queen I was born to be.

For him.

For myself.

"Zeph," I said, my voice low and sultry.

"Aflora," he returned softly, his thumb flicking open the button on his jeans.

I couldn't see him as well as he could see me, but I caught enough of his movements to recognize his intentions. His zipper whispered through the air, lashing my skin with a fresh wave of warmth and anticipation. However, he didn't kick off his pants the way he'd stripped mine.

Hmm, no. He wouldn't.

This was Zeph.

He needed a measure of control, which would come with him being partially dressed while I stood vulnerable and naked among the trees.

I didn't mind. This was what I wanted. And his proclivity for dominance called to the queen within me. I adored the fight, the push and pull, the need to submit while knowing I could challenge him if I wanted to.

It made this so much more sensual and right.

His hands caught my hips, his arms flexing as he hoisted me into the air. "Wrap your legs around me."

I did and moaned at the feel of his hard arousal situating itself right between my thighs. "Yes, Zeph. Yes."

He didn't enter me but teased me instead, his head stroking my clit with expert ease and causing me to shake against him. His mouth sealed over mine, catching my scream as rapture erupted inside me without warning. I hadn't even felt it mounting, too lost to the teasing air and intensity thriving between us.

I panted against him, an apology on my tongue for exploding without his permission, but his tongue refused to let me utter the words. Almost as if he didn't want to hear them. And maybe he didn't, because I could feel his masculine pride vibrating around us, his obvious pleasure at causing me to fall apart without doing much more than stare at me.

"I love when you come," he admitted, his lips tracing mine with each word. "I'm going to need you to do it again, Aflora. But around my cock this time."

He didn't give me a chance to reply, his hips shifting and causing him to line up with my entrance without so much as a hand between us. His body just knew where to go and how, and he proved it now by penetrating me with a thrust that left me winded.

His name caught in my throat, a cry of pain mingled with pleasure tingling against my tongue, and was swallowed abruptly by his mouth.

He kissed me as if he needed my essence to breathe.

And then he began to take me, truly, with his hips pounding against mine.

He'd been right about it being fast and hard, and it did hurt, just like he warned. But oh, it felt so good, too. I welcomed the scrapes against my back, bathed in the masculine growl coming from his chest as he pummeled into me, and tossed my head back on a sound of approval that probably echoed through the park.

If that guard came back now, I'd tie him up with a vine and stuff a flower in his mouth.

Because no one and nothing was going to ruin this moment.

Zeph had me.

I had him.

All I wanted now was his bite.

"Please," I begged him, referring to the pressure growing between my legs and the ache in my veins. I needed him to finish this, to tie us together as one.

His lips feathered over mine, his hands tightening on my hips as he angled me to receive him even deeper. "You feel so fucking good," he breathed.

"You, too," I replied, unable to say more. I had my arms wrapped tight around his shoulders and my ankles crossed over his ass. The rasp of his jeans against my inner thighs heightened the moment, reminding me of my vulnerability with each stroke.

Yet I felt the tenderness in him, too.

The way he held me with care, his guarded energy as he monitored my reactions to his movements and actions. It hurt in the best way, and I made sure he knew that by gazing directly into his eyes and showing him what this did to me.

"Fuck," he whispered, his mouth taking mine again in a brutal kissed underlined in promise. "I don't know what I did to deserve you, Aflora, but I'll spend every day thanking whatever higher power put you in my path."

I arched into him, my limbs trembling with the intensity

growing inside me. "I'm close."

"I know," he said, his tongue tracing a wet path along my jaw to my ear. "I can feel you clenching my shaft, pixie flower, trying to force me to come early with you." He bit my earlobe, sharp enough to pause the mounting orgasm inside me. "Not yet, Aflora."

"Please."

"Soon," he promised, his pace lengthening, smoothing, and drawing out the moment.

I wanted to scream, to beg, to howl in frustration.

But then I felt a burning twist in my gut that curled into the pressure already churning inside me, and power thrummed through my veins. "Ohhh…"

"Yes," he replied. "That's what I want."

The sensation grew, causing my limbs to tighten around him, the ecstasy climbing with each measured stroke inside me. "Zeph," I breathed, my world seconds away from exploding.

"Now," he said, his teeth sinking into my pulse half a beat later and shooting me off into the stars.

My throat burned with the scream I released, Zeph's palm closing over my mouth to silence the echoes of my ecstasy as he followed me into the pleasurable abyss.

His soul intertwined with mine, marrying us in a forbidden manner that felt deliciously right. I felt him enter me in every way imaginable, his mind becoming mine as mine became his. Connections deepened, his thoughts melding and firing signals inside my brain.

I couldn't understand it, similar to my mating with Shade, but somehow I knew that if I tried, I could access whatever history or detail I wanted, just as he could do the same to me.

It was a level of trust and adoration reserved for mates.

A knowledge that I wouldn't enter him uninvited, just as he wouldn't penetrate my mind without my permission.

The door could be closed as well—I sensed it now—but rather than shut him out, I allowed him to *see* me, and he returned the favor in kind.

An opening.

A new beginning.

A relationship underscored in trust and equality.

He craved to dominate me yet desired my backbone and strength as well. All his lessons were meant to empower me, including the ones I hated. Zeph only wanted me to be safe, to be ready for the future, to be aware of my own abilities.

There'd been doubts.

Concerns.

Troubles.

Yet they all came from the right place—his heart.

I kissed him, my own heart lost to his as I embraced our connection and what it meant for us both. There was fear, uncertainty, and dread. But the adoration, hope, and desire outweighed the uncertainties. And that was what I clung to.

"We need to go," Zeph whispered, his Midnight Fae senses picking up on something I hadn't—the approach of humans. "Your screaming caught their attention."

"Why do you sound pleased by that?" I asked him as he slowly pulled out of my body and set my feet on the ground.

"I'm pleased about a lot of things right now," he admitted, and while I couldn't quite make out his mouth, I suspected it was twisted upward into a smirk.

He handed me my sweater, then found my jeans. My boots were last, and by the time I was all ready to go, he had put himself back together as well.

"What about my underwear?" I wondered out loud, trying to find my bra and panties.

"I've got them," he said, causing me to frown.

"Where?"

But the sound of approaching boots silenced his ability to respond. He pulled me behind a tree just before a ray of light hit the area we'd been a second before. His palm caught my mouth again, making me wonder, *Do you just like this position? Or are you afraid I'll make a sound?*

Both, he replied, his lips brushing my pulse. *And your voice in my head is an amazing sound.*

I smiled. *I like yours in mine, too.*

Oddly, it wasn't hard to talk to him without Shade hearing. It was like I had these mental switches that told me whom I was talking to.

That same switch connected to the doors to their thoughts, drawing my attention to Shade's closed one. I hadn't really noticed it before, his mental voice always strong inside my head, but he'd sealed off my ability to see into his mind. Likely because of his Fortune Fae heritage. I'd have to ask him about it later.

Can you use your earth magic to create a safe escape path? Zeph asked. *Preferably one where the humans don't see us.*

You mean you don't want to go invite them to have loaves with us?

He snorted into my mind. *Cute, Aflora.*

Just checking, I replied, smiling against his hand. *Yeah, I can use some tree cover to help us out, but you're going to have to tell me which direction because this place is huge.*

I can do that, he agreed.

Then let's go, I said, already outlining a path through the trees that would take us away from the humans trampling over the earth. *When we get back, I want a shower,* I added, grimacing as I took a step. *My jeans are going to need to be washed, too.*

Feeling a little damp, pixie flower? Too much seed for your lady garden?

I nearly choked out a laugh at the horrible joke. *Don't ever say that again.*

He chuckled into my mind. *Hmm, but I like growing inside you, Aflora. Rooting you so deep you'll feel me all day.*

Stop.

Making you blossom with pleasure around my thick—

I elbowed him in the side. *If you want me to get us out of here, you will stop right now.*

His amusement touched my thoughts, but he ceased his dirty commentary.

Not that I hadn't heard similar puns before. I was an Earth Fae. There was a myriad of sexy statements that could be made using the element as a base.

For the record, I enjoyed you taking root inside me, I told him as we walked. *And I'm open to you doing it again as soon as we return to your flat.*

Good, because I intend to fuck you against the shower wall next, he replied, his puns replaced by his usual crass approach. *And then I'm going to fuck you in my bed.*

I shivered. *Will you bite me again, too?*

Only if you beg.

I glanced up at him and gave him my best innocent look. *Please, Headmaster Zephyrus. Bite me again.*

"Fuck," he muttered, grabbing my hand and yanking me down the path.

I grinned at his sudden haste.

Yeah, begging I could do.

Maybe I'd make him beg, too.

CHAPTER THIRTY

AFLORA

MMM, I LIKE THIS, I thought, stretching against Zeph's soft sheets.

Only, they were the wrong color.

Black, not green. I frowned at them, my fingers drifting through the silk as I glanced up into a pair of silver-blue eyes. "Oh," I breathed, surprised. "I didn't realize I'd fallen asleep." The last thing I remembered was Zeph kissing me thoroughly after taking me for the third time in his bed.

He really did know how to knock a girl out.

My blood heated at the memory of his tongue between my thighs, his scruff tickling my skin in the most sensual way.

"You're blushing," my figment mused, his lips curling at the edges. "Is it your newly bonded mate inspiring those thoughts? Or one of your others?"

"Zeph," I admitted, my cheeks burning hotter. "They all make me blush, though."

"I bet," he drawled, lounging on the pillow beside me in a pair of black pants and no shirt. I tried really hard not to admire his physique.

Tried and failed.

Because he truly was sculpted to perfection, something I blamed my mind for doing.

"Why do you keep visiting me?" I wondered out loud.

"Why do you think I'm here?" he countered, arching a brow. "You created me, right?" There was a hint of teasing in his tone that I probably deserved, because yeah, I did.

"Yeah. For sex," I admitted.

He chuckled, the sound a deep reverberation in his chest that hypnotized my senses.

Why did he have to be so beautiful?

Oh, right. Because my mind made him that way.

"I love how honest you are," he mused, his silver-blue eyes glistening with approval. "So am I here now for sex? Because you seem rather sated at the moment, little star."

His observation heated my cheeks once more. It probably shouldn't bother me that my mind recognized my satisfied state, but hearing it out loud—or in my head, I guess—flustered me a bit. "I'm… I don't know why you're here. Maybe to talk about what happened today?" I'd avoided thinking about the village, so it made sense that my subconscious would push me to consider it.

"What happened today?" he asked as he went up onto his elbow to stare down at me. "Anything I should be concerned about?"

"I think someone tried to trap me," I told him, frowning. "We went to the tavern to see if I recognized the magic used during the attack the other day, and somehow he knew I'd be there. He was waiting for me… and then he attacked me."

His white-blond eyebrows shot upward. "Attacked you?"

I nodded. "Yes. Or that's how it felt, anyway."

"Maybe he was just testing your powers, to see how much you know," he suggested.

"Maybe," I agreed. "But it felt… aggressive."

"That could have been the village reacting to your magic," he pointed out softly. "Perhaps he was actually protecting you from a bigger trap set to catch him, not you."

I considered that angle. "The alarms were going off," I admitted, recalling the cawing and sounds of stones shifting. "But I didn't feel like they were trying to attack me."

"It's possible he deflected it away from you and onto himself."

"Yes, that could be true." My brow furrowed. "But I still think he meant to trap me."

"Or see you, yes," he murmured, reaching out to tuck a strand of my hair behind my ear. "Does he feel ominous to you? Threatening? Do you even know who he is?"

"I feel like I know him," I whispered, glad to be talking to my mind and not to someone else. "His magic reminds me of my past, but I don't know why."

"You're missing memories," he replied. "They were stolen from you to protect you."

"What?" I gaped at him. "How could you know that?"

"I'm in your mind, Aflora. I know many things."

"Or you're leading me into a false train of thought," I tossed back, suddenly tired. "The truth is, I have no idea who he is, just that I feel as though I know him. And he doesn't seem to want to hurt me, but he definitely wants to find me."

He nodded. "All true."

"I just don't know why."

"I think you do," he said softly. "And if you look hard enough, you'll see what's right in front of you. When you're truly ready, the truth will reveal itself. Because every detail you need is here." He covered my heart with his palm, his touch hot against my bare skin.

"You're not very helpful," I accused, sighing.

His lips twitched. "On the contrary, sweet star, I've been extremely helpful. You're just ignoring the obvious."

"You mean your penchant for riddles?" I asked, mock innocence in my voice. "Yes, those are very helpful."

He released another of those chuckles, the reverberation warming my skin as he leaned in to press his lips to my ear. "Do you like riddles, darling star?"

I swallowed, his closeness doing things to my body that I didn't want to acknowledge. Mostly because it was wrong. "Not particularly," I breathed, my voice raspier than I intended. Why did I have to create a male who impacted me so acutely?

"Then maybe you should ask why your mind is so fond of speaking in them," he whispered.

I already knew why. "Quandary magic is all about solving puzzles. You take things apart just to put them back together another way. A riddle at its core."

"Mmm, true," he agreed, running his nose down my neck to kiss the spot where Zeph had bitten me earlier. "But why would your mind choose to operate in riddles when you claim them to be unhelpful? What if I'm not your mind's creation at all, but something else entirely?"

"Then I would have to consider the possibility that I'm going insane." Something I didn't want to do.

"Or consider that I exist." The words were a kiss against my ear, his teeth skimming my lobe. "I'll be back again soon, sweet Aflora." He pressed a kiss to my temple, his sinful gaze glimmering with intent as he forced my eyes to close once more.

Consider that I exist, I thought, repeating his words with a frown. *But that's impossible.*

Or was it?

"There you are," a masculine voice rumbled against my ear, followed by a kiss to my forehead. "I was beginning to worry."

"Kols?" I whispered, slowly opening my eyes to find him lounging beside me on a bed of red silk framed by gold and black fringe.

I blinked, glancing around the opulent room. Floor-to-ceiling windows spanned one wall, a set of doors situated in the middle that led to a balcony overlooking a black sky sprinkled with bright stars.

"Where are we?" I asked him, taking in the expensive fixtures and flickering candlelight.

He followed my perusal, his lips twitching. "My suite at Nacht Manor. It was easier to bring your mind here than to join you since I don't know exactly where Zeph took you. He's not answering my calls."

"He's not?" That seemed odd. "You should wake me up so I can check on him."

"Not needed. I can sense him near you now," he murmured, his fingers clasping my chin to draw my focus back to him. "Are you at his flat in New York City?"

"Yes. He took me to Central Park."

"Did he?" Kols seemed amused. "Well, that's why I'm struggling to connect with him. Our phones don't always work across realms, but apparently dream manipulation does. At least when connecting to a mate." He leaned in to brush his lips against mine. "I missed you today, sweetheart."

"I missed you, too," I replied, feeling warm all over.

"Did you learn anything at the tavern?" he asked, his fingers sliding into my hair to comb through my tangled strands.

Oh, he didn't know what had happened because he hadn't spoken to Zeph yet.

"Um, he was there waiting for us. The one with the magic I recognize, I mean. I… I think he was trying to get to me, but I stopped him. Sort of." I frowned. "It was weird. I could feel his magic, and mine responded to it, then Zeph bit me and I passed out."

"Zeph bit you?"

I swallowed, the intensity in his gold gaze leaving me uneasy. "Yeah. To pull me out of the enchantment."

His gaze went to my neck, a flicker of jealousy flaring in the depths of his soulful eyes. "I'm glad he did," he said, his hand leaving my hair to run his knuckles over my neck. "Protecting you is priority number one. And you're right; whoever the Quandary Blood is that's responsible for these attacks is trying to take you."

The certainty in his tone had me studying his expression. "How do you know that?" I wondered out loud. "And how do you know it's a Quandary Blood?" We'd discussed the familiarity of his power but hadn't decided his fae type. At least, not with the resolve he'd just spoken those words.

"There's a lot I need to tell you, Aflora," he said, sighing and withdrawing his hand. "It's actually why I brought you here. While this conversation would be better in person, I can't leave without looking suspicious, and I didn't want to wait to tell you what I've learned. My father is requiring I stay here through my free days to review some texts that are related to our current situation."

"Oh. I'm not going to like this, am I?"

"No, you're not," he agreed, sounding sad. "I learned today that certain members of the Council and our Elder circle have been hiding several crucial secrets, all revolving around the Quandary Bloods."

My heart dropped into my stomach as he continued telling me all about his meeting today and how they questioned Headmaster Irwin. He told me how he learned that Quandary Bloods were in fact not eradicated, how the Elders had continued hunting them with help from the Council, and how Shade knew about this for months without letting on.

"He bit you because they told him to," Kols added. "Or that's what I thought until I spoke to him later. He's hiding something, and I suspect it's Fortune Fae related because he mentioned *seeing* a future path."

"Yes," I whispered.

"You knew?"

"Not about your Council's secrets or that they told him to bite me, but I know he's working with a Fortune Fae." I didn't know whether or not I should elaborate. It wasn't my story to tell, and while I trusted Kols, I didn't want to put Shade at risk.

"That explains his penchant for being cryptic," Kols muttered, his arm flexing as he shuffled on the bed beside me. It drew my attention down to his chiseled chest. Similar to my figment, he wore only a pair of pajama pants, while I remained nude.

Something about that wasn't quite fair.

And thinking of my white-haired figment reminded me of his final words. *Consider that I exist.*

Do you? I wondered. *Do you exist?*

Then how was he in my dreams? Well, Kols had infiltrated my head without mating. So it was definitely possible. I needed to learn more about how he did it. That would help me determine if I had anything to worry about or if my head was just playing tricks on me.

"There's more," Kols said, drawing me back to our conversation. "It's about your parents."

Ice drizzled through my veins, his tone telling me nothing good would come from whatever he had to say next. "What about them?" I asked.

"There's no easy way to say this, Aflora, so I'm just going to tell you what I learned."

"Okay."

He took a deep breath, his gold irises swirling with remorse. "The Midnight Fae Elders killed them for being known Quandary Blood sympathizers."

I froze, his words not fully registering beneath the thudding in my ears.

No.

No, that couldn't be right.

"They…" I cleared my throat, my voice a rasp of sound. "They were Royal Fae…" I trailed off, my voice still not quite right. It sounded loud now, like a squawk. Or maybe that was just me.

And wow, I was dizzy.

Stars danced around me. Real ones. Huh. That

reminded me of Dream Guy again and his nickname for me. I never did ask why called me *star*, of all things, nor did I know his name. I should probably give him one.

You know, after I figured out the whole dizzy thing.

Because yeah, um, the world was starting to go black.

"*Aflora.*" The urgent tone felt like a slap to my senses, yanking me back into... Zeph's room.

I stared at the windows overlooking the building across the street, tilting my head slightly at the strange exterior. "Is that brick?" I asked. Such an inane question but it seemed easier than facing the tumultuous thoughts in my mind.

Zeph's palms burned into my cheeks, forcing me to look at him. At some point, he'd pulled me beneath him, his elbows braced on either side of my head. "What the hell just happened?" he demanded.

I looked up at him, noted the fury in his green eyes. "What do you mean?" And wow, my voice sounded dreadful. I really needed a glass of water because my throat was killing me.

"You just spent the last five minutes screaming," he ground out. "I couldn't wake you the fuck up and had to put my palm over your mouth to silence you before you alarmed all the damn humans in the building."

"Oh."

"Yeah, *oh*. What the hell, Aflora?"

I opened my mouth to tell him, but I couldn't. The words were trapped in my throat.

And then his phone began to ring.

"Answer that," I managed to say.

"Fuck the phone."

"It's Kols," I said, knowing I'd probably scared him by leaving so abruptly. But there was no way his words were true. "My parents were Royal Fae." The statement was meant more for me than for Zeph. "It doesn't make sense. They wouldn't be able to do that. The Elemental Fae Council..." I trailed off, trying to figure out how the Midnight Fae had gotten away with *murdering* my parents.

And what did Kols mean about them being Quandary Blood sympathizers? I didn't even know what that was until recently.

Except…

I am one.

My eyes went wide. "Of course," I whispered. "They… they were protecting *me*."

But that could only mean they knew about my abomination status. Was one of them really a Quandary Blood?

"Not possible," I continued out loud, oblivious to everything around me. "A Midnight Fae can't connect to the earth source. Unless…" My lips parted, my throat going dry. "Unless a Quandary Blood rewired it…"

I reached for Zeph, his heat having left mine when he went to grab his phone. His hand caught my wrist, drawing my palm to his and linking our fingers. "What is it?" he asked softly.

"What if my parents weren't Earth Fae at all, but Quandary Bloods who rewired the earth source to accept their magic?" I asked him, my heart beating erratically in my chest. "What if they weren't sympathizers at all, but actual Quandary Bloods hiding from the eradication? They were old, Zeph. So, so old."

My mind kept working through the puzzle, the pieces falling into place.

"I was their only heir. An heir they left with a single mother and her very powerful son. *Sol.* Maybe they chose his family because they knew his bloodline was the rightful connection to the source, and that's why…" I met Zeph's gaze. "That's why he's connected to it now."

It was incredibly rare for an elemental source to allow a new entity to tap into the power when it already had a powerful conduit.

"I'd thought the earth source welcomed Sol because of his mating to Claire." She had access to all five elements. It made perfect sense. "But what if it had nothing to do with her, and it was the source realigning itself with the appropriate monarch?"

My entire life had been a lie.

My parents were never Earth Fae.

"I'm a Quandary Blood." Yet that statement didn't feel quite right, and my link to my elemental power screamed at the wrongness of that claim, confusing me even more. "I don't know who I am anymore." My eyes didn't well with tears. My heart didn't break. My mind just kept whirring with theories and possibilities.

But at the end of it all, I knew one thing for sure—I despised the Midnight Fae Council and their Elders.

"They killed my parents," I whispered. "*They killed my parents.*" And they'd gotten away with it.

They'll pay, I vowed, uncertain of whom I spoke to.

They will, a dark voice whispered back.

Just for a moment, I swore it belonged to my figment.

But that wasn't possible.

He only existed in my head.

CHAPTER THIRTY-ONE

KOLS

"SHE'S ASLEEP AGAIN," Zeph said over the line, his voice tired. "Shit, Kols. What the fuck just happened?"

I ran my fingers through my hair and sighed. "A lot. A fucking lot. Hold on."

I cast a myriad of spells around my room to ensure there were no listening devices. After learning what I had today, I no longer trusted anyone, including my own damn family. Because clearly they were holding out on me. At least my father and grandfather were, anyway.

When I finished my spells, I picked up the phone again. "Are we sure this line is secure?"

"Please," Zeph muttered. "The cuffs work, right?"

"Yeah. Fortunately." Because if anyone sensed my ties to Aflora, I'd be royally fucked, and not in a good way. Since the same guy who'd made the band around my wrist also enchanted our phones, I could safely assume our conversation would be private.

I collapsed on my bed and told Zeph about the meeting, ending with the bit about her parents. "That'd been where

I was when she woke herself up."

Zeph had fallen silent, probably from shock. Which, yeah, I'd felt the same when I heard it all in the Council Chambers.

"I think it's safe to say she didn't take the news well," Zeph muttered.

"Thanks for stating the obvious," I drawled, pinching the bridge of my nose in frustration. "She's going to hate me, Zeph."

"She's not," he replied. "She knows it wasn't you."

"Does she?" Because it really didn't feel that way. "I had no idea until today."

"I know you didn't."

"And I couldn't not tell her," I added. "It felt wrong to keep that to myself."

"No, it was the right thing to do," he agreed. "She'll see that. Trust me."

I sighed, my hand falling from my nose to the bed while I stared up at my ceiling. "She said you bit her again."

"Yeah," he replied, clearing his throat. "A few times."

I wanted to hate him, to yell at the unfairness of him taking her before I had the chance to, but my surroundings reminded me why I couldn't take that next step. Not yet. Not until I figured out how to finish the mating without jeopardizing us both. "Good thing the bands work," I said after a beat.

"You're jealous."

"Fuck yeah, I'm jealous."

He chuckled. "It wasn't exactly planned."

"But you're not sorry," I pointed out.

"No, I'm not," he admitted without hesitation. "She's mine."

"Ours," I corrected.

"True."

A comfortable silence fell between us while I considered what a future with her would be like. "Maybe we should run," I suggested. "Take her far away from this bullshit and never look back."

He remained quiet for a long moment before murmuring, "You'd never forgive yourself. And neither would she. The reason you're both so compatible is that you share a sense of responsibility for others, and you won't turn your back on the Midnight Fae. Not even for her."

I despised him for being right. Just for a moment. Then allowed the annoyance to leave me because he was correct. "I can't stop the ascension." The black writhing marks painting my torso and arms were proof of that.

"And she wouldn't want you to."

"I know." I heaved another sigh. "Fuck, I know, but it would be so much easier if I could."

"Want to know what I think about easy solutions?"

"They never last," I said, aware of his thoughts on the topic. "Yeah, yeah."

I could *hear* him smirking. "You want me to coddle your ass and pity you?"

"Fuck you," I muttered.

"Then stop whining."

"I'm not, dick. I'm just telling you my hopes and dreams so you can squash them like you always do."

He snorted. "Whatever, Midnight Prince."

"Don't even start that bullshit with me," I muttered. "We're not going back to the title fuckery again."

"You really hated that, didn't you?"

"You know I did." His whole formality kick had served as a punishment to us both. "The entire situation wasn't our fault. She played us and our cocks, end of discussion."

He fell silent again, making me wonder if he was going to revert into his previous depression and tell me to fuck off. But instead, he quietly said, "I should have seen it coming."

"I should have seen it, too," I told him, owning up to my part in the mistake of our past. "I know my father blamed you as my Guardian for not vetting her, but as the future king, I shouldn't have allowed her to lead me by my cock. As soon as I ascend, you'll be reinstated. Actually, no, you'll be higher because of the whole, uh, quad." That would be unprecedented, but fuck if I cared at this point.

"I've been mad at myself, not at you," Zeph admitted after a beat. "She hurt you under my watch, and that…"

"It happens," I replied softly. "You didn't fail me. *We* failed. But it won't happen again." I thought of Aflora while I spoke, pictured her sleeping beside him. "We're going to do right by her, Zeph."

"Yes," he agreed. "Somehow."

"We'll figure it out." Because there wasn't another choice. "She's ours."

"She is," he murmured, his tone filled with wonder. I could practically see him stroking his fingers through her hair, the vision one that had my lips curling, only to freeze as a shuffle of a foot had my eyes flying to the side door.

The one I shared with Tray's quarters, not the main hall.

I hadn't heard it open.

Nor had I heard it shut.

And Tray stood just inside it, arms folded over his chest, expression furious.

"Shit," I said, sitting up. "I need to go."

"What's wrong?" Zeph asked, immediately alert.

"Tray's here, and from the glare he's sending me, I'm pretty sure he heard most of our conversation."

"Try *all* of it," Tray replied, his tone telling me how he felt about me keeping him in the dark. "You enchanted the entire room but forgot the damn door connecting our suites."

"Seriously?" Zeph sounded exasperated.

"I need to go."

"Fix it," Zeph said, hanging up.

"Yeah, sure," I replied to the phone, tossing it to the side. "Tray—"

"You mated her, didn't you?" he accused.

My eyes widened, going to the door I'd apparently forgotten to enchant. *Rookie move*, I chastised myself.

"I already enchanted it," Tray said, referring to the threshold. "It's just you and me. So no more secrets. No more hiding. Talk to me."

I just gaped at him, unsure of where to begin.

And that was apparently the wrong response.

"You think I'm an idiot?" he demanded. "I've known for a few weeks now what happened in her room that day and the real reason you set it on fire. I could *feel* it, Kols. But I waited for you to come to me, to confirm what I already knew. And I had to hear about it *through our fucking door?*"

"Shit," I repeated, clearly out of decent terms. "I didn't want to involve you."

"I'm your fucking twin," he seethed. "You don't think I can feel these things? We're magically bonded by blood, Kolstov."

I rubbed my hand over my face. "I'm sorry." Two meager words that definitely didn't help the situation, but they had to be said. "I didn't want to risk you knowing too much. You know how bad this is, what they'll do if they find out."

"And you thought I'd turn you in?"

"No," I replied without hesitation. "I was worried about what they'd do to you if they found out you knew and didn't report me."

"You think I'm afraid of them?"

"You should be," I muttered, thinking about what I'd learned today. "They've been hunting down a race and exterminating anyone involved, including Royal Fae like Aflora's parents. You think they'd spare me or you if they found out about this?"

A few months ago, I might have thought they'd forgive us because of our bloodlines. Now? Yeah, now I wasn't so certain.

"She's a Quandary Blood, Tray," I whispered. "Or at least part one. We don't really know, but she has cerulean magic and can undo and rewire enchantments."

He gaped at me. "That's how she knew the song."

"Yes, but she didn't understand the lyrics," I replied.

He started to nod, his shock evident.

When he said nothing else, I softly added, "Now do you get why I hid this from you? From Ella? If the Council finds out…" I didn't need to finish that statement, his expression told me he already knew.

"Fucking hell, Kols."

"Sounds about right," I muttered, rolling off my bed to land on my bare feet. Like me, he had on a pair of pajama pants and nothing else. "Is Ella sleeping?"

"Yeah," he replied, sounding defeated. They'd both joined me and our parents for dinner tonight, but Tray hadn't known the reason for the family gathering. "I can't believe Dad kept all of this from us."

"It's definitely raised a few questions," I admitted. "Like how he's okay with exterminating our own kind. I get that Quandary Bloods are terrifyingly powerful, but Aflora…"

"She can't even kill a burning thwomp," Tray replied.

"Exactly." She wasn't weak by any means, just thoughtful. Caring. "She'd never hurt someone for personal gain. Hell, she wants to turn herself in as an abomination because she doesn't see herself as fit to lead anymore. How could the Council vote to kill someone like that? She's honorable and kind."

"I'm still trying to wrap my head around them assassinating her parents. How the hell did they get away with that?"

I shook my head. "I don't know, but if the Elemental Fae ever find out, we'll be going to war."

"Is that why they kept her alive? Aflora, I mean." He frowned. "Wait, no, you said it was because she's bait?"

Yeah, that was how I'd phrased it to Zeph. "They want me to let her be captured."

Tray grunted. "That's never going to happen."

"No shit." But I wouldn't mind going with her to meet whoever was behind the attacks. Not to fight him, just to find out his motives.

Because one thing had become very clear to me today.

The Council couldn't continue to operate as they did currently. "Things need to change," I whispered. "This isn't the way to lead."

Tray met my gaze, his dark eyes reminding me of our mother's. He dipped his chin. "You have my support every step of the way, brother. Always."

No hint of uncertainty, just unerring loyalty.

I didn't question him, because I'd pledge the same to him.

"I just hope I don't get us killed," I admitted, feeling as if I had the weight of the world on my shoulders.

"You won't," he replied. "Something tells me that mate of yours won't allow it."

My lips twitched. "She's a bit of a badass when she wants to be."

"She'd have to be to put up with your bullshit," he tossed back.

"Jackass," I grumbled, but I couldn't stop my grin.

Because yeah, he was right.

She put up with a lot.

And I sort of fucking adored her for it.

"So now what?" he asked.

"Now I pretend like everything's normal and pray to the fae that Dad doesn't find out," I told him.

Tray gave me a look. "Sounds like a brilliant plan, mate. Top-notch."

"If you think of a better one, I'll be all ears," I drawled.

He just shook his head. "I'm going back to bed. Something tells me I'm going to need all the sleep I can get because Dad said I'm joining you tomorrow for whatever discussion he wants to have."

"Try to act surprised if he mentions the Quandary Bloods."

"Trust me, that won't be hard," he admitted.

Yeah, I imagined it wouldn't be.

"Oh, but there is one positive to all this," he said, starting toward his door.

I arched a brow at him. "Which is?"

"You don't have to mate that bitch Emelyn anymore," he replied, clearly thrilled by the realization. "Silver lining and all that."

I laughed. "Thank fuck for small miracles," I drawled.

"I'd call that a major fucking miracle," he corrected.

I grunted. He was absolutely right about that.

As he undid the enchantment to allow himself to leave, I picked up my phone and sent a quick text to Zeph.

Fixed it. But Tray pretty much knows everything.

Zeph's reply came a few minutes later. *Something tells me he already knew and was just waiting for the right moment to catch you in the truth.*

I considered that with everything Tray had just said and replied, *You're right.*

I usually am, he shot back.

I rolled my eyes. *Take care of Aflora. Tell her I'm sorry.*

Will do, he returned.

I set my phone down and slipped into my sheets. Tomorrow would come all too early, and I needed to be prepared, just like Tray said.

And I also needed a much better plan.

CHAPTER THIRTY-TWO

AFLORA

EIGHT DAYS LATER and I still couldn't stop thinking about what Kols had told me about my parents.

It was like finding out they'd died all over again, except I never really knew about it the first time. I'd felt their souls detach from the source—a life-altering experience for a seven-year-old—and I'd understood what it meant. Yet I'd never known *why* it'd happened. Or how.

And now I did.

The Midnight Fae Elders assassinated my parents.

Because they were Quandary Bloods? Because they were helping Quandary Bloods? I didn't know. But Kols had promised to find out everything he could, including who, specifically, had killed them and how.

I didn't blame him. I knew better than that. Yet that didn't stop me from feeling uneasy around him and his direct connection to the source.

He was their future leader.

The Midnight Fae King who would be in charge of exterminating Quandary Bloods and anyone perceived to be assisting them.

What violent lives these fae led. I missed my elemental home surrounded by thriving energies and a love for spirits and general existence.

However, I couldn't go back to them.

Not in my current form.

Because I was an abomination of unknown origin. Who knew if my parents were even the rightful earth source heirs?

Shade came up beside me, his palm finding the small of my back as he leaned in to kiss my temple. "Want to skip class?" he asked me softly. "I'm sure Zeph won't mind."

I looked at up at my Warrior Blood mate and watched as he stretched beside Kols across the yard. He'd insisted we return to the Academy after two nights in New York City, saying we needed to present a normal front and pretend we didn't know anything about the Council's plan to use me as bait.

I'd argued that it put the students in danger to keep me near them.

My mates had then reminded me that keeping me safe at the Academy would be easier than out in the open world. Because here they had snake vines and other nefarious wards in place that would automatically guard me as a student. Thereby making it less obvious when they protected me as well.

This whole thing resembled a waiting game—one I didn't want to play.

"Aflora?" Shade murmured, his lips brushing the shell of my ear and sending a shiver down my spine. I'd stayed at his place after Advanced Conjuring yesterday. It had provided a nice change of pace and sort of solidified our new existence where Zeph, Shade, and Kols somehow managed to share me evenly. Shade never joined the other two, but Zeph and Kols seemed to enjoy putting me between them. Or sometimes Kols was in the middle. Those were interesting experiences.

"That look in your eyes makes me want to skip class even more," Shade murmured, drawing me around to face him. "Are you thinking about last—"

A blast of magic from across the yard had both of us jumping apart to find the source.

"What the fuck?!" Kols shouted as he caught the ball of fire with his hand and threw it downward to smother with his shoe.

"That's *my* line, Kolstov," Emelyn snapped, her palm already alight with another flame. "Have you forgotten to tell me something, darling *betrothed*?"

My heart dropped into my stomach. *Oh, no. She knows. She knows we've bonded and now—*

"I'm sure there are many things I've *forgotten* to tell you," Kols drawled, somehow managing to sound both bored and annoyed at the same time. "Care to elaborate on which item you're inquiring about?"

Emelyn huffed and threw the inflamed sphere at his head, only for him to catch it again and dispense of it like the first one.

"Do that one more time and I'll show you how to properly use WarFire." The threat lingered in his golden irises, causing a chill to skate down my spine.

So much power, I thought. *So much beauty, too.*

Emelyn was either oblivious to the threat or didn't care. She stopped right before him, giving me her back. "Why did a dress arrive for me today from your mother? I thought we agreed not to go to the Blood Gala together."

My brow furrowed as I glanced at Shade, my mental connection to him opening automatically. *Blood Gala?*

Political bullshit, he replied. *The Nacht family throws the fancy ball annually. I always skip, but Kolstov will be expected to attend with Emelyn.*

I frowned. *Oh. Right. Engagement.*

A vision of Kols taking Emelyn as his date to the event fluttered through my mind, and I didn't quite care for it. Not even a tiny bit.

Kols sighed. "Fuck. I forgot to talk to my father about it."

"Obviously," she said slowly, annunciating each syllable. "Fix it."

"Yeah, I will," he muttered.

"No, you'll fix it right now," she demanded. "I'm not going."

"I said I'll take care of it, Emelyn."

"Yeah, and that's what you said weeks ago, Kolstov. I want it fixed right fucking now." She put her hands on her hips.

Whatever expression she gave him seemed to irritate him even more, because his golden eyes swirled with red power. "Remember who you're talking to, Elite Blood."

"My betrothed," she spat out.

"Your future king," he corrected, his tone holding a chill in it that caused all the hairs along my arms to stand on end.

Power sizzled in the air as the two of them squared off.

My stomach twisted at the dark-source essence, my Quandary magic flaring to life inside me at the familiar call. I winced, trying to shove it down, but it spread like rapid fire through my veins.

Aflora? Zeph's deep voice trickled through my thoughts.

My mind shut down my ability to reply, the magnitude of energy swimming around me, through my soul, and stealing the breath from my lungs.

Shade grabbed my wrist, his voice urgent in my ear. I tried to hear him, to comprehend his words, but I couldn't understand him over the roar of sound inside my head.

Kols's golden irises snapped up to mine, his expression melting into concern as he tried to harness his power, but it was too late. He'd released too much, his connection to the source thriving between us like the day we first joined.

Only this was worse.

It ripped through me on a level I didn't understand, the dark essence searing my being and bringing me to my knees.

Kols shouted, the inky lines climbing up his neck

writhing and stirring a cascade of electricity that sizzled through the air and zapped my skin.

Blue embers flickered across my fingertips, forcing me to lock my fingers into the charcoal blades. Pain shot up my arms and down my spine, causing me to tremble beneath the weight of oppressing magic.

Red fire sprinted across the ground, circling me.

My body reacted defensively, shooting off an array of colors in response. *Blue. Green. Purple.*

How is that even possible? I thought, tears blurring my vision. *Oh, Fae. It burns!*

The blood-red flames fought mine, the power mounting into an array of light that temporarily blinded me.

And then Emelyn was there, her black eyes narrowed with fury as she engaged in a battle I didn't understand.

Everything began to spin, her energy somehow connecting to mine in a savage handshake that rippled through the air. Zeph and Shade yelled inside my thoughts, their collective voices leaving me unhinged and uncertain as a tornado of power swept me up into a cloud, the world disappearing behind a thick smog.

A hand grabbed mine, nails digging into my flesh.

Not one of my mates.

Emelyn.

Her Elite essence engaged mine, battling my power for dominance.

Except, it wasn't my Quandary side that I engaged to fight back, but a new link to unexpected Warrior magic.

Zeph.

I also sensed Shade.

What is happening to me? I asked, suddenly cold and hot all at once. *Stop this madness!*

I threw out my arms, forcing Emelyn to let go of me, and screamed as the cyclone released me from its smoky grip. I landed with a thump, my pants tearing as my knees met the knifelike grass below.

My chest heaved, breaths coming in and out of me in

sharp gusts.

Too much magic. There's too much! I expelled my mounting energy into the ground below, forcing wave after wave of the overwhelming surge to go deep into the earth. Only, I felt Shade and Zeph absorbing it through our bonds. Kols, too.

And a fourth source I didn't understand.

A source that reminded me of home.

My eyes widened as I realized what that had to mean— I was feeding dark energy into the earth source! I immediately pulled back, collapsing onto my side into a ball of shivering nonsense.

Abomination, I told myself. *This is why everyone fears us.*

Because I couldn't control it.

I couldn't stop it.

And I'd just attacked *my home*. My element. My very reason for being.

I reached out on a tentative strand, begging whatever fae gods existed that I hadn't done any permanent harm. But as I poked at my earth energy, I found nothing nefarious or changed. Just my deep-rooted connection to the existence of life.

My brow furrowed. *That's impossible.* I felt the fourth link, the—

"Aflora!" Emelyn shrieked, forcing my attention to her and the threats surrounding us.

My lips parted in shock.

We were no longer in the training yard, but in the LethaForest.

And the encroaching shadows whispered danger.

Emelyn sent a sizzling web toward one, which resulted in a sharp, screeching echo to sound through the black tree trunks.

Hot, acrid smoke billowed in the air.

This was not the same part of the LethaForest I'd visited with my mates, but a deeper section that clearly didn't see fae life often. Because streams of fiery liquid slicked the obsidian rocks, one of which was less than a foot from my prone form. Had I landed just a few inches to the left, I'd have been burned alive.

"Fae…," I breathed, glancing around to gather my bearings.

The sky overhead lacked stars, the inky curtain creating an icy atmosphere that the flame streams heated and illuminated in shades of red and orange.

"Aflora!" Emelyn shouted again, fear etched into her voice.

A rock creature of some kind came toward her, the fingertips long talons of black flames. It lashed out at her, catching her wrist. She cried out in pain, her spells no match for the monster.

I forced myself to my feet, careful of the surrounding terrain, and searched for my wand.

Where did I—

The thing's talons whipped out of its opposite hand, encircling her throat and forcing me to act on instinct. A spell left my mouth—one I had never learned—and hit the being directly in the torso. The creature grated out a loud, crunching growl, then exploded into a mound of pebbles.

Emelyn crumpled to the ground, her neck and wrist charred from the creature's grip. I leapt over one of the fiery streams, then a second one, and knelt at her side. Her eyes rolled into the back of her head, the power zapped from her lifeless form.

Adrenaline spiked through my veins, my mind whirring with solutions I didn't understand. They came from a place deep inside, a foreign strand tied to my Quandary magic. I yanked on it, bringing it to the front of my mind, and sorted through the web of magic before me.

Chaos echoed around me.

Two more rock creatures spurred to life with those deadly claws aiming for me and Emelyn. A spell flew from my mouth that created a defensive wall, more of Zeph's energy surrounding us both while I tapped into the

Quandary line that provided me with a strand of thought underlined in magic.

Words spilled from my mouth that didn't belong to me but to something else.

No, *someone* else.

The Quandary link.

Who are you? I marveled even while I spoke, my mind fracturing beneath an assault of confusion and reality woven together as one.

Don't think; do, a deep voice replied.

Familiar.

Warm.

Underlined in memories and dreams…

A vision of white hair flickered in my thoughts, there and gone in an instant as my mouth obeyed his command.

Yet he wasn't so much talking to me as he was allowing me access to his mind and power and granting me the knowledge I needed to survive this insanity. It also wasn't willing, more like my spirit demanding his compliance for my own survival.

And I felt him trying to pull back, to resurrect a barrier I'd unknowingly knocked down.

Who are you? I asked him.

But Emelyn gasping back to life distracted my focus, drawing my attention back to her and the spell I'd somehow woven through her, healing the marks on her neck and wrist.

"How did you do that?" she asked hoarsely.

I just shook my head because I didn't know, the powers spiking through me a tangled mess of knots I couldn't seem to unravel.

I flinched as one of the monsters shredded my defensive barrier, his fire hot against my senses. I grabbed Emelyn's hand, ready to run, but the clouds engulfed me again and sent us spinning through time and space.

Shade, I realized, baffled and completely thrown by his interference. Only it wasn't him at all, but me, tapping into a dark-source connection created through our bond—a connection I didn't realize existed until now.

That was where all the magic lived.

A dark orb of power fueled by my mates, allowing me access to strands of energy I intuitively understood.

I frowned at it, confused by the four links once more.

Death.

Elite.

Warrior.

Quandary.

The last was deeply rooted, as if it'd been there for years. Because that represented me and my family line? That notion didn't feel right.

I tried to investigate it more, only to spin out of the cyclone and into a darkened grove with a stunned Emelyn at my side. Her dark eyes flashed to mine, alarm in her expression. "You're... you're..."

"An abomination," I whispered, unable to lie to her. Not after everything she'd just witnessed.

She shook her head. "That's not..." She cleared her throat, her delicate hand going up to touch her unmarred throat. "You saved me."

I winced, not because I regretted it but because I couldn't explain how I'd done it. "I..." I didn't know what to say.

A hint of wonder entered her gaze. "I sense Kols in you." She lifted her hand as if to touch me, only to drop it a second later and spin toward the dark forest around us and the moving trees. "Who's there?" she demanded, her wand already in her palm.

I tried to find mine again, this time successfully, and mimicked her defensive stance.

Nothing immediately approached, but I felt the building energy and the hum of familiar magic in the air.

Something was coming.

No, the presence was already here.

Multiple essences.

All woven with magic my soul recognized on some deep, dark level.

"Well, well, the *queen* finally arrives," a feminine voice drawled from the shadows of a nearby burning thwomp. "And she brought us an Elite Blood to play with as a gift. How incredibly thoughtful."

CHAPTER THIRTY-THREE

AFLORA

ENERGY CRACKLED FROM THE DEADLY TREES, causing my defensive instincts to flare to life. Zeph was a strong presence in my head, his magic pouring through my senses to surround Emelyn and me in a protective shield of invisible power, one meant to deflect any untoward spells.

Like the one that came from the darkness, aimed right at Emelyn. It bounced back with an emerald spark, causing electricity to sizzle around us.

"Impressive," the female mused. "Why are you protecting the Elite Blood?"

"Who are you?" I countered, unable to see her cloaked in the darkness.

She stepped forward with several Midnight Fae at her back, all of them raising their wands to illuminate the tips in cerulean magic.

My lips parted. *Quandary Bloods.*

Except for the woman at the front. Her wand glowed with red magic, marking her as an Elite Blood.

"Dakota," Emelyn breathed, her eyes widening. "What

are you doing here?"

"Oh, you mean after your betrothed banished me for playing with his source?" she asked, her lips curling into a smile. "What do you think I'm doing here?" She sent another spiral of magic toward Emelyn, but my net caught it and volleyed it back to her.

I had no idea how I was holding that up in front of us, but I felt the strands of it tied to my fingertips, not my wand. A fresh burst of power flared from my hand to restructure the shield, ensuring Dakota hadn't damaged the exterior.

The woven threads of magic hummed back at me, confirming their integrity.

It all came naturally to me, like I'd flipped on a switch in my mind that allowed me to suddenly envision every strand of vitality around us. The elements were there just waiting for me to pluck and use them as I required. Which I did now as I reinforced our blockade, the invisible net pulsing with ominous intent, ready to engage at will.

"That's a bit of an irritation," Dakota said after dealing with her backfired spell. She polished her nails against her shirt, then lowered her wand. "I don't understand. Why are you protecting the very being who wants you dead, Aflora?"

"I don't want her dead," Emelyn said quickly, her widening dark eyes looking at me. "I know I've been a bitch, but—"

"Not *you*, but Midnight Fae like you," Dakota interjected, sounding bored. "Emelyn and her betrothed are the future queen and king of a Council that has hunted and killed Quandary Bloods for over a thousand years. How could you guard someone destined for such evil?"

"I can't hold Emelyn responsible for a history she had no jurisdiction over," I replied, not bothering to point out the sexist nuances that would forbid she even be part of it as the Midnight Fae Queen.

"And for a marriage I have no interest or say in," she muttered, causing me to glance at her. She'd lowered her wand, but I sensed her awareness of our situation, her tense limbs ready to fight as needed.

"Condemning Emelyn would be similar to classifying all Quandary Bloods as evil just for being born into a certain bloodline, as I believe it's her father's lineage that made her a match for Kols," I said, thinking out loud.

"It is," she admitted, her eyes holding a touch of respect as she looked at me. And a glimmer of fear.

"Then why wouldn't I defend her?" I asked, returning my focus to the dark-haired fae who seemed to be the leader of the others. "Destinies change every day, and she's not the one pointing a wand at me right now. You all are."

"They're pointing their wands at Emelyn," Dakota drawled. "As I said, she's the future queen."

"And as she pointed out, it's not by choice." A discussion I'd love to revisit with Kols later. "What do you want? Who are you? Why are you here?" But I already suspected the answers involved the recent attacks and the trap from the village.

They were here for me, to take me to someone.

But who?

Because this female wasn't the source of magic I'd felt at the Academy during the assault, and while the others were familiar to me, they weren't responsible for the events of that day either.

"Where are we?" Emelyn added to my list of questions.

"In an alternate paradigm within the LethaForest," Dakota replied, sounding amused. "We were only supposed to take Aflora, but you came with her. Would you like to be sent back? Because I can arrange that for you."

"And what would that require?" Emelyn asked, arching a black brow.

"Leaving Aflora behind, of course." Dakota sounded so nonchalant, as if the terms of my kidnapping meant little to nothing to her.

"Yeah, I'll pass," Emelyn drawled. "Aflora and I are a package deal."

We are? I thought, shocked by her statement.

"Oh? Are you one of her three mates?" Dakota asked, cocking her head to the side. "I thought they were all male." She glanced at the fae around her as if seeking confirmation. "What were their names again?"

My stomach twisted. How did she know about my quad?

"Shadow, Zephyrus, and Kolstov," one of the Midnight Fae replied. He was a shorter male with long black hair— or at least, it appeared black in the night and with the light of his cerulean-glowing wand flaring before him.

"Kolstov?" Emelyn looked at me. "You mated *Kolstov*?"

"Oh, did you not know?" Dakota asked, not sounding the least bit guilty. "Yes, it does cause a certain perplexity, but we plan to teach Aflora how to undo the bond with him, so he'll be free again shortly. Of course, he's going to die in the process, but that's neither here nor there, yes?"

"You mated Kolstov?" Emelyn repeated, her tone not necessarily angry so much as startled.

"I, uh, yes." There was no sense in denying it or explaining how it happened or telling her it wasn't done yet. This situation required honesty and quick responses, not dwelling on things I couldn't change. We'd deal with the nuances later.

"Does that change your stance on the package deal?" Dakota wondered out loud, her enjoyment in our situation palpable.

Emelyn held my gaze as she replied, "No, it doesn't change a damn thing."

My eyebrows shot upward. She couldn't really mean that.

Maybe she only intended for us to remain in this together until she saw a better escape, because I doubted that Dakota's offer to let her go came without caveats. Emelyn must have sensed the same duplicitous notion as well, therefore not trusting the proposal.

"Huh." Dakota sounded amused. "Well, I'll be. Then I

guess you're both coming with us."

"Not so fast, Dakota." The new voice came from the surrounding woods, echoing all around us as if the trees spoke rather than a person. Yet the feminine tones resonated in my thoughts from a single source—a powerful one.

The Midnight Fae before us all raised their wands in a new direction, their expressions grim as another group of fae entered the grove led by a female with long black hair, and a male on each side.

Emelyn gasped beside me, clearly recognizing the trio.

I studied their features. They appeared only a few years older than me, but I could almost *taste* the ancient air surrounding them. And the male to her right had a Fortune Fae Alpha appeal to him with his silver hair, larger build, and enhanced jawline—suggesting he had fangs. Yet his eyes weren't slit like a Fortune Fae Alpha's.

The male on her other side held up a wand lit with purple magic, indicating his Death Blood heritage, and as it illuminated his features, I caught sight of a pair of startling blue irises.

Blue irises that reminded me of Shade's.

Thinking of my mate had me automatically opening my mental channel to him.

Where the hell are you? he demanded immediately.

In some sort of paradigm, I replied. *And I'm pretty sure your dad is here.*

That's impossible.

Well, he looks like you, I whispered, swallowing. *Same eyes. Thick, nearly black hair. Chiseled features. Death Blood magic.*

Silence. Then he softly asked, *Is he with a dark-haired female?*

Yes.

And a man with silver hair?

Yes.

Those are my grandparents, he replied. *You can trust them. I'm coming.*

How will you find me? I wondered.

Just keep the connection open, Aflora. And never shut me out like that again. You scared the shit out of us.

I winced. *I didn't mean to.*

We'll work on it, he promised.

"What are you doing here, Zen?" Dakota asked, sounding wary.

"You know exactly why I'm here," Shade's grandmother replied, sounding regal and in charge. "This is not the way." She turned to address the others with Dakota. "Retribution isn't the only path. We can do this without spilling more Midnight Fae blood."

"She's right," the silver-haired fae replied. "Reformation will allow us to lead without the unnecessary loss of lives."

"Unnecessary," Dakota repeated. "You know what was unnecessary? The Midnight Fae Elders killing my parents for helping Cassandra escape the kingdom. You know what else was unnecessary? The Midnight Fae Elders killing Tobias's entire line because a grandparent was a Quandary Blood."

"Violence cannot be countered by more violence," Zen replied softly. "If you continue down this path, so many more innocents will be wrapped up in a war of blood and retribution. How is that a rightful solution?"

"They deserve to bleed for what they've done to our families," one of the Midnight Fae hissed.

Another grunted in agreement. "The Nachts were never meant to rule. They've destroyed our source and polluted it with their false superiority."

"Blood for blood," a female said softly.

"Hear, hear!" the male beside her cheered.

Zen shook her head. "I understand you're angry—we all are—but to kill the lineages entirely will dwarf Midnight Fae kind."

"It's what they did to us," someone pointed out, his voice gruff and lost in the darkness. "It's what they bloody deserve."

"We've chosen our side, Zen," Dakota murmured. "Perhaps it's time you join us once more. I'm certain Zakkai would welcome you home."

"It's not the path I choose," Zen replied sadly.

Aflora? Shade's voice trickled through my thoughts.

I'm here.

Yes, I feel you, he replied. *I'm about to penetrate the paradigm, and I need you to grab onto me as quickly as possible. There's a fleet of Warrior Bloods waiting out here to attack.*

What about your grandparents? I asked, suddenly worried for their safety. Odd, considering we hadn't really met, but I felt a kinship to Zen, sort of like I'd met her in another life.

They'll be fine, he whispered. *She's already seen what's coming.*

My lips parted in understanding. *Because she's a Fortune Fae.*

Yes, he replied. *Ready?*

What about Emelyn?

Ajax will take care of her, he promised.

Ajax? I repeated.

He's with me. And trust me, he'll make sure she's safe.

But he hates her. And while I didn't have a lot of like for the woman, I didn't wish her ill will. Especially after her show of solidarity here, even if it was for her own survival.

Ah, sweet little rose. Hate and love are so closely connected. Surely you understand that by now?

You mean—

I'll explain later, he inserted, an urgency entering his voice. *I need to come in there now. Are you ready?*

I glanced at a pale-faced Emelyn, then took in the growing tensions outside our shield. The Quandary Bloods had begun arguing, with Zen and Dakota on opposite sides squaring off, their postures a strange mixture of defensive and broken at the same time. There seemed to be pain, coupled with a sense of rightness.

Because they couldn't agree on a path forward.

Retribution on one half, reformation on the other.

A Midnight Fae faction driven apart by the greed and violence of the rest of their kind.

The question became, what side did I fall on? The Elder Midnight Fae had killed my parents. "Will the Elders pay for what they've done?" I asked, cutting off whatever some had been saying. "With reformation, will they pay?" I restated, wanting my direct query answered. "They killed my parents."

"Yes," Dakota replied. "They did."

"Will they be punished? My parents were Royal Earth Fae. That assault can't go unanswered."

Zen sighed. "My child, there is so much you don't understand regarding the circumstances and the consequences of our actions. It's not as simple as one might predict."

"That's a riddle that doesn't answer my question," I replied, ignoring Shade's roaring commentary in my head. He'd asked if I was ready, and the answer was no, not without additional information. "Will the Elders pay for what they've done?"

"We will ensure they pay," Dakota said, her expression gleaming with approval. "And you will lead us as queen."

I had no idea what she meant by that. "I don't want to be your queen. I just want the Elders held accountable for their sins."

"What punishment would you give them?" Zen asked me. "How would you see them properly reprimanded for their actions?"

"How would you?" I countered. "By restoring the balance, yet allowing them to live? They didn't afford my parents the same consideration, so why should I give it to them?"

"Because it's our responsibility as the architects of the source to ensure the survival of Midnight Fae kind, not act as jury and executioner," the silver-haired male beside her said, his voice deep and kissed by darkness. "As the last remaining Earth Fae Royal, I would expect you to understand that sense of duty."

"Am I an Earth Fae Royal?" I asked, arching a brow. "Or were my parents Quandary Bloods in hiding?"

Zen's eyebrows lifted in surprise while her counterparts stared at me in confusion, making me wonder if I had deduced that incorrectly. But before I could ask, the ground began to shake, causing the Quandary Bloods to curse and weave their magic through the air in hypnotic shades of cerulean blue.

Shade's grandparents vanished, the world shifting around Emelyn and me in a delirious dance of excessive light, blinding me momentarily before revealing the similar surroundings of the LethaForest once more.

Burning thwomps released an explosion of smoke and fire, causing me to cringe.

And chaos descended as magic wove through the air in a colorful eruption.

Emelyn grabbed my hand, yanking me to the side. I nearly shook off her grip, not wanting to fall into another enchanted *paradigm* with her, but then I saw Ajax on her opposite side, guiding us out of the field as his wand produced a thick black smog that hid the three of us from view.

He took off at a clipped pace through the woods, leaving the war behind us as the Quandary Bloods fought the Warrior Bloods—or I assumed that was the case. I hadn't actually seen who fought whom, my focus primarily on following Emelyn out of the insanity.

Ajax didn't stop until we were under a blanket of darkness, the trees in this area of the LethaForest boasting leaves.

I squinted.

No.

Not leaves.

Bats.

So many that they completely blocked the moonlight above.

If they were bothered by our presence, they didn't show it. Only one seemed to care, his little feet moving along the trunk of the tree as he carried himself down until he was a few inches from my face. I slid my wand back into my pocket and studied the adorable little creature with intelligent eyes. He seemed to be doing the same to me.

"Good job, Draco," Shade said from the darkness, startling me. He stepped forward, and the bat landed on his shoulder with a little clicking chirp. Then his icy blue eyes met mine. "We need to go. Now."

"I've got Emelyn," Ajax said. "Go."

I glanced at the pair, who were locked in a hug that spoke volumes about their relationship. It left me wondering what their history entailed, because clearly one existed here.

Shade grabbed my wrist, a thick cloud enveloping us before I could ask for details or even voice my approval, and a moment later, our meadow appeared. My shoulders immediately relaxed, the flowers and sunshine calling to my element. I wrapped my arms around him, breathed in his familiar peppermint scent, and sighed.

Just for a moment, I allowed myself to calm.

To release the last however many minutes or hours of chaos.

To exist in a world that was me and Shade, surrounded by the familiarity of home.

Only, I sensed another presence, one that had my brow furrowing in confusion.

That was when I realized Shade's arms weren't around me, his body stiff against mine.

I pulled back to study his eyes, noting the coldness lurking inside. *Shade?*

No reply.

My lips pulled downward as I tried to access our link and found it closed, just as he'd done before when keeping me out of his mind.

I shook my head. "I don't understand."

"I know," he replied, his attention on something over my shoulder.

No, not something. Someone.

Because I could feel him.

The familiarity of his magic.

The hint of an ocean kiss.

The faint memory of several sleepless nights.

I turned slowly, already knowing whom I'd face—the white-haired male from my dreams. "You're not real," I whispered.

He stood leaning against a tree, his silver-blue eyes glinting with amusement. "We've had this discussion before, little star. And I suggested you reconsider that thought."

I stepped backward into Shade, begging him with my mind to whisk us away from here, but other than place his hands possessively on my hips, he did nothing.

"Why are you here?" I asked, terrified of the answer, praying he said anything other than what I feared.

"Because this was where Shadow and I promised to meet for the exchange," he replied, killing all my hopes.

How could you? I asked Shade. But our link remained closed, the willow stump doing the one thing he told me not to do only minutes earlier—he shut me out.

Zeph! I called, quickly opening another channel.

Silence.

But not in the same way as Shade's.

Zeph felt... *unconscious.*

"What did you do?" I asked, shivering uncontrollably despite the warm sun overhead. "What did you do, Shade?"

"What fate required me to do," he replied against my ear, his lips brushing my temple. "I warned you that you would hate me. Now you know why."

"Because you're working with *him*?" But I didn't even really know what that meant. This male had attacked the Academy, seduced me in my dreams, tried to trap me in the village, and now stared at me with almost illicit intent.

"Who are you?" I asked him. "Why are you doing this?"

"I'm Zakkai," he replied. "As to why I'm doing this, well…" He smiled, pushing off the tree to saunter toward me.

Shade held me in place when I tried to step to the side.

Energy kissed my fingertips as my powers ignited in automatic defense, only a wave of Zakkai's hand calmed my power. I pulled out my wand to try again, and he smiled fondly at the item.

"Ah, I've been looking for that," he murmured, plucking it easily from my palm and twirling it between his fingers. "I should have known those figments at AcaWard would give it to you." He chuckled and canted his head to the side, his silver-blue eyes holding mine as he slid the wand under his cloak. "Thank you for keeping my wand warm for me."

"Your wand?" I repeated, my mouth dry.

His lips curled again, causing little dimples to appear at the edges. "Yes, sweet star. My wand."

"I-I don't understand," I whispered. "How?"

He reached out to tuck a piece of my hair behind my ear, then stepped into my personal space, trapping me between them, with Zakkai in front of me and Shade behind me. "Close your eyes," he whispered.

I didn't want to obey him, but my eyelids slipped shut as if he'd drawn them down with a spell. And then I felt him in my mind, untwisting a strand of magic that led to the root of my mate bonds.

One that finally allowed me to understand and see the connection at the end.

The missing link I'd failed to comprehend all this time.

The real reason I had access to Quandary Blood abilities.

It was never my parents or my own heritage or my lineage.

It was *him*.

Zakkai.

My Quandary Blood mate.

EPILOGUE

SHADE

"YOU HAD BETTER BE RIGHT ABOUT THIS," I muttered to the white-haired male standing in the place Aflora had just stood thirty minutes ago. Before Zakkai took her. Before I betrayed her in the worst way possible.

"How many times must you live the same history to believe my method?" Tadmir asked, his black eyes flickering with a millennium of secrets. "This is the only way. Even Kyros agrees, and he rarely agrees with anything."

"It doesn't feel right," I admitted, pressing my palm to my heart.

"Sacrifices rarely do," he replied softly. "But the outcome will prove our pain worthwhile. Trust me, Shadow."

"The last time I trusted someone, I bit an Earth Fae, fell in love with her, and watched her destroy the world in seven different ways," I said, recalling each version of our lifetimes together.

They all linked back to that pivotal moment in Kols's

suite when Aflora threatened to break the bonds. I'd been living the same reality over and over again, several different ways, all of them ending in war no matter what I did to avoid it.

So this time I gave Zakkai what he wanted—our mate.

Which had been the plan all along.

He was the reason I'd bitten Aflora, after all. He'd warned me she would be beautiful, that I would crave her, but that she wasn't mine to take.

Yet I did this time.

Because she bit me and I couldn't help but claim her in return.

I'd expected him to try to kill me after I told him, but instead, he'd shrugged and said it only empowered her more. Which was why I'd guided Zeph down a similar path, providing him with the opportunity to finish the bond with Aflora.

I knew the Council would convene to tell Kols the truth on our first break day—as they'd done every time during the last seven iterations of this sequence.

But unlike before, I hadn't voiced discontent with Aflora and Zeph going to the village. However, I hadn't counted on Zakkai's interference—an error that had almost destroyed everything.

Only, it led to Zeph taking Aflora to the Human Realm and finishing the bond.

That left Kols, who, unfortunately, never took the opportunity to finish the mating before his duty to the source.

Thus leaving Aflora with only two of her anchors and a sadistic third mate.

"I hope it's enough," I whispered to myself. "I hope we can pull her back."

"It's never been just about her, Shadow," Tadmir replied. "That's the piece you've failed to *see*—her fate is tied to Zakkai. To win this war, and to ensure the future we both desire, she needs to convince him to take the

313

appropriate path. That's the key."

"And there's no going back this time," I added.

"Yes," he agreed. "Not without risking your memories and hers, and then we'll be right back where we started when I first approached you about fate."

That seemed so long ago now.

And yet...

"Has that happened before?" I asked him, curious just how many times he'd used his Paradox Fae abilities to yank us through the circle of time. The purple sword on his hip glinted at me, as if in agreement with my thought process.

"You'll never know," he replied, but by the gleam in his gaze, I suspected it had happened least once.

Which explained my inexplicable connection to Aflora.

Our souls had linked many times before, just as she'd bonded Kols and Zeph to varying degrees. I'd witnessed some, but perhaps not all.

And I'd seen what happened when she cut them off indefinitely as well.

Those were the worst iterations of fate.

The ones I never wanted to experience again.

"Aren't you exhausted?" I asked Tadmir. "So many hundreds of years of masquerading as a Malefic Blood while traversing the realms of time and space in unending loops?"

He lifted a shoulder. "I do what I need to do to ensure that fate follows the correct path."

His existence baffled my mind. He was half Midnight Fae Quandary Blood and half Paradox Fae—the true definition of an abomination—and he'd used his Quandary skills to rewrite his abilities to appear as a Malefic Blood after skipping into the future and witnessing the demise of his kind.

And he'd been plotting for this moment ever since.

The one where Aflora aligned with four mates to right the wrongs of the Midnight Fae Elders and the Council.

I'd originally joined the wrong side, choosing to listen

to Zakkai's rhetoric about the need for retribution.

Then I saw where that path ended several times over.

Now it was time to walk in a new direction, one Tadmir had tried to drive me down multiple times before. Only, on this attempt, I'd finally listened.

And broke my heart in the process.

I'm sorry, Aflora, I thought, wishing I could open our connection and tell her everything. But Zakkai was in her mind. Which was why I'd blocked her initially. If he found out what I'd hidden, all the fates I'd lived, the futures I'd *seen*, we'd be doomed.

Keeping Aflora in the dark was the only way we'd have a chance at winning this war before it truly started.

I just hoped she'd be able to forgive me in the end.

The trilogy concludes with *Midnight Fae Academy: Book Three*...

Midnight Fae Academy: Book Three

Retribution.
Reformation.
Two sides of a revolution, both vying for my allegiance.
Well, I pick neither side.

I'm an Earth Fae Royal bound to four Midnight Fae. My powers
are growing stronger every day, and I'm tired of being a pawn in
a war I don't understand. Now that I know all the players
involved and the risks at stake, I'm ready to ascend.

No more tricks.
No more lies.
No more deadly secrets.

My name is Aflora.
Your future Queen of the Midnight Fae.
And I'm done playing your games.

Welcome to the new reign, boys.
I make the rules here.
And I will not bow.

Author's Note: This is the conclusion to the dark paranormal
"why choose" Midnight Fae Academy trilogy. It's strongly
recommended that these books be read in order.

You met Gina in *Midnight Fae Academy: Book One*. Find out what she's really up to in *Fortune Fae Academy…*

I never asked to be an Omega.

I'm a Fortune Fae—I see the future. But I didn't see this coming.
My Alpha will stop at nothing to possess me until he drags me all the way to Fortune Fae Academy to join the other wide-eyed Omegas-in-training. He believes I'm strong enough to survive— and I hope he's right.

He also believes I'll kneel at his feet.

He couldn't be more wrong about that.
I don't need three broody Betas and an asshat Alpha telling me what to do. I'm going to keep running until he realizes he's chasing the wrong girl.

Except there's one slight problem. My Alpha has seen the future too… and he knows something I don't.

Whatever he thinks is going to happen, his cruel smirk says I'm not going anywhere.

Fortune Fae Academy is Book 1 in a Reverse Harem Omegaverse Romance. Be warned there are obsessive males who will stop at nothing to claim their fated mate. Trigger warnings include dub-con, strong language, and violence. As this is a series, book 1 ends on a cliffhanger.

ACKNOWLEDGMENTS

Thank you first and foremost to all the readers following me on this journey. Aflora comes from a very special place in my heart, and I truly love this world. I can't wait for you all to see how it ends.

A special thank-you to my husband for your constant support of the voices in my head. You always know when I'm daydreaming, and you don't hold it against me. Sorry I keep cheating on you with Shade. I promise it's not sexual. I just love his cryptic mind.

To Jen, for making this all possible. Our co-writing adventure just keeps growing, and I'm loving every minute of it!!

To Louise & Diane, thank you for all your support. You seriously keep my life going every day, and I appreciate you both more than I can say.

To my Alpha team, Katie & Jean, thank you so much for reading my raw notes and chapters and helping me keep my brain straight with all the time-jumping behind the scenes. My brain still hurts.

To Bethany, my editor extraordinaire, thank you for working with my book in pieces again. I swear I'll send you a full MS one of these days. Like in 2025 when I have more time. This is why I need a Paradox Fae in my life. Just sayin'. To Lori, thank you for the gorgeous cover and title page. I love them!

To Heather, thank you for the chapter headers! They

capture the characters perfectly.

To my ARC team and reader group, I love you all! Thank you for encouraging me to be the best that I can be.

And last, but certainly not least, a heartfelt thank-you to my PR team for keeping me sane, organized, and on schedule.

Until next time… xx
Lexi

ABOUT LEXI C. FOSS

USA Today Bestselling Author Lexi C. Foss loves to play in dark worlds, especially the ones that bite. She lives in Atlanta, Georgia with her husband and their furry children. When not writing, she's busy crossing items off her travel bucket list, or chasing eclipses around the globe. She's quirky, consumes way too much coffee, and loves to swim.

www.LexiCFoss.com
https://www.facebook.com/LexiCFoss
https://www.twitter.com/LexiCFoss